P9-BAW-383

THE
RADIUS
OF
US

ALSO BY MARIE MARQUARDT

Dream Things True

THE
RADIUS
OF
US

MARIE MARQUARDT

ST. MARTIN'S GRIFFIN ❧ NEW YORK

This is a work of fiction. All of the characters, organizations, and events portrayed in this novel are either products of the author's imagination or are used fictitiously.

THE RADIUS OF US. Copyright © 2016 by Marie Marquardt. All rights reserved. Printed in the United States of America. For information, address St. Martin's Press, 175 Fifth Avenue, New York, N.Y. 10010.

www.stmartins.com

Designed by Steven Seighman

Illustrations by Carlos Alfredo Morataya

The Library of Congress Cataloging-in-Publication Data is available upon request.

ISBN 978-1-250-09689-0 (hardcover)
ISBN 978-1-250-09690-6 (e-book)

Our books may be purchased in bulk for promotional, educational, or business use. Please contact your local bookseller or the Macmillan Corporate and Premium Sales Department at 1-800-221-7945, extension 5442, or by e-mail at MacmillanSpecialMarkets@macmillan.com.

First Edition: January 2017

10   9   8   7   6   5   4

This one's for you, Mom
(for so many more reasons than I could ever put into words).

THE
RADIUS
OF
US

CHAPTER ONE

GRETCHEN

I WAS SITTING ON a bench in the Place Without a Soul when it happened, another one of my episodes. The ones that shove me so deep inside of my crazy head that I can't see out. This one was the worst yet, because I'm not even sure it actually happened. I think I might have hallucinated the whole thing.

So, yeah, I'm pretty much certifiable.

The Place Without a Soul—that's what my best friend, Bree, and I decided to call this neighborhood. It's only a mile or so from my house, but it feels like a completely different world. It's as if someone comes in to paint the grass green at night, when all the perfectly formed nuclear families are sleeping in their enormous houses. And the flower beds. Who lines up flowers that way? Do they use rulers? I think they must, because every little flower is almost precisely three-point-five inches from the one next to it.

Here's the thing: six months ago, I would have hated this subdivision with all of its pointless order. Now it makes me feel safe. Or at least it did make me feel safe, until this afternoon.

There I was in the neighborhood's private park, babysitting my little cousins. I was hanging out on a bench that's made to look like wood but is actually plastic. Luke and Anna were climbing up the corkscrew slide, and it looked like Anna might fall. I jumped up and hurried toward her. By the time I got there, she had already tumbled halfway down, knocking Luke to the ground. Of course, he burst into hysterics. Luke's five, and a total spaz. I scooped him up and carried him back toward the bench.

That's when I noticed.

There's a little creek at the other side of the park. No one is allowed to go down there. All the parents in the neighborhood worry that the water's too dirty, and they say the rocks are dangerous. I saw something rustling in the bushes, and at first I thought maybe it was a coyote. There are a bunch of coyotes in the neighborhood, which is sad, if you think about it. I mean, they must be pretty desperate for a place to live if they're in the Place Without a Soul. Not a whole lot of vegetation, unless you count the neatly aligned crepe myrtle trees.

I may be afraid of a lot of things these days, but I am *not* afraid of coyotes. Humans can coexist with coyotes just fine. I shushed Luke and called quietly to Anna, pointing in the direction of the bushes. I was hoping maybe we would see it—a real live coyote, hanging out in a rich subdivision three miles from downtown Atlanta.

But that's not what we saw. Instead we saw *that boy*—his arms wildly shoving the bushes apart. That boy who was not yet a man, the one whose features I knew too well, whose face was etched into my mind, the shape of whose hands I couldn't seem to forget. That boy with light-brown skin, deep-brown eyes, short dark hair.

My mouth went dry and my hands started to tingle. This wasn't real. I knew this wasn't real. Why would he be *here*, crashing through the bushes in the Place Without a Soul? I took a few steps back, trying to shove his image out of my mind, trying not to let my body remember the grip of his hands.

"Gretchen?" I barely heard Anna's voice, small and faraway. "Gretchen, what's happening?"

And then, before I even knew what I was doing, I grabbed her hand, slung Luke onto my hip, and took off. I rushed the kids across the street, stumbling toward their house. My heart was beating fast. Too fast.

I threw the door open and we tumbled into the foyer. Feeling dizzy, I looked up at the chandelier that barely filled the cavernous room. I tried to focus on the light refracting through its crystals. I tried to let the light take me to a "peaceful, safe place." I did exactly what my mom's friend, the meditation instructor, told me to do. I tried to imagine that those shards of light were actually rays of sun, sparkling across a blue sea. I tried to place myself on the edge of a dock, shaded by palm fronds and suspended over still water. I tried to visualize those palm fronds rustling in a salty breeze. But all I could hear was my heart, beating too fast, shoving blood through my body.

I was not finding my "peaceful, safe place." I was suffocating. Even in this two-story entryway filled with empty space, I felt like the walls were closing in. I gasped and turned the dead bolt, peering through the etched lines of the frosted-glass window. I watched as a fluffy little dog darted across the lawn. The kind Bree calls a kick-dog.

Definitely not a coyote. Definitely not *him*.

I collapsed onto the hardwood floor, sucking air deep into my lungs. I wanted to go back to that safe place—really, I did. But the light ocean breeze kicked into a powerful wind, and I started to worry that a tsunami was forming on the horizon. And then, across the choppy, whitecapped water, Luke was calling my name, but his voice was distant.

I felt Anna's small hands, cool against my searing hot skin, shaking me. But they couldn't bring me back.

"Dad," I whispered. I managed to hand Anna my cell phone as my body curled into the fetal position. "Call Dad."

———————

It's forty minutes later, and Anna and Luke's mom is home from work early. I'm climbing into the passenger seat of my dad's car, feeling like a nutcase. Again.

"Are you sure you're okay, Gretch?"

"Yeah," I say, reaching down to adjust the seat. "I think maybe I just need to lie back for a minute." *And come up with a new "peaceful place."* Clearly, Bora Bora's not working for me.

"Sure," he says. "The lever's in the front, sweetheart. A little to the left."

Dad got a new car—a Nissan Leaf. He's so proud to be the first in the neighborhood with an electric car. He drives it like a badge—a merit award for his progressive politics.

I find the button and ease the seat into a reclining position.

"I'm sorry you had to come over and rescue me like that. Is Aunt Lauren upset?"

"She understands."

Understands what? I wonder. That I probably shouldn't be trusted with her kids? Not in my condition. But Luke and Anna are family, which must be why she took pity on me and gave me a job in the first place. Aunt Lauren and my dad are cousins—the kind who basically only have genetic material in common. For instance, until she asked me to help out with her kids, my dad wouldn't be caught dead in this neighborhood. Apparently, there was a big controversy fifteen years ago, when the suburban developer came in with a backhoe and plowed down hundred-year-old hardwoods. Dad was on the front lines, protesting the intrusion of McMansions into his quirky old neighborhood. After a long community battle that included forty-year-olds chaining themselves to trees, the huge houses went up practically on top of one another, and Dad vowed never to enter the subdivision again. Except now he's here all the time. He's kind of like my designated driver. I haven't been behind the wheel of a car in months—not since the incident.

"I called Dr. Cohen," Dad says.

Dr. Cohen is the person who was supposed to make me feel better. But all she did was give me some stupid "diagnosis." A "disorder" with a meaningless acronym. Then she handed my dad a prescription for drugs that made me feel—well, drugged. I hated it. I hated her. I convinced my parents that I was well enough to quit, but only under the condition that I would try alternative therapies. Thus my mom's hippie friend and her guided meditations.

"Dad," I say, "please."

"Maybe we jumped the gun, Gretchen. You were doing so well—"

"I'm okay," I tell him. "It was nothing."

"We need to consider going back on the meds for a while, Gretch, just until you're feeling stable again."

"We didn't jump the gun," I say. "I promise. It was just—I don't know. I don't really get what happened."

"Will you tell me about it?" He is using his concerned voice.

No, I won't tell him, not that I may have seen *the boy*. I can't. How could I explain to my father—to anyone!—how I always look for him through the car window, at the grocery store, how I almost *want* to see him? Maybe after so many months of looking, I have finally imagined him into being. Because how could he have been in the Place Without a Soul? He must have been in my head. But, God, he was so real. Which is a clear sign that I have completely lost my marbles.

Dad does not need to know this. Dr. Cohen absolutely does not need to know this.

"There was a dog in the bushes, and it sort of spooked me."

"You weren't 'sort of spooked.' You had a panic attack—a debilitating one."

"I know," I say. "I get it. But everything is okay."

"Really?" he asks, wrapping his hand around mine.

"Yes," I say, giving his hand a little squeeze.

When we pull into our driveway, Mom steps out through the side door, which is strange—she's usually not home this early. But I'm guessing she's been home for a while already, because she's wearing the fur-lined clogs she uses as house shoes and the big cashmere sweater that she likes to climb into after a particularly long day at work. She's rubbing white lotion into her hands, wringing them back and forth.

"I'm canceling the meeting with the prosecutor," she says.

Well, hello to you too, Mom.

"You're not ready to do this."

She's referring to *the incident*, which probably only lasted two minutes—one hundred and twenty seconds, maybe less. But it changed my life. Every single one of those seconds runs through my head all the time. Since I'm unable to escape them, I might as well talk to the federal prosecutor. Though it's still a mystery why she cares, so many months later.

"Gretchen?" Dad puts his hand on my shoulder and leads me up the stairs to our house.

"I want to talk to her," I say.

The three of us are now standing on the top step. The warm air from the house spills out through the open door. I breathe in the lavender scent of Mom's hand lotion. She always says it's a natural stress-reducer. Which makes me wonder what she would be like without the lavender . . .

"It's all good," I say, sliding past my mom and into the house. "I'm fine."

Big fat honking lie.

CHAPTER TWO

PHOENIX

I CAN'T GET THAT girl out of my head—the one that ran away from me in the park like I was a deranged rapist or something. I was walking Amanda's fancy dog through this weird neighborhood that looks like a movie set. It feels like one too, come to think of it. It's so quiet and empty during the day, it's like nobody actually lives here.

But, yeah. The last thing I need is for a bunch of strangers to be afraid of me.

Maybe I did something to freak her out without knowing it. *Christ*, it's been months since I've even talked to a girl, unless you count Sally and Amanda, who are, like, fifty, or Ms. Pérez, my lawyer. She's probably younger than fifty, but she is one scary woman.

I'm hoping the judge will be as terrified of her as I am.

And that girl in the park—she didn't look like any girl I'd ever seen. I mean, not even on TV. I think it was her hair. It was superstraight and shiny. The color was like a little bit orange and a little bit blond. Her skin was white-white, like a statue. She was looking at me like I was a ghost or zombie or something, and then she grabbed those kids and took off, running and stumbling.

Damn. That girl was crazy. I mean, crazy beautiful, but crazy all the same.

I've been in this place for fifteen days, and I'm already scaring away the white girls. What the hell is wrong with me? Back in El Salvador, I spent five long years working as a guide for visiting church groups. They called themselves missionaries, but they were pretty much tourists. Those groups had tons of white girls, and I never had any problems with them. So what did I do to scare away this one?

Ni mierda.

"Phoenix, dinner!" Sally is calling from the top of the basement stairs.

When I get up to the kitchen, Amanda is already at the table, pouring herself a glass of white wine. Sally and Amanda love to drink wine, which, until coming to this house, I had never actually *seen*. Plenty of people drink back home, just not wine. A bottle of that stuff costs, like, twelve dollars, which is the same as a couple of bottles of vodka. I'm pretty sure vodka is way stronger. So, I think most people figure: *What's the point?*

I don't really drink—not since a bad night a long time ago. I was a *cipote* back then—just a stupid kid.

"Hey, you!" Amanda says, cheerful as always. "How was your day?"

"Nothing to complain about," I reply. "I'm alive, right?"

She laughs nervously. I don't think Amanda really gets my sense of humor. Sally does, though. She grins wide. "And you're living with two of the most fantastic women ever to walk the earth, yeah?"

Amanda and Sally got married a couple of years ago in New York City. They told me they had to go there because, back then, women couldn't marry each other in Georgia. They had a big party here, though. They have photos all over the house. They both wore white dresses. I don't know how long they've been together, but I know Amanda has an ex-husband and grown kids, and I'm pretty sure that this obscenely big house is a holdover from those days.

I won't lie—the whole thing took a little getting used to when I first came home with them.

First off, I'm staying in the basement, which is about three times the size of any house I've ever lived in. I think it's called a basement because you have to go downstairs to get there. I guess I knew what a basement was before I showed up here, probably from horror movies. Those missionary kids loved their horror flicks. We watched them all the time, after their parents and counselors went to bed.

But Sally and Amanda's basement isn't, like, scary or dark or anything. It looks exactly like the rest of the house: Big windows with heavy curtains, fancy leather couches. There's even a pool table down there, like the kind you see in bars on TV, and a dart board, too. The pool sticks are lined up on the wall and there's chalk laid out on the table. Sometimes I'm sort of tempted to try playing pool, but I don't want to mess anything up down there.

Amanda said the basement is where her sons stay when they come "home" to visit. But they're adults now, with their own homes. They live in Seattle and Los Angeles, but I guess they visit pretty often, because they have this big empty apartment that looks like a bar, always waiting for them.

Well, almost always. Now I'm here, taking up space.

And then there's the whole lady-couple thing. Amanda and Sally are great, and they're trying hard to make me feel like I belong here. But, I mean, it's a little weird hanging out with them, just because it's not every day you see two old women hugging and kissing. They hug and kiss a lot. Where I'm from, there aren't many married couples living together at all, since one of them's usually over here working in the U.S. The couples that *are* together don't exactly go around hugging and kissing. They're also not gay. I think it will be a century or so before gay people can get married in El Salvador.

We pass around a big bowl of salad, some rice, and grilled fish. Their food is insanely good, and every day it's something different. I definitely don't miss the food back in Ilopango—except maybe *pupusas*. I could eat about twenty *pupusas de loroco* right now.

"The grouper is brilliant, Amanda. Just brilliant."

Sally's from England, so she has a funny accent and she says "brilliant" a lot—it took me a few days to figure out that she wasn't talking about how smart everyone is. I'm not used to British accents, either, so I sometimes have trouble understanding her. I'm pretty sure England doesn't send missionaries to El Salvador. At least, I've never met any.

I nod vigorously and shove in another mouthful of rice.

"Any word from your brother?"

"Not today," I say. "Maybe he'll call later." My stomach does a weird sort of twist, and I look down at my almost empty plate, trying not to think about what my brother is eating tonight. He's in Texas, living in some sort of group home for kids. I think it's better than detention—anything is better than that hellhole. But still, it must suck. It doesn't seem fair that I'm here, and he's still over there. Plus, the stupid kid refuses to call me. We haven't talked once since I got out, which worries the hell out of me. I feel like crap when I think about it—me being here, eating this awesome food, while he's over there, alone.

Christ, I live with a lot of guilt. Maybe it's a Catholic thing. Maybe I should be Lutheran, like Sally and Amanda. They don't seem to feel guilty about much of anything. Honestly, I didn't even know what Lutheran was until a couple of months ago, when Sally showed up across that glass divider in the visitation room, picked up the phone, and told me she was a visitor with the Lutheran Church of the Redeemer. I sat there in my stupid blue prison jumpsuit and stared down at the floor, pretty much incapable of forming any reply as I listened to her try to make small talk. Sally thought maybe I didn't speak English, even though the people who sent her to visit me said I was totally fluent.

I am.

I was just so completely—I don't even know how to explain it. Tongue-tied? Freaked out by being in a place that felt like prison? Crazy worried?

But then she said, "Tell me about Ari. He's your brother, right?"

I looked up into her blue eyes—they were so intense, even across the glass divider.

"How do you know about him?" I asked her.

Her eyes got wide and then they wrinkled a little at the edges, because she was smiling.

"You *do* speak perfect American English," she said. And then: "I already learned about your case, Phoenix. The nonprofit I volunteer with, they explained before they sent me to you."

I had no clue who'd sent her to me, but somehow those eyes told me it was okay to do what I was about to do. So I did it. I cried like a goddamned baby. I cried and cried, and I told her our sad, sad story. The guys in the little booths next to us leaned back to look over at me, maybe to make sure that I was okay, or maybe to see who the major asshat was, talking to the white lady with frizzy hair and crying his eyes out.

Anyway, when the guard showed up to tell her to leave, Sally went straight out to hire a lawyer, just because she wanted to do me and Ari a favor. I mean, that stuff really happens. Who knew?

Three weeks later I was leaving that hellhole with Sally, Amanda, and Ms. Pérez, who looks like a normal lady lawyer but apparently is a miracle worker. Because here's the thing: I came to Georgia on a plane packed full of guys just like me—two hundred of us, caught at the border, running away from the hell that's breaking loose in El Salvador. I am the only one of those two hundred guys who walked out of detention. The rest of them are still in there, or maybe they've already been sent back.

I can't even think about what's gonna happen to some of those guys when they get off that plane. I'm not trying to be overly dramatic or anything, but a bunch of *gangueros* back in El Salvador want people like us dead. And they're not afraid to kill. Believe me. I've seen it with my own two eyes. Those guys kill people for the stupidest reasons—like walking across an invisible line into their territory or trying to hook up with one of their girlfriends. The lucky ones are the ones sitting in detention—the ones who got away before getting a bullet through the skull.

No. They aren't lucky. There's nothing lucky about being in that place. I'm the one with the crazy good luck. Sally and Amanda and my kick-ass lawyer have bought me a little time. So here I am, eating fresh grouper in the middle of Georgia, a thousand worlds away from my *pinche* hometown, and a thousand miles away from my stupid-ass little brother.

This isn't how it was supposed to go down.

CHAPTER THREE

GRETCHEN

"WHAT AM I GOING TO DO?"

"About what?" Bree asks. "The fact that you've temporarily lost your mind?"

"You're so sympathetic," I say, turning the page in my enormous calculus book.

I don't go to school anymore. Well, technically, I'm homeschooled. So Bree drops by every afternoon to remind me that I'm a mess. Or maybe to keep me updated on what's happening out there in the real world. It depends on her mood, I guess. She's got plenty of time on her hands, since she already got into her dream school, early admission. (Wellesley, of course—because it has graduated more successful female politicians than any other university in the country.) I, on the other hand, haven't even thought about college, which is stressing my mother out.

I'm sitting cross-legged on the rug in my room, a neat stack of grid paper on the floor in front of me. Bree walks over to my makeup table and starts fiddling with a tube of mascara.

"This mascara is dried out," Bree says. "Want me to toss it?"

I shrug. We both know it's been six months since I've worn it. She drops the tube of mascara into the wastebasket.

"Seriously, Bree," I say, nervously tapping my thumb against the tip of my pencil. "I see him sometimes."

Bree has moved on to the lipsticks, also untouched for months, but still neatly arranged inside a clear plastic container. She picks one up, uncaps it, and twists the base. "See who?" she asks absently. She's running the lipstick along the top of her hand to check out the color.

Sushi Kiss. That's what the color is called. I picked it out with Adam last spring to go with the cobalt-blue dress I wore to his graduation party. After I tried the lipstick on at the MAC counter, I kissed him right on the lips. I told him I wanted to see how it looked on him, since the color was bound to end up on his perfect pout sooner or later.

It did, many times. Until it didn't.

I don't wear lipstick anymore, either. I also don't kiss Adam, even though we're still "together," whatever that means. Adam gets it. He understands that, these days, I can't even think about another body against mine. So he's away at college, waiting patiently.

Bree holds out her hand to show me the coral stripe she marked across her skin.

"Oh God," she says. "This color looks truly horrendous on me."

"It's not bad," I tell her. "You can have it, if you want."

"Thanks but no thanks" she says, glancing at the label. "These lips were *not* made for sushi kisses."

Bree points to her own face, which is so dark that she and I have trouble getting good photos together. Cameras can never decide whether to overexpose my pasty-white face or to underexpose her brown one. Especially at night.

"You should give it to your mom." She hands me the tube. "So *who* is it that you keep seeing?"

"*That boy,*" I tell her, turning the lipstick over in my hand. "I saw him on the playground yesterday, in the Place Without a Soul. I'm not even sure he was real."

"You think maybe you were, like, imagining him?"

"He was *right there*," I say, looking up at her. "I scooped up the kids and ran into the house, and then all I saw when I looked out the window was a stupid dog. How messed up is that?"

"Honey," she says, with a voice that makes me look right at her, "you saw someone who looked like *that boy* and it made you feel anxious. It's perfectly normal. No big deal."

"I'm such a mess," I hear myself whisper. "Maybe my mom's right. Maybe I need to try acupuncture or something."

My mom thinks psychology is "horseshit." She doesn't get how talking about problems can fix them. She does, however, fully believe in the powers of: acupuncture, herbal remedies, Reiki energy therapies, and guided meditation (to name a few). It probably seems a little inconsistent that my parents will send me to a shrink who puts me on meds, but they won't take me to a run-of-the-mill psychologist. Dad's the one who believes in the effectiveness of medical science, but he's not really all that into talking about problems either.

Since I gave up on Dr. Cohen and her drugs, Mom has put me through at least five forms of "alternative treatment." The only one I even remotely enjoyed was the month I spent in art therapy. Dad took me twice a week to a little yellow bungalow a couple of miles away from our house, where I sat around a metal folding table with five or six kids. They were all younger than I was, which made me feel silly—like Will Ferrell in the movie *Elf*. Honestly, even the molded plastic chairs were not easy for me to squeeze into, and when I pulled up to the table, my knees had nowhere to go.

Janet, the woman who ran the group therapy sessions, was sort of amazing. She had this calm way of talking to us, getting us to pull up our memories and make art from them. There was a girl in there who always carried a ratty pink stuffed bear, even though she was probably eight or nine. That little girl never used color, even when Janet was instructing us to. It was incredible, though—what she could do with a charcoal pencil.

When I turned eighteen, Janet invited me to join a group for adults. She said it was mostly refugees and also a couple of war veterans. I didn't ever tell Mom and Dad about that group. It seemed so wrong to even think about comparing my issues to all that they've been through. So I stopped doing much of anything, except for the occasional visualization exercise.

"You're making too big a deal out of this," Bree says. "There's a simple solution. That neighborhood is pretty small, so you'll have a chance to prove to yourself—and to him—that you're not an idiot or a total freak. The next time you see him, just go up to him and start a conversation."

"Yeah," I say. "I could totally do that."

Assuming he is not a figment of my imagination, all I'd have to do is find him and be friendly with him. I wouldn't want the poor guy to think that—just because he looks like he might be from Mexico or Central America or wherever—I'm afraid he's dangerous. Of course I wouldn't be that way. I'm *so* not that kind of person.

"So it's all good," Bree says. "Oh, and you're also going to a basketball game with me Friday night."

"A what?"

"Basketball. You know, people running around trying to throw a ball into a little net stuck to the top of a long pole?"

For a moment I wonder whether someone has finally convinced her to play basketball. People are always coming up to us in public and asking whether we play together on a team, which is hilarious. I mean, as if all tall people in the universe have basketball hardwired into their genes or something.

"I know what basketball is—I mean, basically. But why in God's name would we go to a basketball game?"

THE RADIUS OF US 17

"It will be good for you. It's very *high school*, you know?"

"A boys' game?" I ask.

She shrugs, and a strange grin spreads across her face. This is a very un-Bree grin.

"Oh good lord. Please tell me this is not what I imagine."

"Ty," she says. "That's his name. Isn't that a cute name?"

"Ty Pennington? You mean the kid we've gone to school with since, like, birth? He bit me in preschool—many times. I think I know who he is."

"Awww." She grins even wider, which is freaking me out. "That's so adorable."

"No, I mean like rabies-shot bites," I tell her—pointing to the spot on my forearm where Ty Pennington generally aimed. "He broke the skin once. I *bled*."

"Ooooh, maybe he's a vampire." She arches her eyebrows. "That's kinda sexy."

"Blood-sucking is so not sexy."

"Yeah," she says. "I'm kinda over vampires. They're a bunch of misogynists."

Misogyny has been Bree's favorite word since the seventh grade. Which makes me wonder why she's acting all giddy over a boy.

"Anyway," she says, "he plays basketball, which means I watch basketball. Because Ty Pennington looks crazy hot in that uniform."

"So you want to go to a basketball game to *objectify* Ty Pennington?"

"If by *objectify* you mean check him out in public without seeming creepy, then *yes*."

"I'm sorry," I say, "I'd love to contribute to your objectification of men, but I can't. This is *me* we are talking about. I can't even go to the grocery store without having a panic attack."

Her face softens and then goes all serious. "Gretch, it's been a long time. You have to get back out there. You need to *try*."

I look down at the neat stack of grid paper next to my calculus book, at all the solved equations that stack represents. I've become a little obsessed with math. I won't deny it. I work the most complicated calculus problems I can find, writing out the answers neatly, each number and letter filling a small block on my favorite grid paper. And when I'm finished, I go over my answers again, because I love the feel of my finger running along the clean sheet. When I'm doing this insanely hard math, I'm not thinking. I mean, I *am* thinking, but only about how to form a solution. And the solution, it always comes to me. It takes shape in my mind, and all I have to do is put it down on paper.

On those blue lines, everything makes sense. Why can't the rest of it be so simple?

I need to grow a spine. I need to stop with the crazy talk. I need to be *normal* again.

"I'll think about it."

CHAPTER FOUR

PHOENIX

WHO KNEW MY MAD SKILLS would be so handy here in Ivywood Estates?

I'm standing outside, in an empty lot, with a group of ten clueless American girls and their dads, trying to teach them how to hammer a nail into a two-by-four. What's weird about this, besides the strange green dresses all the girls are wearing, is that it makes me feel like I'm back in El Salvador.

I stand beside one of the girls and fold the hammer into her hand. I think they're called Girl Scouts or something. That's what Amanda told me. This one's about my brother's age. She's wearing turquoise nail polish that sparkles. When my hand touches hers, she looks up at me, all goofy.

"Thanks," she says. "You're such a good teacher."

I give her an innocent grin and move on to the next clueless kid with a nail in her hand.

I'm showing this *cipote* how to hold a hammer, but I'm having trouble focusing on it, because cold wind is cutting right through my sweat shirt (well, technically, it's the sweat shirt some nice stranger donated to me). I'd give just about anything to feel the sun on my face right now. Honest to Christ. Sally keeps saying that spring is the most beautiful season in Atlanta, and I keep thinking she's got a pretty messed up concept of beauty. The sky is always steely gray here, the sun never comes out, and almost all of the trees are missing their leaves. And then, there's the wind.

I mean, *damn.*

I guess it doesn't feel all that much like being back in El Salvador, except for the fact that I'm out here helping a bunch of very enthusiastic volunteers on a construction project that they have no idea how to do.

This whole thing was Amanda's idea. She was worried I might get depressed or something if I didn't get out and "have a purpose." She wanted me to "breathe fresh air." She knew about my work with the church groups in El Salvador, so she convinced me to launch her lifelong dream of building a community garden in Ivywood Estates. I'm pretty sure this is Amanda's way of being a rebel. As far as I can tell, she and Sally aren't really a typical couple for the neighborhood. Most people around here seem happy to go out in their huge cars and buy their vegetables at Whole Foods—they don't want to get their hands dirty.

Whole Foods. That's the crazy-ass grocery store where people pay eleven dollars for a *piña* that's already cut up. Eleven dollars! The first time Sally took me there, I wandered around, my jaw hanging open. Where do these *bayuncadas* get all of their money? And why *en el nombre de Jesús* would they spend it on a cut-up pineapple, when there is a perfectly good whole pineapple sitting right next to it for one-third the price?

Completely nuts.

So, anyway, Amanda was worried I might get depressed while waiting around for my court date. Depressed? I wanted to remind her that: one—my brother and I are alive. Two—I am not in the hellhole that some people refer to as a "detention facility." Three—my brother is safe in Texas, in a heavily guarded shelter for kids that's a long way from the guys who want to hurt him. So there's not really a whole lot to be depressed about, is there?

I mean, bored, yes. Insanely bored. But I'm not depressed. That's for sure.

I'm thinking about all of this, minding my own business, when a dad shows up next to me, wearing an enormous tool belt that looks like it just walked out of Home Depot. They have those stores in San Salvador, too. Sister Mary Margaret used to send us there to get supplies.

This guy's tool belt is in pristine condition, so I know what's coming.

"What are we working on over here, young man?"

"Uh, well, I just thought we could make some smaller raised boxes here, just at the entrance to the garden, you know?"

"Sounds like a fine idea to me." He squints at me with a challenge in his eyes. I know exactly what's about to happen. I have no idea why guys like this one feel the need to prove that their *cojones* are bigger than mine, but they do.

"Your measurements are completely off," he says, whipping out a brand-new measuring tape. Give him a tool belt and a plank of wood, and he thinks he's just captured his inner tough guy.

"I think they're fine," I say.

Over the years, I've worked with dozens of *bayuncos* just like him. Those American church groups loved to build—libraries, water cisterns, community buildings, soccer goals. You name it, they built it. Or at least they tried. The problem was, even though they pretended to know what they were doing, they didn't. I mean, not at all. I didn't blame them. They were, like, accountants and salesmen and stuff, so they probably never *needed* to build anything, not until they decided to spend a week as missionaries.

Yeah, they were usually only around for a week at a time, which wasn't exactly long enough to build a whole library. But I appreciated all of those missionaries, for real. I learned how to speak almost perfect

English, hanging around them all the time. When I was a little kid, there used to be enough of them to keep a bilingual school running in my neighborhood. Once the neighborhood started going to shit, they decided to shut down the school, but Sister Mary Margaret helped me get a scholarship for the International School over in San Salvador. So, I'm pretty much bilingual. And, just for the record, I never touched a single one of those American high-school girls. I'm not a complete idiot. My ass would have been back on the street in two seconds flat if I'd tried to have a thing with an American. They were *off-limits*—which was fine by me. I didn't even think of them as girls. They were missionaries, and I was their guide.

Mr. Tool Belt pulls out a brand-new level and waves it in my face. *Who needs a level to build a wooden box?*

"Step aside, son." The brand-new measuring tape goes back into the tool belt. "Why don't you just work on the edging over there and let me figure out these dimensions for you?"

"Sure," I say. "Let me know if you need some help."

It might seem like a wussy thing to do, walking away like that. Maybe it makes me look *bien güevon*. But I'm not afraid of this guy. And I'm definitely not lazy. It's just that if I make any trouble, this whole thing with Amanda and Sally could go to shit and I could end up back in detention. So I turn and wander off. Not too far, though. I have to keep an eye on the damage Mr. Tough Guy is going to do.

That's the difference between me and my stupid-ass little brother. I can let things go. Ari, though, he's got a temper. I'm telling you, he's always been that way. Even when I was, like, twelve and he was a six-year-old little pissant, he used to come at me, arms flailing, every time I did the smallest thing to make him mad. I mean, I would accidentally pull the covers off him when we were sleeping at night, and the next thing I knew, he'd be wailing on me. I used to think it was funny, little

Ari's temper. But that was before it got him in real trouble and sent us both running for the border.

I step back and look around, trying to decide which of these little girls I need to help next. It's kind of amazing, watching all these people at work—even if they don't know what the hell they're doing. When I first saw this piece of land, it was covered in weeds. Hard to believe the people around here let it go like that, since the yards in this neighborhood are so perfect, they look like they're made from plastic. Yesterday I tilled the soil for the first time. The color is so strange. In Ilopango, dirt looks like dirt. It feels like it too. Black-brown and soft, easy to dig around in. Stuff grows really fast over there. They say it's because the town is located on the edge of a volcanic lake. The thing is, even though it's easy to make things grow, no one really does it much anymore. My grandmother did. She had a little courtyard with some fruit trees, and we used to plant beans and corn. But most people, they get jobs at factories, unless they're too busy dodging bullets. Or shooting them.

Anyway, the dirt here is this weird orange-red, and it sticks together in big clumps. It smells different too—like maybe it has some metal in it. To build a garden, we had to go out and buy big bags of soil—like the kind back in El Salvador. Christ, for all I know, the dirt we're about to pour into these raised beds *came* from El Salvador. Home Depot probably sent people down there to dig it up for free, and now they're selling it to me in Atlanta for eight dollars a bag.

That's messed up.

I'm thinking about all of this as I help the girl with the goofy grin. She's finally getting used to using the hammer, and I can tell she feels proud. After a while, and exactly as I predicted, Mr. Tough Guy loses interest in arranging the two-by-fours and moves on. I tell the girl how great she's doing and then head back to undo his damage.

The girl follows me over to the raised beds, which is fine. I set the two-by-fours where they belong, and we both start hammering away at them. And then a small miracle happens. The sun burns through that dense layer of gray clouds and I feel a ray on my face. It's still cold, and the wind is still blowing a little, but there's a sun up there, and it's warm on my skin. I stop to pull off my sweat shirt. I can feel that little girl watching me.

"Oh my God," she says, and giggles. "You have a tattoo! That's *sooo* cool."

Mierda.

Heat starts to spread across my chest and neck. I can feel it rising.

"Nah," I tell her. "It's just like—uh—a scar."

I'm tucking my T-shirt into my jeans, cursing myself.

Jesus, Phoenix. What the hell were you thinking? You need to be more careful.

Here's the thing about this stupid goddamned tattoo. When people see it, they think they know all about me. They think this tattoo means something, but it doesn't. I got stupid drunk and let somebody ink me. That's all it means. At least that's what I keep telling myself.

The girl smiles big and winks at me—she actually winks.

"It's okay," she says. "I can keep a secret. I promise."

I smile back and shrug. And then I make a little prayer to the *Virgencita*, begging the sweet Virgin Mary to make that kid keep her promise. Because if she doesn't, all hell could break loose.

CHAPTER FIVE

GRETCHEN

"SO, WHEN ARE YOU going back to school, *mon chou?*"

Adam calls me *mon chou*. It literally means "my cabbage" in French, but it's also a term of endearment. At least, that's what our French teacher told us. I used to love it when Adam called out *mon chou* from down the hall at school, or when he leaned over to whisper, "I've missed you, *mon chou*," after I climbed into his car at the end of my shift at the restaurant. Now it doesn't seem quite right; maybe because it never was. I don't even like cabbage.

Luke and Anna are finally asleep, and I'm sitting in front of Aunt Lauren's home computer, which has a screen so enormous that Adam's face is larger than in real life. So when he asks me that question about school, it feels larger than life too.

"I haven't really thought about it. I mean, I'm fine at home with Dad."

"Really? It's your *senior* year."

Yes, really. School's not really going to work out, Adam, since I barely have the courage to leave my house.

That's what I want to say. Maybe that's what I should say. But I don't.

"Yeah, I know," I tell him instead. "I'm working on it, Adam."

We used to constantly make up new pet names for each other: my squash, my artichoke, my Brussels sprout. *Mon chou* was just the one that stuck. It made us both laugh like crazy, coming up with those names. But we don't laugh much anymore. Or maybe we don't ever laugh. I'm not really sure.

"Come on, *mon chou*, it's just—"

Loud music overtakes Adam's voice. He lifts a finger, gesturing that I should wait, and then stands up to walk away from the screen. I hear him slam the door to his dorm room, which has the basic effect of making the music just as loud but sort of muffled.

Adam appears on screen again. "Sorry." He shrugs.

Last fall, only a couple of weeks after I fell apart, Adam left for college. He offered not to go, but I kept telling him that he wouldn't be very far away. He's in Athens, at the University of Georgia. Even though Athens is only an hour-and-a-half drive from where we live in Atlanta, whenever we talk, it feels like he's in a different galaxy. We never see each other, and his life is so—full.

"Listen, *mon chou*, I gotta go soon. But New Catalan is playing at the 30 Volt next weekend. Remember how amazing they were live? You should come up."

Yeah. Right.

We went to see them last spring. Adam picked me up from work at ten, his car already packed with people. Back then I was a hostess at a funky restaurant in the Old Fourth Ward. All night I had been so excited to see the show, I kept forgetting to give people their menus when I took them to their seats. It was a great place to work—the kind of place that served breakfast all day long. It had the most amazing apple butter. God, I used to love that job—I loved the independence of it, and all the weird people that worked there.

But I haven't gone back. That entire life feels like a distant dream.

"I can come get you after my last class, if you want. Maybe you could stay over?"

Adam is so completely out of touch with my reality that I feel like crying.

"And they keep saying there's gonna be a surprise guest, you know? A legend. Michael Stipe's supposed to be in town these days. So maybe—"

I hear a rowdy group burst into his room. Two girls appear on the screen, shoving Adam aside. I don't recognize them. I watch one of them take Adam's arm and yank him out of his seat while the other calls out, "We're gonna miss the opener!"

They're wearing ripped jeans and dark-red lipstick. One of them has pale streaks in her hair. The other's hair is dyed bright pink. They both look so beautiful, and so—*alive*. I wonder what Adam thinks when he sees them, what he feels. Does he wish I still looked more like them? Does he wish I weren't part of his life anymore, so that he could be with one of them?

For a moment I see myself, six months ago. I suddenly remember so clearly what it felt like to stand in the restaurant's cramped bathroom and apply my lipstick before leaving work. I remember the crack in the mirror, and the feel of the tube in my hands, the way I'd duck a little to avoid the broken glass and then lean in. I remember the chalky smell of my favorite lipstick, how I always started at the center of my mouth and then worked my way out. I remember how much I loved to push those new red lips against Adam's smooth cheek.

But then I start to feel it. It's like my body is lifting out of itself, like I'm moving away from reality, pulling away or up to someplace distant, looking down onto that moment. My heart is starting to beat fast and I am remembering another red mark, the one smeared across the brown skin of *that boy's* forearm.

Instigator.

I squeeze my eyes shut—so tight that my eyeballs tingle inside their sockets. And I make myself forget.

"Gretchen?" Adam says from somewhere offscreen, his voice anxious. "Are you okay?"

I open my eyes and look directly at him. "Mmmhmm."

I lick my bare lips. Always bare. I can't exactly remember the last time I put on lipstick, but I know it must have been that night, just before leaving work. Since then, I haven't worn earrings, either, or eyeliner, and my hair is always yanked into a ponytail.

The girl with streaked hair looks at me from the screen, like she's trying to work something out in her head. Her eyes are pool-blue and rimmed with tons of black eyeliner.

"Oh, hi!" she says brightly. "You're Gretchen?"

Adam's dorm room goes quiet.

I nod, silent, acutely aware of how dull and lifeless I must look. "Come to Athens!" she says. "We all want to meet you."

The pink-haired girl nods. Her face has gone all somber.

I shrug. "Can't," I say quietly. "I promised Bree I'd go to a basketball game with her."

"A *basketball game?*" Adam says. "Why?"

"I don't know, Adam. Bree just wants me there."

"Blow off the game and come with us," the pink-haired girl croons. "I bet it would do you a lot of good, you know? To get out of Atlanta."

I need to get out of this conversation.

The other girl keeps nodding, a sympathetic smile across her glowing, flushed face.

Maybe I should feel angry—that these strangers presume to know what I need. Or maybe I should be pissed at Adam for telling them what a mess I am. Maybe I should feel jealous, or maybe relieved, that even though she didn't mention the unmentionable, she at least acknowledged it. I don't feel any of those things, though.

I just feel alone.

"Y'all go on," Adam tells the beautiful, alive girls. "I'll catch up to you."

The girls lean in, waving at me, and then they're gone.

Adam looks back at me and smiles. I know every one of his smiles, which I guess happens after a couple of years together. This is the forced one, the one that shows he's trying a little too much to make everything all right.

"I'll come see you," he says. "On Saturday night. My mom has been begging me to come down for my sister's piano recital Sunday—I'll come early."

"Yeah, okay." I nod.

"We'll go out, or . . ."

"Maybe, yeah. Maybe we can go out."

"Or we can just stay at the house, order Thai."

"I'm sorry," I tell him. "I want to come to Athens. It's just—"

"No worries, *mon chou*," he tells me, glancing toward the door.

In his mind, he's already outside. I can see it. But he stays with me for a few moments longer, because he's Adam—*My sunchoke. My kohlrabi. My broccoli. My asparagus.*

I want to say something, to give him a name. But none of them work anymore.

For the rest of the week, I make myself do it. I look for the guy with the dog. It seems important. I feel like if I find him and talk to him, I might prove something to myself.

I drag Luke and Anna away from their screens and I force them to ride their scooters around the Place Without a Soul, in and out of every cul-de-sac. (And why do they even call them that? *Cul-de-sacs.* They're dead ends, for God's sake!) Luke keeps getting tired and making me carry him, so I end up hauling him around on my hip, dragging the Batman scooter behind us. Anna asks why we can't ride scooters on *their* cul-de-sac. Every time I hear her say *cul-de-sac* it makes me feel sad, wandering these streets that are going nowhere, in the Place Without a Soul.

Anyway, no boy. No fluffy white dog. Just a bunch of empty streets, emerald lawns, and dead ends. By day three, I'm feeling almost certain that Bree was wrong—that I am, in fact, losing my mind completely.

But then we turn onto a dead-end street near the neighborhood playground, late in the afternoon on our third day of cul-de-sac wandering. I see him, sitting on a pile of wood, in the middle of a big torn-up field. Part of me is thinking how strange it is that this empty lot is still here, since it stands out against all of the perfect homes and neat lawns. But most of me is thinking this: *Oh, thank God and all the angels in heaven. He is real. That boy is real.*

And he is not *the boy*. He is just *a boy*, which means I am not crazy. At least not completely off-my-rocker crazy. He's about the same build as *the boy*, strong and lean, and his hair is dark brown and cut close to his head. But his skin has more copper in it, I think, and his face looks a little stubbly, not smooth. All of his features are so defined, almost sharp. He has high, broad cheekbones and a long, straight nose. His eyebrows are thick and full. His ears, they stick out a little, in a way that's kind of sweet. They make him look young, probably younger than he is.

I know I'm staring, but I can't stop.

I walk toward him, preparing to make normal conversation. He looks right at me, his eyes big and dark and penetrating. His hand is resting against his lower lip, like he's thinking about something. And maybe I'm imagining it—maybe it's all in my crazy head—but the way he looks at me, it's like I'm scary. Like I'm the dangerous one.

CHAPTER SIX

PHOENIX

THAT CRAZY GIRL from the playground is heading right at me, like she's coming over to have a chat, and the two little kids are trailing behind her, dragging their scooters.

What the hell?

She's wearing jeans and big black boots. They look like work boots, but they aren't scuffed. She has on a bulky sweater that hangs almost to her knees, and it swings around her when she walks. She smiles—a big, broad smile. I feel myself smiling back, but I don't want to do that, so I lift my hand to cover my lips.

I cannot be smiling at this girl.

This girl cannot be pretty.

This girl is way off-limits.

She's white. And she's nuts. And she's still waving. At me.

I take my hand from my lips and wave, casually. I'm hoping she sees I'm harmless, hoping she isn't going to bolt again. I almost stand up, but she was so skittish the other day that I figure it's best if I don't make any sudden movements. So I sit as still as I can and watch her approach.

"Hey," she says. "I'm Gretchen."

Gretchen. I know a lot of American names from the missionary groups, but this one I've never heard.

I figure it would be rude to stay seated, so I go ahead and risk standing up, very slowly. She holds out her hand and I take it.

"I'm Phoenix. Like the city." I pronounce it the American way. "I'm sorry I scared you the other day at the playground. I was just, uh, looking for a dog."

The girl sighs, all deep and heavy, and then she looks right at me. "I'm the one who should apologize. I was sort of, I don't know, sort of out of it, I guess."

"No worries," I say. "How are you now?"

What am I doing? I'm asking this crazy beautiful girl how she is. I'm not supposed to care about these things. And then I realize I'm still holding on to her hand. It feels soft and powdery. Truth be told, I don't want to let go, but I do anyway.

"Oh, I'm fine," she says. "I mean, whatever."

She doesn't look fine, not anymore. Her eyebrows are crunching up and she's squeezing her eyes shut.

"Really?" I say.

She gives me a strange look, like she's trying to solve a mystery or something. Then she smiles, really big. And, *derecho que sí*, this is a problem. Because seeing that smile makes me feel dizzy. I try to focus on her eyes instead. They're green or blue. It's hard to say. It's like they couldn't decide. And then to add to the confusion, one of them has a little brown spot, just to the left of the pupil. It's like a freckle, right in the middle of all that blue-green.

Those strange eyes are not easy to look away from. Maybe they aren't confused. They're just sort of *everything*, all at once.

She reaches back and tugs on her ponytail. The way she does it makes me think it's something she does a lot. Maybe when she's thinking. But she keeps looking right at me. "I'm not fine," she says, shaking her head slowly. "And—the other day—I was kind of a mess."

"That's okay," I say, gesturing toward my clothes. "I'm kind of a mess too." And I am. I am filthy. I've been dumping bags of dirt into raised beds all day, and I'm 100 percent positive that I stink. "Wanna sit?" I ask.

What am I doing?

She doesn't answer, just plops down on the edge of the vegetable bed. I try to keep some distance between us so she won't have to smell me. That would not be good.

We don't say anything. We're both looking at the kids instead. They have abandoned their scooters and are walking along the edges of the new flower beds, their hands outstretched like they're on a balance beam. The boy's acting all crazy, calling out, "Whoa, whoooa," like he's gonna fall. But the little girl is serious and focused, carefully placing one foot in front of the other, watching the plank of wood like she's studying it.

And then it comes to me: I need to be nice to this Gretchen girl. Right? I mean, wouldn't that be better than being standoffish and having her get all weirded out, again? Like I said, the last thing I need is for people in this neighborhood to think I'm some sort of criminal or something. I've got enough problems as it is.

It's decided. I'll just be friendly, make her feel comfortable. I can do that.

"So, I'll start," I say. "I'm a mess because I have been helping girls in green uniforms build this vegetable garden all week, with their nice—but also kind of clueless—dads."

"This is going to be a vegetable garden?" she asks, looking around. By now the little boy is digging around in the fresh dirt and the girl is standing over him, telling him he's gonna stain his pants.

"Yeah," I say. "A community garden for the neighborhood."

"Wow, Ivywood Estates doesn't really strike me as a community garden type of place."

I shrug. "Places can change."

If anyone knows how places can change, it's me. Ilopango, where I grew up, it used to be a tourist destination. *Honest to Christ*. People would come out there from the city center of San Salvador on the weekends. They used to hang out by the lake and sit around in the restaurants, drinking *batidos*. Even bird watchers came from, like, Germany and shit, just to stare up into the trees outside of town. That was before the *maras* took control. Needless to say, not a whole lot of tourists are risking being caught in a gang-war cross fire just to see a rare bird, or to get a nice view of the lake.

"Yeah," she says. "I guess places *can* change. It's great that you're helping with it."

"I don't really have much else to do."

Ni mierda. That was a stupid thing to say. I don't want to get into why I don't have anything to do. I mean, most guys my age would have, like, a job, or they'd be in school or something. I have a feeling that telling her the truth—that I just got out of detention, that I'm not allowed to work or go to school, that I'm in her neighborhood because I'm running away from a stupid *pinche* death threat—none of that would make her feel more comfortable.

"Anyway, that's my messy story," I say, hoping she won't ask more questions. "What's yours?"

"Are you sure you want to hear it?"

"I asked, didn't I?"

"Okay, well . . . are you really sure?"

I don't know. All I know is that I want for her to keep sitting here— to keep talking. And I definitely don't want to talk about *me*.

"I'm sure," I say.

She tugs at her ponytail and looks away, not toward the kids this time. She's looking out across the street, but I don't think she's really seeing what's over there.

"Six months ago I was leaving work. It was pretty late. I used to work in a restaurant." She turns to look at the kids again. "I was a hostess." Then she hugs her legs up to her chest and reaches down to touch the laces of her boots. "It was after closing. And I had to stop for half-and-half for my mom. I mean, she can't drink her coffee without it. So she texted me and asked me to get some."

She's playing with the laces of her boots, winding her fingers so tightly into them that her skin turns red. I watch, not saying anything, sort of wondering what half-and-half is.

"Oh my God," she says, looking over at me. "That's so strange. I completely forgot that until now." She goes back to wrapping the bright-yellow laces around her fingers. "I mean, about the half-and-half." She's not wearing nail polish, and the edges of her fingernails are ragged, like maybe she bites them. "I guess I was distracted, looking at the text from my mom. I didn't see him coming."

"Who?" I ask. I'm starting to worry that whatever she's going to tell me is bad. She looks back at me with those everything eyes. They're getting shiny, like maybe she's gonna cry.

Oh Christ. What do I do if she cries?

She releases one hand from her shoelace and wipes her eyes. "I think maybe we should stop talking about this. I get these, uh, panic attacks?"

She says this like it's a question, like she's waiting for me to tell her *Yes, you get panic attacks.* I don't think I've ever heard *panic attack,* but I'm pretty sure I know what she means.

"Did seeing me give you one of those . . . attacks?"

"You didn't do anything," she says. Her voice has gone wobbly. "I feel terrible about it. That's why I wanted to find you."

She has been looking for me? Is this why she's telling me this stuff? I don't even care why. I'm just relieved that she's sitting here with me and she's not looking at me like I'm a murderer. She smiles again and my lungs fill with air. Looking at that smile, I feel like I can breathe better, like the air has just changed to pure oxygen.

"What's it like?" I ask. "I mean, when you have a panic attack?" I really want to know. Honestly, I think maybe I already do.

"You know what?" she asks. "You're the first person who has ever asked me that. Everybody just wants me to snap out of it—they don't want to hear about it."

"Snap out of it?"

"You know, like, get over it."

"Oh. You'll get over it sometime," I say. "But until then you might as well be straight about it, right?"

She nods once, like she's concentrating on something. God, she is so pretty. With absolutely no makeup on at all and her hair pulled back into a ponytail and that enormous sweater swallowing her up, she is really beautiful.

"So, okay. Here goes." She slides a little closer to me. "First my heart starts beating fast. Then I feel sort of tingly in my arms and legs, and then I can't breathe—I mean, I am breathing, but I feel like I can't take in enough air. I keep sucking it in, and sometimes I start crying, like freaking out, sobbing. But other times, I curl up into a ball, or I just bolt. I mean, I run away, like I did the other day." She tugs on her hair again, and she's moved so close to me that her elbow brushes my shoulder. "After a while it ends."

"That sucks," I say, trying not to think about the last time I curled up into a ball like that. It wasn't that long ago.

"Do you feel better?" I ask her. "I mean, after it's over?"

I do, I'm thinking. Sometimes.

"I guess," she says. "But I'm afraid to go anywhere or do anything, because I never know what's going to set it off."

"Maybe you should, like, do something that makes you feel calm first. I mean, before you go out and try something new."

"Like visualizations?" she says. "Or breathing techniques?"

Visualizations? Techniques? I don't have a clue what she's talking about. "No, like *pupusas*. Whenever I'm about to face something kind of scary, I eat *pupusas*. They make me think of when I was a kid, and of my grandmother."

"What's a *pupusa*?" she asks.

"*Damn, girl.* You don't know what a *pupusa* is?"

She shakes her head and shrugs. *What am I thinking?* Of course she doesn't know what a *pupusa* is. They're impossible to find around here. I've looked, many times.

"You're missing out," I tell her. "They're like a thick tortilla filled with cheese and stuff, and they're the best food ever invented."

"I guess I need to try them," she says. "I mean, if they're the *best food ever invented*."

"Let me know if you find some," I tell her. "I'm dyin' for one."

We both laugh, and Gretchen leans in toward me.

"Anyway, you seem pretty brave to me," I say. "You came over here and talked to me, didn't you?" I wipe my dirt-stained hands on my filthy jeans. "And I look a little scary, after working in this garden all day."

"You're right." She smiles at me. "I mean—not about looking scary, but . . ."

That makes me laugh. "I get it."

"So I know this is really weird," she says. "But I'm going to hug you now."

And then that girl climbs halfway onto my lap and wraps her arms around me, folding us both into her enormous sweater.

I hear myself talking to her, but I have no idea what I'm saying anymore. All I can hear is my heart, running like a goddamned freight train. It's like *la Bestia*'s barreling through my chest. Where I'm from, people always say the road to the American Dream runs through the Mexican Nightmare, but it's not a road. It's a train track, and if you're poor and stupid like me, the only way through that Nightmare is on the back of *la Bestia*. If you're lucky—if you find the tracks after you cross into Mexico, if you get space up on top of the train and something sturdy to grab on to, if you have a strong enough grip to stay on the roof when the Beast jolts to a start and the wheels begin to squeal, if you're awake enough to hold on through the night, or if you're smart enough to have remembered a belt or rope to tie yourself on, if you survive the rain and the sunburn and the bandits and the kidnappers, *la Bestia* will take you all the way to the border—all the way to the edge of the Promised Land. But if you're not lucky, if you let go for even a second, you're done. Crushed under the rails. Or worse. Torn apart, limb from limb.

I've seen it.

I'm not gonna let myself fall off this train. So I don't move. I grasp tightly to my stupid beating heart and I let Gretchen hug me.

Then, *gracias a Dios y a la Virgencita*, a single clear thought enters my head. I decide to imagine that she is Sister Mary Margaret. They're about the same build, both tall, so it isn't impossible. Of course, Sister Mary Margaret is about sixty years older than this crazy beautiful girl, but I figure thinking about the nun will help keep me from going completely haywire.

"Thank you," Gretchen whispers in my ear.

That about does me in. It's like I'm way up on the roof of that train again, in the very front. Hot steam is hitting my face, the loud thump and high-pitched squeal of all those metal wheels is growing faster and louder.

I'm holding on for dear life, and a wild thought speeds from my stupid heart into my stupid head: *I cannot let go.* Because even though I'm terrified, I have this strange feeling that maybe we're both on our way to someplace better.

And then I'm thinking about other things, like: *Damn. Sister Mary Margaret does not smell this good.*

CHAPTER SEVEN

GRETCHEN

"I DID IT."

Bree and I are sitting across from each other at a metal picnic table in Woodruff Park. It's the first time either one of us has ever been here. There's really no reason to come to this part of downtown, nothing but ugly office towers and this dingy park with a fountain and a big statue in the middle of it.

"Did what?" she asks.

"I talked to him," I say. "The guy from the playground."

"Seriously? You saw him again?"

"Yesterday the kids and I were on a walk in the neighborhood, and he was there alone in that empty lot—I guess they're turning it into a community garden."

"A community garden?" Bree leans back on the rickety metal bench. "In the Place Without a Soul?"

"Uh-huh."

"Well, that's unexpected. I didn't think they *did* community in Ivywood Estates."

"I know. It's weird, right?"

We both look at the fountain for a while, not saying anything, waiting for Mom and Dad to show up. Bree brought me down here to meet my parents, for the thing with the prosecutor. My mom had to come straight from a luncheon she was working in Buckhead. She's an organic florist. Everybody around here seems to be going green, and she's the only person in town who can give them "bright bouquets bursting with color" that don't rely on exploited third-world workers and scary baby-disfiguring chemicals. She's always busy, and she usually works nights and weekends.

I think that's why, at some point, Dad decided to quit his job. He must have figured someone needed to be around to change my diapers and pick me up from preschool—and then later, to help me with homework and drive me to piano lessons. For fifteen years he was a stay-at-home dad with some contract work on the side. When I finally got old enough to drive myself, he applied for teaching positions, and last year he nailed his dream job—teaching history at a super-liberal private school just down the road, where all the kids call teachers by their first names. But then I fell apart, and he had to pick up the pieces. So Dad quit his dream job after only one year and went back to teaching online classes to homeschoolers. The only difference is that now I'm one of those homeschoolers. My dad not only teaches me, but also chauffeurs me, since I'm still not ready to get behind the wheel. Today Dad has an appointment with the eye doctor that he couldn't change, which meant Bree had to step in as my driver.

He told us to park in a pay lot nearby and wait for him by the fountain. So here we are. The water smells a bit skanky, like chlorine mixed with algae, and nobody else is here, except for a couple of homeless guys with shopping carts.

"So, what was that guy doing there?" Bree asks. "I mean, does he live in the neighborhood?"

"I don't know. I didn't really ask."

"You didn't ask?" Her voice is going in that direction—the one that tells me she's about to launch into critique mode. "Okay, so what exactly *did* you talk about?"

"I told him about the panic attacks."

I glance away, toward the huge metal statue lurking over us, but I know Bree is looking right at me. I don't even have to look back at her. I can feel the judgment coming on.

"Oh no. No—you—did—*not*."

"What? What's wrong with that?"

"Um, hello? You just unloaded your crap onto a complete stranger. That's what's wrong. He must have thought you were a lunatic. I mean, did *he* run away?"

I remember what it felt like to lean against him, to feel him solid against me. I think back to the feel of my arms around him, and the way he sat so still, how he apologized for being covered in soil.

"No," I say. "He was sort of amazing, actually."

"Amazing?"

Bree leans across the table that separates us. "Um, what is this I'm hearing in your voice right now? Because you're kinda freaking me out."

"He listened. And he asked the right questions, you know?"

"Not really." Bree shakes her head. "But I guess I'm proud of you, I mean, for doing it."

"Yeah," I say. "Me too. It sort of feels like I've turned a corner or something, like maybe I'm getting better."

We sit together in silence for a while, looking up at the statue. It's beautiful, actually, when you really look at it. It's huge, like, two stories tall. There's a woman holding on to the feet of this enormous bird, and it's lifting her up off the ground, beak pointed directly into the sky, wings jutting forward. I don't know what kind of bird it is, or what it's supposed to mean, but it looks like it's going to lift that woman right up off the ground, with no effort at all.

It makes me feel peaceful, seeing that bird about to take off, a woman holding tightly to its claws.

My dad arrives, wearing those stupid plastic glasses that they give you after the doctor dilates your eyes. Bree stands up and reaches out to give him a hug. "Looking good, Dan."

"I do my best." He smiles a goofy smile. Then he looks at me, and his face goes all concerned. "Ready?" he asks.

"Not really," I say.

Bree shoves me gently. "You've got this. Remember? You've turned a corner."

"Yeah." I wrap both of my hands around the cold metal armrests and push, propelling myself to a stand. "Corner turned."

Here's the thing about going down to have a little chat with the assistant U.S. attorney in charge of "major crimes." You think you're heading to a fancy courthouse—marble columns, mahogany desks. I mean, that's what these places always look like in the legal thriller movies. But actually, you're going to a dumpy high-rise in a questionable part of downtown Atlanta.

They have just taken away our cell phones and we're stripping off our shoes and belts when my mom launches in. Again.

"This is just so infuriating. Where were the Atlanta police when all of this happened? Absent. Couldn't have cared less." She thrusts her phone into the little plastic basket and shoves it toward the X-ray machine. "They barely even filled out a police report. And now, suddenly, they're so interested that they're putting us through all of *this*."

Mom marches through the metal detector and takes her salmon-colored flats from the bin. She's tall, like me, and she almost always wears flats. I guess she spends most of the day on her feet, which means that heels don't make much sense. Even without the heels, people tend to watch her when she walks by. I've seen it so many times, at airports, in restaurants. My mom is beautiful and confident—lean and long, with thick gray hair cut into a stylish bob. She wears big, bold earrings and pencil skirts, lots of color, but always in the perfect combination. All of her clothes are "finds," since she loves to shop at upscale secondhand stores.

We used to do that together—it was one of our Saturday afternoon mother-daughter bonding rituals. But not anymore. I think she knows I want to be invisible now, and I must be doing a good job, since she never says a word about what I'm wearing. We haven't been on one of those "hunting expeditions" in months.

Dad and I quietly remove our belts and shoes and walk through the metal detector behind her. There isn't much to say. Sure, she has a point. The police were outright bored by my story. They did nothing to investigate, and then a few months later we got a call from the Feds and suddenly everyone cares.

I pull my shoes from the bin. It's just like at the airport, except here they keep your cell phone until you come out of the building. Oh, and we aren't exactly going on a vacation.

We ride an elevator to the sixth floor, where we have to show our driver's licenses to a receptionist, who sits behind a Plexiglas window, not even looking at us. Then we're handed stickers and told to put them on our shirts. They read: VISITOR: MUST BE ACCOMPANIED AT ALL TIMES. After checking us in, the receptionist sends us (unaccompanied) back down to the fifth floor, where we wait in a lobby that looks like a dentist's office. Except everything is red, white, and blue. No joke. Blue carpet with thick red stripes, red vinyl couches that look entirely uninviting, white walls that really need a paint job. There are several doors around, but they're all closed tight. One of them has a big sign in red, white, and blue that reads: PLEASE DO NOT KNOCK ON THIS DOOR.

Patriotic.

I don't know how long we wait. I'm flipping through the frayed pages of a magazine, but I don't really see them. I don't even know whether I'm looking at *Us Weekly* or *House Beautiful*. I guess I'm starting to get anxious about all of this, because all I see is *that boy* standing in front of me.

The door we're not supposed to knock on flings open, and a woman about my mom's age steps out in a black suit with a pink scarf. My parents stand, and the woman holds out her hand to introduce herself. Next to my mom, she looks short. She tells us to call her Karen.

"Thanks so much for coming today, Gretchen," she says, reaching out to shake my hand. "I wish we could have met somewhere else—somewhere more comfortable—but things are just so busy right now."

I guess when your job is to investigate "major crimes," you get busy.

We follow Karen down a long empty hall and then stop at a red door. She types something into a keypad and the door opens, revealing another long, empty hall.

"Welcome to our glamorous offices," she says. "You know, we Federal employees really get to live the good life."

We walk into her office, and I head straight for the window. I think all of those interior halls and windowless waiting areas were making me feel claustrophobic.

"You have a nice view," my mom says absently.

It doesn't look all that nice to me. Her office overlooks an abandoned train track, a bunch of graffiti everywhere.

The prosecutor laughs. "True story," she says. "A few months ago a film crew went out there to film some zombie movie and they actually had to *clean it up* before they started."

My dad laughs and I decide I like this woman. She seems kind. I wonder how a kind person can end up in her line of work. Or maybe what I mean is: How can a person stay kind after doing this sort of work for a while?

My mom did a little research after Karen called us. She told me Karen investigates stuff like human trafficking, child pornography rings, gangs. Which makes us all wonder: What are we doing here?

CHAPTER EIGHT

PHOENIX

"WHO KNEW MY LITTLE pissant brother was such an artist?"

I'm sitting on my bed—well, not really *my* bed, but the bed I've been sleeping in for three weeks in Amanda and Sally's basement.

"And he's still just sending pictures?" Sister Mary Margaret asks.

Even though she's all the way in San Salvador, she sounds so close. I forget sometimes, how far away I am from her. She was sort of like my boss, or maybe more like my mom. It's complicated. I call her every morning, from the phone that Sally and Amanda gave me. It's expensive, but I don't really have anyone else to call, especially since my stupid little brother doesn't want to talk to me.

I'll never be able to repay Sister Mary Margaret for all that she's done, so the least I can do is call her to check in.

"Have you tried to talk to him again?" she asks.

"Yeah, like, every day. I call and he just sits there on the other end of the line. It totally sucks, Sister. I can't keep doing this."

"Well, you don't have much of a choice now, do you, Phoenix?"

I keep my mouth shut. I know Sister Mary Margaret well enough to get that it wasn't really a question.

"You're just gonna have to *hacerse güevos* and keep trying."

Hacerse güevos roughly translates as "suck it up" in English. I guess that's not the sort of thing that nuns typically say, but Sister Mary Margaret isn't exactly a typical nun.

"Yeah, okay," I tell her. "I will."

"Well, keep your chin up," she says. "And call me tomorrow."

"All right," I say.

"And watch your language around Sally and Amanda, Phoenix. You can't go around telling your hosts that things 'suck.' Do you understand?"

This, coming from the nun who just told me to suck it up.

"Got it," I say.

I hang up the phone and look down at the drawing my brother, Ari, mailed to me.

It's all tropical—palm trees, ocean, dolphins jumping out. He drew it with a pen, on a piece of white paper, but I can sort-of see the red sunset, even without any color there. It looks good—especially the palm trees. They've even got coconuts hanging from them. I'm guessing central Texas doesn't have a whole lot of coconut palms, so I figure this is Ari's way of telling me he misses home.

Which makes me want to break his scrawny little neck, since it's kind of his fault we're in this situation in the first place. If he hadn't decided to go all badass, I'd be sitting in my sociology class right now, and he would be doing whatever kids back in Ilopango do these days to stay out of trouble.

But who am I kidding? The truth is, it's not really Ari's fault; it's mine. After our grandmother died, I was the only one he had to watch out for him. And then, when the head of my *colegio* told me I could go to the UCA—the university in San Salvador, and somebody else was gonna pay for it—all I could think of was how crazy the world is, how completely insane it was that I, Phoenix Flores Flores, who never knew his dad; whose mom took off to take care of somebody else's kids in Arizona; who lived the first thirteen years of his life with his grandmother in a concrete block house with no windows, that this same Phoenix Flores Flores was going to university? Even after all the stupid mistakes I made when I was Ari's age?

So I went. Of course I went. Who wouldn't go?

But Ari didn't go. He stayed back and had to fend for himself in our *barrio*. Sister Mary Margaret promised me that she would watch out for him, just like she had always watched out for me and the other guys who worked for her, but I guess she was getting too old or something. Maybe her eyesight was going, because a month into my little fantasy life, the one where I got to pretend I was the kind of person who went to university, she called to tell me that she had run into Ari at the community center, that he was sporting a big black eye and a broken wrist and telling anybody who asked how he was wasn't going down without a fight.

Stupid Ari thought he was gonna fight back. He thought he was a hero.

I knew what would come next, and I was not going to let that happen. So I went back there, and I got him. Kidnapped him, basically—my own brother—and we headed north. Ari fought me the whole way, telling me I should live my own stupid life, telling me that the *federales* were all over the neighborhood these days—that they would protect him. But I knew too much about the so-called protection offered by the federal police, and I wasn't gonna live with that on my conscience. So I dragged his scrawny ass all the way through Mexico. Ari punched me in the gut, like, twice a day the entire time I was hauling him toward the border. Kid's got a temper.

That's why it doesn't make any sense—what that lady told me on the phone a few days ago. Sally was out and Amanda was trying to teach me how to play a card game called solitaire. Yeah, it's pretty pathetic. I know so few people in this place that Amanda has been teaching me how to play cards with myself. I need to do *something* to keep from thinking about that girl I met in the garden—Gretchen. I *want* to think about her, but I know it's pointless to go there. Still, I can't figure out why I felt so jumpy around her—I mean, not in a bad way. It was like the way you feel when you know something good's about to happen. Like when you're a carefree little kid and it's the last day of school before Christmas holidays, and you keep looking at the clock in the back of your classroom, waiting for the holiday to start.

I don't know much, but I know that nothing good is gonna happen with that girl, because I'm probably never going to see her again. So feeling like that when I think about her is pointless.

Anyway, I was trying to distract myself, watching Amanda deal the cards, when this nice lady called me from that place where Ari is staying. She told me her name was Ms. Rosales, and that she was trying to help my brother. I'm pretty sure she called herself a social worker.

Anyway, she said that Ari seemed "lethargic," and she asked me whether he was "mute." I told her I didn't know what those words meant, so she started explaining in Spanish. She said, "Does he talk?" And I said, "*Yeah,* he talks. The kid won't shut up." Then her voice got all concerned and she told me he wouldn't speak a word. She said not to worry, that it was probably a result of the "trauma" he experienced while we were traveling through Mexico.

Not to worry. I feel like I'm gonna puke when I think about the "trauma"—or maybe the fact that I'm the one who made Ari leave home in the first place.

The thing is, it's supposed to work out for my brother. That's what the lawyers keep telling us. That's what I keep reminding myself. Those lawyers call Ari an "unaccompanied minor," which sort of pisses me off, since *I* "accompanied" his scrawny ass all the way through Guatemala and Mexico, kicking and screaming. Anyway, as long as Ari will tell some judge why we left and that our parents abandoned us a long time ago, he'll probably get permission to stay in America. That's pretty easy to do, since we haven't heard a thing from our so-called mom in, like, ten years, and we don't have a dad. We never did, neither one of us.

But what if Ari refuses to speak? Then what? How are they gonna let him stay if he won't even talk to them? He doesn't have to tell them *everything*, but they need to know *something*.

Sally shows up in the doorway. I don't know, maybe she was there all along, but she says something that makes me look up.

"A letter from Ari?"

"Yeah, well, a picture, really."

I turn it around to show her.

"Wow," she says. "He's a good artist."

I shrug. "Who knew?"

She takes the piece of paper from my hand and studies it. "Is that what it looks like there? I mean, in El Salvador?"

"Not in Ilopango, where we live," I say. "It kinda looks like a bomb dropped in the middle of town and nobody bothered to clean up the mess."

"Sounds charming." She comes to sit on the edge of the bed, still holding that piece of paper.

"The tags add color."

"Tags?"

"You know, like, gang tags. Graffiti. People mark their houses and stores and stuff with gang signs. That way, the gangs won't mess with them. At least, that's what they hope."

"Oh." Little creases run across her forehead. "It's really like that? I mean, I thought maybe they exaggerated it all—you know how the news can be."

"It's not like that everywhere," I say, leaning against the headboard. "But, yeah, in Ilopango. It's bad. There was, um, a truce a couple of years ago. I guess the gangs decided it would be a good idea to stop killing each other. My town was part of it, so things got better for a while but . . ."

"They're bad again?" She's tracing the edge of the paper with her finger, back and forth.

Worse than ever. "Yeah, the federal police got involved and, I mean, they're a little trigger-happy, you know?"

I'm pretty sure Sally doesn't know. She's from *England* for chrissake. I heard the cops there don't even carry guns.

"I'm sorry," Sally says, handing Ari's drawing back to me.

"Me too," I tell her. "But I shouldn't be so hard on my town. Ilopango's a pretty place. It's on a big lake with a volcano on the other side. I mean, not an active volcano, but, uh, it's nice—or it used to be."

"Are there beaches nearby?"

"Yeah," I say. "You can take the bus. I mean, it's only, like, an hour to La Libertad, on the coast."

"Do you like the beach?" she asks.

"Ari likes it more than I do." I close my eyes and think of Ari swimming out past the breakers in La Libertad. "He's all proud that he can swim. He rides the waves."

"Do you swim?"

"Barely." I figure with Sally I don't need to hide how much of a coward I am. She already knows my story—most of it, anyway. "I'm scared to death of those waves. They're big, and the current is strong. It's the Pacific."

"I'm like Ari." She leans back on her elbows and smiles. "I love to ride the waves. It's really quite brilliant—the water surging below you, and you sort of fly for a few seconds."

"Until you crash. And your face hits the sand."

"Well," Sally says, chuckling, "there's that. But you don't always crash. Sometimes the wave takes you right into shore and you land softly on the sand, the water washing around you. It's lovely."

She closes her eyes, all serene, like she's imagining it.

"I'm gonna take your word for it," I say.

"For now you are." Sally sits up straight and looks at me. "Since no ocean will be found within a few hundred miles of this place! Atlanta's so bloody landlocked."

"It doesn't matter." I take Ari's drawing and start to fold it so it will fit back into the envelope. "I'm happy here."

"Good," she says. She reaches over and grabs my other hand, squeezes it lightly. "We're so glad you're here, Phoenix. We feel lucky to have you."

"Yeah, you're lucky," I reply, nodding. "How else would you two get your community garden built for free?"

We both laugh, and it feels good.

"Speaking of that . . ." Sally stands up. "I need to stop gabbing and head over to the nursery for those plants. Are you up for it?"

"Sure," I say.

I decide not to put the drawing back into the envelope. Instead I walk over to the desk and pin it up on the empty corkboard.

"Can I—"

"Of course," Sally says. "It's your room, Phoenix."

And I guess it is, but not for long. I know the statistics. It's pretty much impossible for people like me to get permission to stay in the United States. Since I'm not a minor anymore, they told me I'm an "asylum seeker." That's the technical term. In the Atlanta court, where I'm heading soon, not a single person "seeking asylum" from all the stuff happening in El Salvador has been allowed to stay. Not a single one. I don't really expect to be the first. That's not my kind of luck.

CHAPTER NINE

GRETCHEN

KAREN PULLS SOME CHAIRS in from the hallway, and we all sit in a tight circle.

"Would you like a cup of tea?" she asks, heading toward an electric kettle shoved between several enormous piles of paper on her desk.

"Yes, thanks," Mom says. "That sounds lovely."

Lovely. None of this is lovely. This is all very unlovely.

Karen takes four mugs from a drawer and arranges them in a line.

"I'm the lead attorney in a federal criminal investigation of gang activity in Georgia." Her voice is serious, but she doesn't look at us now. She's fiddling with the mugs. "We are examining a major crime that took place in the Old Fourth Ward on August fourteenth, around eleven p.m. Our investigators found record of an assault robbery around the same time of the event, and we believe the two may be connected."

"You mean *my* assault robbery?"

I know that's me, asking the question. But I think I am beginning to have an out-of-body experience.

"Yes, Gretchen." Karen sits down and crosses her ankles. I focus on her feet, hoping to pull myself back into the conversation. She's wearing black heels that look like they've probably been in her closet since

1983. She offers me a piece of toffee from a cut-glass bowl on the coffee table. I unwrap the toffee and slowly put it into my mouth.

"Can you tell me in your own words what happened, Gretchen?"

"Well, I was leaving work, walking to my car. It was parked on the street. And a guy came up to me . . ."

And then what happened? The toffee sticks to my teeth, almost forcing my mouth shut, so I can't tell this nice woman how I felt that night. How I walked toward my car, on legs exhausted from a double shift at the restaurant. How I went alone through the dark August night. How humid the air felt—so humid that its heaviness pressed down on my bare shoulders. I didn't want to stop to get my mother half-and-half. I didn't want the smell of fried chicken clinging to my scalp. I needed a cold shower. I wanted to drink a kombucha. I was too tired, even, to text Adam and ask him to meet me at my house. I wanted Netflix and air conditioning. I wanted my feet up on three pillows. I wanted *rest*.

I do not want to tell this nice woman how I was halfway to my car, the only car left parked against the curb. I don't want to tell Karen how I had been late to work twelve hours earlier, how I had barely squeezed my economy car into the only remaining spot on this now-abandoned street. I do not want to tell her how I heard him first, his feet pounding, and how I turned to see him running toward me, with crazed eyes. How my legs launched into a run, trying to close the distance to the car.

I didn't see his body when it slammed against my back. I only felt it, hurling us both to the ground. And then he pressed my face against the cracked sidewalk and wrenched my hands above my head. I felt his knee in my back, smelled his stale breath, warm against my cheek. He dug his hand into my pockets, and I freaked. I felt his hand near my crotch, and I knew he would try to pull off my pants. I bit his arm and he flinched. My red lipstick smeared across his forearm. I saw it there, part of me on him. That's when I tried to break free. I flipped my body over and struggled to stand. He punched me in the gut. I was on the ground, lying on my side, folded over myself. He kicked me, maybe twice, until I was flat on my stomach. Then he dug through my pockets.

"Please don't hurt me," I heard myself beg quietly, over and over.

I think what I really wanted to say was, *Oh please, God, don't rape me. Please don't.* He was on top of me again, holding me down with his body while his hands roved. I could see his face, his smooth skin and his wide brown eyes. I couldn't look away, because his eyes looked terrified. They looked as scared as I felt.

"Be still," he said. "Don't make me hurt you."

I squirmed, feeling his hands there.

"I don't want to hurt you. I need money."

Could that be true? I wished I'd had a purse so he could just take it and go, but my money was shoved into my front pockets. Tips— ones and fives, split with the waitstaff. He pulled my phone from my pocket and threw it aside. He found the cash and pulled me to my feet.

"Leave," he said. "Run!"

And then he was gone. Just like that. I watched him sprint away, a wad of my money in his hand.

He told me to run. *Why did he tell me to run?* I could not run. Everything hurt. I wasn't even sure I could stay on my feet. I reached for my phone.

"Gretchen?" My father's hand is on my knee now. I am back in the prosecutor's office, staring out the window, onto the wasteland.

My dad speaks my name again, softly. "Gretchen?" His arm wraps around my shoulders, and my mom leans toward me, holding a steaming cup of tea. The prosecutor looks down at her hands, waiting patiently. She must have poured the tea. The water must have boiled already. I still taste toffee in my mouth, stuck between my teeth. I think it's coconut flavored. Yes, coconut. It smells like suntan lotion.

"Is this too much, Gretchen?" my dad asks. He looks so tired and sad. It's his eyes. I think maybe his eyes are telling me that it's too much for *him*, that he can't bear the thought of hearing it again.

Karen gives me a cup of tea. I take it and wrap my hands around the mug. It feels warm but not hot. I'm not sure I can speak, but I do.

"No," I say quietly. "I'm fine."

My mother stands and walks toward the window. She looks out over the abandoned track and sips her tea.

"He came up to you and what happened, Gretchen?" Karen asks.

"He took my money," I say. "I had cash in my pocket—tips—and he took them out and ran away. That's all."

A lie. I lie to my mom, staring out the window. I lie to my dad, gripping my knee. I lie to the nice prosecutor, Karen, and to myself. I lie because there's *more*. This isn't even the most disturbing part, the part I've forbidden myself to think about or acknowledge. The part I can't even tell myself.

"What exactly do you need from my daughter, Ms. Wells?" my mom asks, her consonants clipped. She is still looking away from us.

"I'd like for you to describe the man who attacked you," Karen says. "Please know I wouldn't do this without a very good reason."

I know his face so well. I'm not even sure the English language contains enough words to describe every little detail—all the things I see when I imagine him back into being. *How sick is that?*

I sip my tea and begin. "He was Latino; I guess light to medium skinned. He looked pretty young. His face was against mine for a minute, and it was smooth." *God, that sounds messed up.* "I mean, he didn't have whiskers or any facial hair. His hair was cut really short, like a buzz cut, and it was dark. Black hair."

The tea is mint. It tastes good. I want to stop talking and drink the tea. I want to think about the other face I've memorized—Phoenix's face. I want to remind myself how different it was from the face of that boy, of how stupid I was to think he might be that boy. I want to see Phoenix again, smiling, his finger touching the edge of his lip.

Yes. I will think about this. I will breathe, and I will think about sitting on a pile of wood in that torn-up field that's supposed to become a garden. I will think about leaning against his side and I will breathe.

"Gretchen?"

I look up.

"This is good," Karen says. "Can you tell me more?"

"Like, what, exactly?"

"What about his build?"

I push away the image of Phoenix and return to the memory I so desperately want to avoid. "He was tall, about my height," I say. "And thin but not skinny, you know, just sort of healthy looking, I guess. He was strong."

I think maybe I am starting to shiver. I try to feel the warmth of the tea, moving through my hands and into my body. I lift the cup to take a sip, but my hand is shaking so violently that I worry the tea will spill.

My dad reaches over to steady my grip. "I think that's enough," he says to Karen.

My face feels wet and cold. I think maybe I am crying.

"I understand that this is difficult, Mr. Ashland. If Gretchen could just tell me what she recalls about his clothing—"

"That's easy," I say, determined to go on. "He was wearing a bright-blue football jersey, with a number on it. Someone had drawn on the shirt with a marker. Black letters. And I think I told the police this, but he had a homemade tattoo on his finger. It was a four-leaf clover." I actually thought about that—how he had an unlucky number on his jersey and a symbol of luck tattooed on his hand. It's so messed up, that I thought all of these things. That I still think of all these things, all the time.

Karen nods while I wipe my eyes. I can't even look at my dad. His pain is washing toward me in waves. I think he feels like he should have been able to protect me, like it's all his fault.

"We may have a match," she says. "But we need to be certain."

The prosecutor stands and walks toward her computer. She clicks around for a bit, and then she turns to look at me.

"I'm going to show you a photograph, Gretchen. I want to warn you that this may be disturbing. I need for you to tell me whether this is the man who assaulted you."

And then he is there, on the screen in front of me, his eyes wide open and lifeless, his blue football jersey pushed up around his neck and the skin of his chest marked with a black tattoo—an ugly, gnarled hand, ring finger curled in toward the palm. Thumb tucked. Two fingers stretch out like horns, long sharp fingernails at their tip. The nails are black.

The tattoo is riddled with tiny bullet holes.

"It's a gang sign." Karen is pointing at the tattoo. She keeps talking, naming some combination of letters and numbers, but I'm not really hearing her anymore. "This particular gang was founded in Los Angeles by immigrants from El Salvador. It's everywhere now—all over the United States and Central America."

I'm trying so hard to focus on her words.

"They're notoriously brutal, but they usually only target members of other gangs—or deserters. The young man in this photo, he was seventeen—a Salvadoran immigrant. He came to Atlanta as a young child. He didn't have a criminal record—"

I close my eyes, wanting to push away the image. Her words are faraway, so faraway.

"Which is why your case is baffling us a little. I mean—"

"Oh God," I finally say, feeling my body start to shiver again. "They killed him."

My mom lurches toward the computer. "This is enough—this is too much," she says, planting her body between me and that terrible image. "Gretchen needs to leave *now*."

"Who killed him?" the prosecutor asks.

I can't speak. My legs curl into my chest and I close my eyes. Even with my eyes closed, though, I am still staring at the bullet-riddled chest of my attacker. Why isn't there blood? And the holes, they are so small, scattered across his bare chest, across the gruesome hand tattooed there. Long, gnarled fingers. Sharp nails.

He is dead. How did I not know this? Except I think I did know this. *Oh God. I knew this. I know this.*

"What do you mean, Gretchen?" Karen says. "Who killed him?"

"Those people," I say. "They shot him."

I feel my dad's hand on my back, rubbing in small circles. I try to imagine it—the look of my father's hand on my back. But all I see is *his* hand, *his* face, *his* chest. And then I remember the sounds.

Pop. Pop. Pop. So loud.

I can't breathe.

"My daughter has nothing to do with this," I hear my mom say loudly.

Pop. Pop. Pop. Ringing in my ears. I hear those sounds, like they're happening here and now. But I know this isn't happening. None of it is happening. It is six months later. But those tiny black holes across his chest. Those lifeless eyes. That terrible, awful tattoo. I see them now. I can't *not* see them.

"She has been through enough already," my mom whispers.

And then I am gasping for air, and my dad is lifting me from the chair, cradling me in his arms like I'm a child, rocking me back and forth, heading quickly for the door.

I have not turned a corner.

CHAPTER TEN

PHOENIX

AMANDA IS IN THE KITCHEN. I can hear her moving around, opening and closing cabinets. It smells pretty good, too, like she's baking. I come up the basement stairs and watch her pull two eggs from the refrigerator. She's wearing a fitted shirt and the same faded-out jeans she wears almost every day. Her bright-red clogs make loud thuds across the floor. Those shoes are weird—huge and chunky. I only know they're called clogs because Amanda's always calling out to Sally, "Sweetums, have you seen my clogs?"

It's weird, how Sally always knows where to find those shoes.

Amanda cracks an egg into a bowl. Then she turns to look at me though her red-rimmed glasses. Who knows? Maybe she bought them to match the clogs.

"I'm going out for a little while," I tell her.

She looks at me all funny—probably because she doesn't think I'm capable of going anywhere on my own. But I start to worry that maybe she sees right through me—that she can tell I don't want her to know what I'm up to.

"Where?"

"I just thought I'd wander around a little," I say, looking away from her quickly. I suck at lying. That's why I stay so quiet most of the time.

I grab a piece of paper from the printer. "I found a bus schedule."

"Do you want some company?" she asks. "I'm just finishing up in here."

Yeah, I want company. But I was thinking maybe a girl with everything eyes and orange-yellow hair, not my fifty-year-old guardian in red clogs. I really wish I could get Gretchen out of my head. It's not like I'm thinking of her in a dirty way, or anything. But I can't stop thinking about her—how her hair smelled like soap and honey and almost-too-ripe pineapple, and how her skin felt so warm through that enormous sweater.

"Thanks, but, uh, I—"

"I understand," Amanda says. "Do you need some money?"

Mierda. How did I not even think about that?

"Yeah." I nod. "I guess I do. I mean, for the bus and all."

Amanda walks over to her purse, which is sitting on the counter by her car keys, and pulls a twenty-dollar bill from her wallet. Seeing her with that twenty makes me think of my grandmother. I wonder what Abuela would think now. Of me, taking a twenty from a lady I barely even know, living in her house, eating her food, not doing a thing to repay her.

I take the twenty.

"Thanks," I say. "I'm gonna pay you back for all of this."

"Please don't worry, Phoenix," she says, looking at me with gentle eyes. "It's nothing. Really."

And maybe for her it's nothing. But to me, it's everything.

Riding the bus is crazy. The routes are really complicated, and I have to change three times. It takes, like, an hour and a half to get to where I'm going, even though it's only a few kilometers away from Amanda and Sally's house. I walk a couple of blocks through this town called Acworth, looking for a place called Georgia Boyz.

I learned about Georgia Boyz from the Internet. It was easy—I just searched "tattoo removal in Atlanta" and this YouTube video popped up. It was like a news show, or something, and the reporter was interviewing this big white guy who looked like he was in a motorcycle gang. The guy said he had a free tattoo-removal program for ex-convicts who want to start over.

"Because of the road I traveled, I want to help them out. I just want to give people a second chance." That's what he said on the news show. I'm not a convict—not exactly—but right about now, starting my life over sounds pretty damn good.

The streets here are empty, and the sidewalks are all busted up. Still, the neighborhood doesn't look so bad, not compared to what I've seen. I mean, a few of the stores could use a fresh coat of paint, but at least it doesn't smell like piss.

Then I see the sign: GEORGIA BOYZ. Next to the words is the shape of a naked woman, kinda like the ones you see on all those eighteen-wheel trucks on the Pan-American Highway. I'm feeling glad that Amanda didn't come along. I'm pretty sure this place wouldn't go over well with her.

I stand there for a minute, looking at the sign. A rough-looking white guy with a shaved head comes out of the place with a bleach-blond woman. She probably isn't much older than I am, but she looks a little spent. I'm starting to wonder whether people like this are gonna help a brown-skinned guy from El Salvador. I mean, I don't wanna judge, but they look like the type of people who join those crazy-ass white supremacy groups.

But what the hell? I have to try. So I head through the door before I lose my nerve.

The room is small, and it smells like rubbing alcohol. The walls are painted in bright colors that don't really seem to go together. The big guy from the YouTube video is standing over a woman with a needle in his hand.

"Shut the fuckin' door," he says. "It's cold out there."

It's not all that cold, but I turn around and shut the door.

Nobody says anything. He goes back to inking the woman's arm.

I watch him work, his tattooed arm moving the needle across her skin. I'm sorry, but the dude has about ten more piercings on his face than anyone should have. There's a shelf behind the big black chair where she's sitting. It has a jar of candy on it. Lollipops, I think. I wonder about those lollipops—does he give them to his clients when he's finished, like the nurse used to do for kids at the free clinic in Ilopango?

After a long time he stops and glances up at me. "Well?" he asks. He has a really strange accent. "What do you want, boy?"

I feel like a boy, suddenly—like I'm back in my *abuela*'s house and she's giving me shit for forgetting to feed the chickens.

"Um, I heard that you remove tattoos."

"Yeah, okay," he says. "You heard right. But for ex-cons. You're not an ex-con."

"Uh—I—" I stare past them, at that jar of lollipops.

"Check him out, Barbie," he says to the woman in the chair.

She turns and looks at me. "Nah, Bo," she says. "Too sweet." That woman is big. Aside from her face, most of her body is covered in ink.

"Barbie and me," he says, "we know what being behind bars does to a person."

I shrug, feeling like an idiot.

"You ain't been behind bars, kid." He looks down at her and smiles. "Ain't that right, sweetie?"

Barbie nods and smiles at him, all gooey. I take two slow steps toward them, my arms still crossed.

"Detention. I was in detention," I say, wishing I didn't have to prove to this guy that I deserve to get my tattoo removed.

He squints his already squinty eyes. "Where you from?"

"El Salvador," I say.

"Figured." He puts the needle back into its cradle. "Either that or Honduras." He says Honduras really weird. Like *Hon-duuurrrus*. He stands up and wipes one hand on his grungy jeans. "I've heard some messed-up stories 'bout those places."

I sort of want to stand up for my country, to tell him about the old colonial towns beside big blue volcanic lakes, about the beautiful beaches and rain forests, about all the cool birds. Or maybe I could tell him about all the brave people who fought during our civil wars, the martyrs and stuff. But I don't say anything. Because, *puta madre*, look where all their sacrifice got me.

"I need this," I whisper. I hate the way my voice sounds, scared and weak.

"I already said it, El Salvador. If you ain't served time, I don't take off the tat."

I'm not sure how being in that hellhole of a detention facility doesn't count as serving time, but I don't want to talk about all of that. "Look," I say. "I want to pay you, but I don't have any money."

"Sucks for you." He goes over to an ink-stained sink and washes his hands.

"Yeah, okay."

I turn around and open the door to leave. But then I feel my eyes begin to water. A hot lump tightens in my throat. It might seem stupid, to cry over a tattoo, but this isn't some lame-ass heart with an old girlfriend's name in it or something. It's way more complicated than that. *Coño*, how is it possible that some black ink on brown skin makes me part of a group? It doesn't make me a part of anything.

I'll never forget how it felt, when we all showed up at the hellhole. The guards at that detention facility made all two hundred of us take off our clothes, down to our boxers, and then they sorted us. They looked at the marks on our bodies and they sorted us into groups, like a bunch of cows, or something. Not a single one of those guards spoke Spanish, so they made me translate for them—they made me tell all those guys that they were doing it to keep people safe, to keep the gangs from fighting inside.

Those guards—they thought they knew who I was, because of a stupid tattoo. But a few lines carved into some skin will never, *never* be enough to send me back into that brutal world. I will die before I go back. I am more sure of that than I have ever been of anything. But until I get this thing removed from my body, anyone who sees it will think I'm one of them. They'll think they know me, but they don't.

I am *nothing* like those people. I am covered in skin.

I swipe my hands across my eyes, suck in a deep breath, and turn around.

"Maybe I can help out around here. I mean, sweep and stuff." I look right at him, watching his pierced eyebrows arch high. "And I'm good at building things. Fixing things."

He chuckles. "You lookin' for a job, boy? Cuz I ain't hirin'."

The big woman in the chair laughs too. "Damn straight he's not hiring. We're flat broke already."

"You don't have to pay me." I shrug. "Actually, you can't pay me. It's kind of against the law."

"Check it out, sugar!" Bo says. "I got myself a volunteer. I'm like the friggin' Salvation Army or somethin'."

I don't say anything, because I haven't got a clue what the Salvation Army is—and also because my eyes are starting to water again, and I'm afraid my voice will crack if I talk.

Barbie is watching me closely. Her face gets all soft, like sad or something. Then she tugs on Bo's arm.

"Give us a sec, hon," she says to me.

I watch as she hauls herself out of the chair. They walk over to a junky blue desk, where Bo keeps an appointment book that looks as old and worn as he is. She whispers something in his ear and then he wraps his arms around her waist, resting his hands on her ass. She gives him a big wet kiss. I'm starting to feel embarrassed. Like maybe they're about to go at it right here.

Barbie gives Bo a nudge, and then he turns toward me, looking me up and down, real careful. "All right, El Salvador. You know how to replace a faucet?"

"Yeah."

He heads over to a door in the back. The paint is chipping off, and the hinges stick when he tries to open it. He tugs harder and reveals a storage closet. It's a disaster in there. Looks like a hurricane blew through. He digs around for a while and then pulls out a shiny new faucet with the handles attached.

Easy. I've done this a dozen times.

"Have at it," he says, nodding toward a big sink in the corner.

"Thanks, man." I say. I want to say more, but I can tell he doesn't want me to gush all over him.

It doesn't take long to replace the faucet. I do the work quietly, mostly keeping my head down. But every once in a while I look up. I can't help it. Above the sink, there's a wall of tattoo designs, all displayed in flimsy black frames. They're drawn with black pen on white paper. All kinds of stuff—hearts and birds and dragons. They're really good. I wonder if Bo drew them.

When I finish, I set the old faucet on the counter.

"Done," I tell him. "Want me to clean out that closet for you?"

Bo shrugs. "Why the hell not?"

I go back over to the closet and pull everything off the sagging shelves. Paper towels and nails and sandpaper. Rusted-out tools and ink and needles. I find a toolbox that's in decent shape. I take out a hammer and the least rusty nails I can dig out. I use the nails to secure the shelves back into place. Then I get a roll of paper towels and clean up all the dust. I put everything back, trying to arrange it in a way that makes sense. When I'm almost done, Bo walks over and looks in, over my shoulder.

"Not bad."

I turn away from the closet and start gathering up the dirty paper towels. I find a garbage can and throw them in. It's really full, so I go ahead and pull the bag out.

"Where do I take this?"

"I got it." Bo grabs the bag from me. "Let's see the thing," he says.

"What?"

"The tat."

"Oh." I feel my heart starting to beat faster. "Yeah, okay," I say quietly.

I lift up my shirt and push the waistband of my jeans down, far enough for most of it to show. I hate this fucking thing. *Christ, how I hate it.* I'm guessing he won't know what it means, though—what it's supposed to say about me.

Bo puts down the garbage bag and pulls on my skin a little.

"Yeah," he says. "I seen that one. You're gonna want to get rid of it fast, El Salvador."

I nod, looking down at my shoes, trying not to let my eyes go watery again. I guessed wrong.

"And you're done with those assholes?"

I look right at him. "*So* done."

"And they're not gonna come lookin' for you or nothin', right?"

"Not here." I shake my head.

"'Cuz I gotta watch out for my girl over there, and we've got two kids at home who mean the world to us. You understand, don't you? A man's gotta protect his family."

I nod, but I can't say anything because my throat has this huge lump in it. *God, why am I such a wuss?*

He shoves me gently on the shoulder and grins. "Dude wasn't much of an artist, was he?"

"Nah." I look up at him, feeling grateful that he doesn't say more, or maybe relieved that he doesn't seem afraid of me.

"I'll take care of it," he says. "Lemme see the top."

I lift my shirt higher. I watch as he examines the gnarled hand that spreads across my abdomen, the black nails on each thin finger, two of them curled, and the other two reaching up toward my heart.

Coño, *that is one ugly tattoo.*

"You'll need a few rounds, and I'm warning you, El Salvador, it hurts like hell."

"I can handle it," I say. "I'll come for a while to help you out, and then you can start. I mean, I wanna earn it first, okay?"

"All right, kid. Whatever you say."

"But I need to have it done before April fourteenth."

"That when you turn into a pumpkin?"

I think he might be talking about the princess story, *Cenicienta.* So I go ahead and try a response.

"Yeah, I don't think anyone's comin' to look for me with one of those glass shoes."

"Christ, don't I know it?" he says.

And then that girl Gretchen is showing up in my head again. I don't really dance—but if she wrapped me up in her arms, I'm pretty damn sure I wouldn't run away at the stroke of midnight.

Bo gives me a jab on the shoulder, the nice kind. "What's your name, anyway?"

"Phoenix."

"Well, lemme tell you something, Phoenix: you gotta make your own happy ending."

CHAPTER ELEVEN

GRETCHEN

OBVIOUSLY I AM TRYING to *pretend* I have turned a corner, because, not three hours after staring a dead boy in the face, I am back in Bree's car, on the way to a basketball game. A basketball game! *Why?* To convince my parents that I am fine. To prove to them that I do not need to go back to the creepy psychiatrist who drugged me.

When we got home from Karen's office, Mom told me it was actually better—knowing he wasn't out there anymore. Knowing he couldn't hurt me again. I said yeah, because I needed for her to think I was okay. I kept saying it: "Yeah, I feel better."

Then she started talking about acupuncture, and how she was going to make an appointment with someone in Duluth named Li Kang. I have absolutely no problem with acupuncture, in theory. I understand entirely the long and significant history of Chinese medicinal traditions. I respect them. Really, I do.

But those needles are *long*.

So I made myself put on a little mascara from a new tube that Bree bought for me. I even put on clear lip gloss. And before I left the house, when my dad told me that we should maybe talk to the prosecutor again when I was feeling stronger, that we should help her get "those people" off the streets, I told him, "Yeah, I'll feel stronger soon. I want to help."

———

As soon as Bree and I get out of her car and start walking toward the gym, it is 100 percent clear to me that I am not feeling better. I am feeling like a nutcase. And I am not feeling stronger. I am feeling weak and alone.

"You can do this, Gretch." Bree is walking beside me.

I head down the sidewalk with my best friend for life. She has her arm around me, like she's holding me up, or maybe to remind me that she's *here* for me, that she's not going anywhere. I don't want to lose her, but I'm worried I will. Or maybe I'm worried she will lose me—that she already *has* lost me.

We enter a gym filled with hundreds of people. A few of Bree's friends come up to say hi, and I say hi back, but I'm not really here at all. I'm observing it through a thick fog, like I'm half awake but still mostly in a dream. We climb the stairs and shove ourselves into a row of bleachers, next to a bunch of kids I barely know. When I was actually going to high school here, I basically only hung out with Adam and his friends, and they all graduated last year. Besides Bree, there's really no one left for me in this place.

"There he is," Bree says, pointing toward a guy running out onto the court.

"Who?"

"Ty. See? He's number twenty-six."

"Oh," I say.

Before tonight I had been to exactly two-and-a-quarter basketball games. The ones before the winter formal. And last year Adam and I bailed after about ten minutes and went to see a concert.

God, that was a perfect night. Just the two of us at the Tabernacle. He was still in his tux shirt and pants and I had on a strapless black dress. We were up on the balcony, screaming and clapping, singing along. We both knew every word to every song. When the lead singer came running up to the balcony, he passed right by us. We both reached out to touch him, and he looked right at us, sang the words to our favorite song. He leaned out over the crowd below and we leaned in toward him. His bodyguards didn't even stop us when we reached out to hold him up. Adam and I, we kept him from falling over the edge, and he sang his heart out, for us.

It was so loud in there that when we left, our ears were buzzing. I could barely hear a word Adam said the rest of the night, but it didn't matter. We walked over to Centennial Park in the freezing cold. We lay down on the grass, and he wrapped us both in his enormous quilted coat. We had bought it together that afternoon, at our favorite thrift store. It still smelled like the back of someone else's closet. But we didn't care.

The stars were astounding that night—so many of them. We never see stars in Atlanta, because of all the smog. So it felt like we had gone somewhere else, somewhere perfect.

"Your boy's got the ball!"

Someone I vaguely recognize is leaning across my lap to talk to Bree.

Bree shifts forward in her seat and then—honest to God—she starts to clap and bounce up and down and cheer for "her boy."

I don't think anyone has ever called Adam "my boy." He's not really the kind of person who belongs to someone else. Or maybe I'm not the kind of person who has someone belong to me.

Earlier this afternoon, after I got home from Karen's office, I wanted to call Adam. I felt like I should tell him about the photo of my attacker, and his bullet-ridden chest. I tried, twice. But I couldn't push call. I think I was afraid he would ask the question he always asks. He would say, *Are you okay?* and I would lie to him, the way I always do. I didn't have the energy for more lies, so I never called.

It doesn't matter, I tell myself. *He's coming to see you tomorrow night. You can tell him everything when you're together.*

Or not, because I probably won't.

And then I remember how completely normal it felt to tell

Phoenix—a stranger!—about that night, and the half-and-half, and the way it feels to panic. Maybe there's a name for this, like, a syndrome or something. Maybe it's totally typical to talk like that to perfect strangers when you're in my condition. Or maybe it was just him, the way he made me feel okay about being a mess, the way he listened to me instead of telling me I'd eventually get better.

I wonder where Phoenix is, and if I'll see him again. I also sort of wonder if I'll ever find a reason to hug him again, because he felt so *solid*. And that was good.

I nudge Bree, who's still jumping up and down and clapping. I'm starting to worry she might bust into a full-on cheer, spelling out *defense* with her arms or something.

"I'm going to get some popcorn," I say. "You want anything?"

"A Coke. Thanks."

Then she returns to bouncing and yelling and clapping.

It's a relief to stand in line by myself. I keep my head down and move forward slowly, and when I get to the front, I order a Coke, a bottle of water, and a large popcorn. It feels like a triumph, standing in line alone, ordering food and paying for it. I'm breathing steadily, I'm smiling at the cashier—some nice mom who is volunteering at the concession stand to raise money for the booster club. I don't know her, and I'm grateful for that.

"Enjoy the game!" she says brightly.

I smile and turn away from the counter. The popcorn smells like salt and butter and that weird orange oil that looks gross but tastes fabulous. I'm trying to figure out how to get a handful of it into my mouth while navigating through all of these people with two drinks balanced in my arms.

Then the horns start up. It must be halftime. Or is that football? Is there a halftime in basketball? That's what I'm thinking when it happens.

Pop. Pop. Pop.

Three loud thuds, reverberating through the gym. Suddenly I'm struggling to focus on the path back to the bleachers, back to Bree.

Pop. Pop. Pop.

But my heart is racing and my eyes are blurring and I'm not in the concession area anymore. I feel the taste of metal on my tongue, and the blood, hot and red, is seeping into my eyes. I'm back in the Old Fourth Ward, on that empty street, reaching across the asphalt for my phone, trying to make sense of what that boy told me.

Run!

I hear the squeal of tires, and a car is coming around the corner, fast. It's full, beyond full. Two Latino guys are hanging out of the windows—maybe three. And there's a white girl with dyed-red hair sitting on someone's lap.

God, how many people are in that car?

I run. I stumble toward my own car and crouch behind the rear wheel. I watch the boy, sprinting fast. His chest pushes forward, his arms pump hard and his legs stretch out long. His face is looking up at the sky, and he's calling out, begging. He's crying out to heaven, and I'm crying too—sobbing. He turns the corner and I watch through the blood and tears as he sprints away from me.

I see a man lift himself from the sunroof of the car. His skin and hair are almost the same color as my attacker's, but he's wearing red, not blue, and he is not a boy. He is a man. I watch his tattooed arm extend. I see the black handgun, so small, pointing toward the boy, toward the place where he disappeared from my view. I see the girl with the dyed-red hair screaming and tugging at the man's waist from inside the car, trying to pull him back in. I see the car take that corner, fast. I hear the sound.

Pop. Pop. Pop. And then a girl screams.

I do not know whether it is her voice or mine.

CHAPTER TWELVE

PHOENIX

PART TWO OF SALLY AND AMANDA'S plan to keep me from getting "depressed": American basketball. They decided this morning at breakfast, over scrambled eggs and this really amazing apple-flavored sausage. Amanda said football would be better—for the whole American experience and all—but unfortunately, it's not football season. Plus, their neighbor's son plays on the basketball team and he's about to graduate. I guess they've been promising his mom they'll go to a game and cheer for him, and time is running out.

Sally said they'd kill two birds with one stone, take me out to see how the "Yanks" spend their Friday nights *and* appease the neighbors. Amanda told Sally that she hated that expression, about killing birds. She said it was so violent. But she agreed with Sally that they needed to get me out of the house.

Then they both looked at me really carefully and Amanda asked if I was feeling "down."

I told them, *again*, that I'm not depressed! That I'm not even close! But they ignored me and pressed on with their master plan.

Which is fine by me. I've got nothing else to do. Plus, I figured it might be cool to see a real American high school, just like in all those movies.

This place, though, it's nothing like the movies. I mean, there is a big fancy gym, and there are basketball players and even cheerleaders, but the gym is half empty, and the basketball team is a joke. Even I can tell they pretty much suck, and I have no idea what's going on out there. Not a clue.

I pretend to pay attention to the game, but instead I watch all the people. There are a few families in the bleachers around us, with moms and dads and little kids, all sitting together, having fun. I like watching them.

But the game is a blowout. When the score gets to 56–24, Sally suggests maybe I should try an American hot dog.

We're standing in the concession line together when the horns start up. They sound pretty great, actually.

"What's going on?" I ask, turning toward the sound.

"Halftime. Must be the other team's pep band," Amanda replies. "Ours never sounded this good."

I motion toward the gym. "Can I go check it out?"

"Sure," says Sally. "We'll get your hot dog and meet you over there."

It is amazing—a bunch of people standing together in the bleachers, swaying together and blowing on their horns. Then the drums start, these huge-ass drums hanging from guys' necks. They are beating the crap out of them, with enormous sticks.

Pop. Pop. Pop.

The sound fills up the stadium. You can probably hear it all the way back in Ivywood Estates.

Pop. Pop. Pop.

I feel those drums in my gut.

I turn around to motion to Sally. I figure she needs to see this, since she is from England and all, and I'm pretty sure this stuff doesn't happen in England, either.

"Sally," I call out. "Check it—"

But it isn't Sally who I see. It's Gretchen—the girl from the garden. She's pushing her way out of a long line. A water bottle falls from under her arm, and she doesn't even notice. She's still holding a huge bag of popcorn and a large fountain soda. Her eyes are really wide, and she is elbowing people out of the way. She runs into some kid, and then she drops the popcorn. He tries to pick it up and give it back to her, but she keeps moving.

Then she screams, loud.

Everyone is stepping aside and staring. It's like she's in her own little world. And it is not a happy world.

I walk toward her, very slowly, but she doesn't see me, even though she's looking right at me. I keep moving toward her, while everyone else moves away. By now she's sort of half bent over, and heaving.

Madre de Dios.

I stand in front of her for a few seconds, my arms held up, like in surrender, like someone is pointing a gun at me. Eventually she looks up. I put my hands on her shoulders, and she blinks. Her hand opens and she drops the drink. Coke splatters across the floor and a bunch of people step back. She stares at the floor, puzzled, like she can't figure out why there's a big brown puddle spreading at our feet. Then she looks into my eyes, and that crazy beautiful girl, she throws her arms around me.

I hug her as she shoves her face into my chest. I pull her in tight, trying not to worry about all the strangers staring at us. There's an old white lady with silver hair digging through her purse. She pulls out her phone and starts to fumble with it, like she's ready to call the police or something. I'm starting to worry that all these people think I'm trying to hurt Gretchen, not help her.

They know I'm not from here. They think I don't belong. I can see it in the way they're looking at us. *We've gotta get out of here.*

I lean back a little and whisper, "Let's go outside. You need fresh air."

The insane drums are still going, and my heart is beating out of my chest, but I think Gretchen still hears me through it all. She lets me take her hand, still cool and soft. I pull her around the spilled drink and through the crowds. I want to yell at everyone who is staring at her to mind their own fucking business, but I look down at the ground and watch our feet move forward, one step at a time. Because if I do what I want to do, if I shove them all away, if I take a swing at the stupid kid in a hoodie who is pointing at her and laughing, I'll probably get arrested. And then it will all be shot to hell.

All of it pretty much is shot to hell already, but at least there is still some tiny sliver of hope that things can work out, that Gretchen will be okay, that I can really be *meant* to be here.

When we're alone outside, she shoves her face back into my chest. "I need you closer," she says.

She actually says that to me. I let myself hold her closer, even though I know I shouldn't. Because my heart is beating like crazy, and I know she can hear it. And then, after I don't know how long, we're sitting together on the curb and I have my arm around her shoulders. She's finally breathing normally.

"So, yeah," she says, smiling weakly at me. "That was a panic attack."

I laugh. I mean I really laugh, doubled over and all.

"Thanks for making that clear," I say.

She leans her head on my shoulder and I squeeze her a little. "Do you feel better?"

"I guess," she says. She turns those blue-green eyes away from me and starts to cry, really soft. *Christ,* I hate the sound of it. "I just need to get out of my head, you know?"

Yeah. I know.

"Wanna hear a funny story?" I nudge her.

"Sure," she says.

"Okay. So I'm afraid of heights—like, terrified."

"Really?" she asks, turning to face me.

"Yeah, really," I tell her.

"Have you always been scared of heights?"

"Nah. When I was a kid, some asshole used to pick me up by my feet and hold me out over the roof of a building. You know, to scare me. I pissed in my pants—no joke. And ever since then—"

"That's horrible, Phoenix."

"It wasn't all that bad," I say. "Well, I mean, pissing myself—that was bad."

She laughs. Which is awesome.

"Yeah, so the first time I flew in a plane, it was to come here, and there were all these guys sitting near me. The plane was packed."

I don't tell her that we were all handcuffed—like criminals, even though none of us were. I know she'd freak out about that—in her present condition.

"And when the plane took off, I couldn't breathe. Honest to Christ, I thought I was gonna die."

"Seriously?" she asks.

"Yeah. I stood up and started screaming, like at the top of my lungs. I was all, like, 'Let me off! Get me off this thing!' and all the guys around me were laughing their asses off."

"Oh my God." She pulls away and looks up at me. "What happened?"

"I shoved my way into the aisle and started sprinting toward that door at the front of the plane, and everybody on the plane was going crazy, laughing." I shake my head, remembering how bad it was. "And there were these, like, guards, and they came and tackled me."

"That's *insane*," she tells me. "You could have been arrested."

I shrug, because I have no idea how to respond to that. There's more I should say. I know that—I'm not a *total* idiot. But I don't want Gretchen to be afraid of me. Because there's nothing for her to be afraid of. I'm pretty sure she will be, if she hears any more of my story. So I leave it alone, at least for now.

"You know," she says, with a crooked smile, "you probably should have eaten some *pupusas* before you got on that plane. It might have calmed you down."

"Yeah," I say. "A couple of *pupusas de loroco* would have done the trick."

"Are those, like, the super-special-calming variety?" She leans back into me and I wrap my arm around her again.

"Nah," I tell her, squeezing her shoulder. "They're just my favorite kind. They're stuffed with cheese and these tiny flowers, called *loroco*. I'm pretty sure you don't have those flowers around here."

Damn. I'm dying for one of those things, hot off the *comal*. I can almost taste it, sitting out here freezing my ass off in a parking lot in Georgia.

People start pouring out of the gym, so I guess the game is over. We watch them going out to their cars for a while, and then Amanda and Sally find us sitting there on the curb. I try to introduce them to Gretchen, but it turns out they already know her. Something about Gretchen's mom working at their wedding. They're hugging like old friends and talking and I'm not really paying that much attention, because I'm starting to get pissed about all the people walking by, pointing and staring at Gretchen. I can tell she's trying to ignore them, but it's not easy.

Sally and Amanda head off to get the car, and Gretchen leans in toward me.

"So how long have you lived with Sally and Amanda?" she asks.

"About a month, I think." I'm starting to worry about what they told her, and how I'll explain it all. I really don't want to explain any of it—not to Gretchen.

"They said they're like your guardians for a while, until you get permanent residency?"

"Yeah." Something like that, I guess. "They've been great."

The kid with the hoodie—the one who watched Gretchen drop the Coke—walks by with a bunch of his friends. He shoves his friend and then points right at her, laughing again.

"God, I feel so embarrassed," she whispers. "I can't believe I melted down in front of all those people."

"Fuck 'em," I say, finding that brown freckle in her eye. "They don't know what you know."

And it's true. All of those people—they don't know what we know.

CHAPTER THIRTEEN

GRETCHEN

"I'VE MISSED YOU, *mon chou.*"

Adam lets himself in, like always. That's the first thing he says to me when he comes through the front door. Mom and Dad have gone out with friends. I'm relieved they're gone. I don't have to pretend anymore—I don't have to lie to them.

When I came home last night, my dad asked me, point blank: "Gretchen, did you see that boy die?" I answered that part honestly. I told my parents that I didn't see him die, but I *did* see someone shoot at him. My father rubbed my back and explained that we needed to let Karen, the nice prosecutor, know what I saw. I told him okay.

My mom, though, she paced the living room and said maybe it was time for me to "talk to someone." I told her that I *was* talking to someone. I was talking to her and dad, and that was enough.

I guess that's the part where I wasn't 100 percent honest.

I didn't tell them anything about Phoenix, and how easy it was to talk to him. I obviously didn't tell them how I felt a constant urge to touch his skin last night, how I even felt that little flutter in my chest when he put his arm around me. Maybe I'm supposed to think that's bad, that I wanted to feel his skin against mine. But honestly, I don't feel bad about it at all. It's been so long since I've craved anyone's touch.

So it made me hopeful—like maybe I could feel that way with Adam again. That would be so great, to want Adam's touch.

Now I'm standing in the kitchen, studying Adam. He's lanky, with creamy white skin and black hair. His eyes are piercing blue, made even more striking by his thick eyelashes and dark eyebrows. He's handsome, in a sort of alt-rocker-that-never-sees-the-sun way. But something is different about him tonight. Maybe his hair?

Adam walks up to me and touches my face. Then he kisses me gently on the lips.

"You taste like strawberries," he tells me, stepping away. "Or maybe vanilla."

"It's the lip gloss," I whisper.

I was fifteen the first time we kissed. Adam and I were hanging out with a bunch of his friends at this weird playground in Inman Park with enormous seesaws and big metal arches that you could climb to the top of and then catapult off. I think some of his friends might have been high, but we weren't. We were just falling for each other. He followed me up a ladder to the top of one of those huge jungle gyms. When he got to the top, I sat down on his lap, wrapped my arms around him, and kissed him.

After that, we just *were*. We were always Adam and Gretch—everyone's favorite couple.

"Where are Dan and Lisa?" Adam asks.

He's called my parents by their first names since the very beginning.

"Out," I tell him, grabbing my wallet from the basket by the door. "They wanted me to tell you to stick around till they're back. They want to see you."

"Yeah," he says. "Okay."

Adam looks out toward the living room. He glances at the wool

Kilim rug, my mom's best bargain find from the antique market downtown. He looks at my dad's favorite leather chair. Nothing has changed about this place, not in years. Nothing but us.

"Little Bangkok?" he asks, suggesting our favorite restaurant.

"Sounds good," I say.

"Do you need to change or something?"

He doesn't mean anything by it. He's dressed to go out—in black skinny jeans and a fitted jacket. He looks great; he looks like Adam. And we both know I do not look like Gretch.

"No," I say. "I'm ready."

But I'm not really sure I'm ready.

On the drive to the restaurant, Adam and I barely talk. We snake our way through the back roads to get to Midtown. Adam prides himself on knowing how to avoid Atlanta traffic. He's the kind of person who has the inside scoop on everything—back roads, dive restaurants, new bands. Winding through neighborhood streets I don't recognize, Adam talks about a band he discovered in Athens. He plays a couple of songs for me. They're not bad, but I don't love them.

When we get to Little Bangkok, we park in front of the body shop across the street. We walk over to the run-down strip mall where the restaurant is located and step under the ornate gold arch that frames the otherwise nondescript door. There's a wait, which is not unusual. There's always a wait on Saturday night. We decide to hold out for our favorite table, the one under the photos of the owners with a bunch of really random famous people. We used to laugh about that, coming up with ideas for the next photo they would put on the wall: Kris Kross, maybe, or some obscure winner of *American Idol* from 2003. Tonight we don't even try any of that.

When we sit down, Adam orders for us both. Nua num tok for an appetizer, shrimp lad-na, pad kee mao with tofu. As always, he says the Thai words, not referring to the dishes by the numbers beside them. I usually like that about Adam. But tonight, honestly, it annoys me. He casually orders a beer, and the waiter doesn't card him. I order sweet tea.

Adam loves spicy food—I mean insanely spicy. The food arrives, and it only takes a few bites to set my mouth on fire. He scoops rice noodles into his mouth and tells me more about the bands he's seeing in Athens, about his classes, and his new friends. I can barely focus on what he's saying, though, because of the burn. I use my spoon to pick out chunks of tofu, hoping that they, at least, will taste bland. They don't. Those squares of tofu are covered in little red flecks of pure fire. I give in and ask the waiter for a glass of milk to cut the heat. Adam continues to talk, describing his creative writing class and how great the professor is, how he's been encouraging Adam to do more writing— song lyrics, maybe. As I gulp down the milk, I hear him talk about writing songs, but I'm only half listening because my mouth is still burning and all I can think about is this:

I wonder if pupusas *are spicy.*

The next morning I decide that Luke and Anna need to dig in the dirt.

Their mom is completely in agreement with me. When I tell Aunt Lauren about my plan to take them to volunteer in the community garden after school, she says that's a fabulous idea—that maybe Luke and Anna finally will understand where their food comes from. (The two of them subsist almost entirely on Goldfish, and I'm not sure Goldfish really come from gardens, but I think I'll leave that one alone.)

I meet the kids at the bus stop, their snacks packed in a cooler. They tumble out of the bus, sucking in the fresh air. There's something great about watching the kids get off the bus. They look so *alive*, or ready to live, or something.

Typical afternoon, except it isn't, because fifteen minutes later, the kids are shedding their jackets and rushing toward the garden, where Phoenix stands watching us, a shovel slung over his shoulder. The sleeves of his T-shirt are pushed up, and his arms are glistening in the sun.

I try to look away, but I can't.

"Hey," he says.

"Hey," I tell him. Suddenly I'm feeling sort of shy—a little out of place. Maybe showing up here wasn't the best idea.

"We thought maybe we'd come see if you need any help." I'm tripping over my words, and I think I might be blushing, too.

"That's great." He smiles. Then he wipes his forehead slowly, sending a streak of dirt across it. He turns toward the kids, who already are inside a flower bed, knee-deep in dirt. "Thanks for coming to help!" he calls out.

"Don't thank *us*!" Anna replies. "Gretchen made us do it."

Phoenix looks down at the ground, like he's trying to conceal a smile. I guess maybe I'm not the only one feeling awkward.

Phoenix tells Luke and Anna to follow him to the shed. He gives them each a shovel and tells them they need to dig a really big hole. Remarkably, they do it. They keep digging until the sun starts to set, and we finish the day filthy and exhausted, but happy, too.

For the rest of the week, as soon as they tumble off the bus, Luke and Anna beg me to take them to work in the garden. Honestly, I want to go too. It's peaceful there.

By Friday, though, our hands are blistered and we have all grown tired of digging holes. When we arrive at the garden, Phoenix greets us with the same big smile as always.

"Guess what, guys!" he calls out as we approach.

"What?" Luke and Anna ask in unison.

"We finally have some trees to put in all those holes you've been digging!"

Phoenix calls us over to a tree and starts unwrapping burlap from the root ball. "Get in there and shake the dirt from the roots."

They follow his directions. *How does he get them to do that?*

I help him lift the tree and place it in the hole. We hold it steady, while the kids dump loose dirt back into the hole. When we've finished, Phoenix waters the tree, and the kids wander off to play. I sit on the grass, watching Luke chase Anna with mud on his hands. They're laughing and screaming—having a great time.

"I owe you," I tell Phoenix. "You've been so good with the kids."

"You don't owe me anything, Gretchen," he responds, looking down at his feet. "It's fun having you and the kids around."

"Still," I say. "I'll find a way to pay you back."

CHAPTER FOURTEEN

PHOENIX

THE DOORBELL IS RINGING. At least, I think that's what it is.

It's Saturday morning, and I'm alone because Sally and Amanda are running errands. I'm thinking maybe I should pretend not to be here, because there's this really nosy neighbor lady who has been coming around and asking Sally and Amanda a lot of questions about me. She's, like, the unofficial neighborhood watchdog or something. Amanda told me she has a surveillance camera on her mailbox, and that she's always telling people they're not "abiding by the neighborhood covenant." Then Sally and Amanda laughed about that lady—they said she would go crazy any time she saw "violations," like dry patches in the grass, trash cans left on the street for a few extra hours, stuff like that. I laughed too when they told me about her. But I was really thinking about how great it would be to live in a neighborhood where the big worry is whether a trash can is blocking the sidewalk.

The doorbell rings again, and I hear a voice calling my name. It's a girl's voice. *Gretchen?*

Nel. No way.

"Phoenix! It's me."

Maybe I'm losing my mind, but I decide I'm gonna have to open the door and find out. So I do, and—honest to Christ—*she's* standing there. Gretchen. Alone on the stairs, smiling a big, beautiful smile.

"I have a surprise for you," she says.

Madre de Dios.

I'm completely unable to produce any sound. I remember I'm wearing my pajamas—not really *my* pajamas. Every piece of clothing I have here was donated by charity, so I'm standing in some other guy's flannel pajama pants and a white undershirt—at least the undershirt came to me new, in a three-pack.

"Let's go," she says. "I mean, you should probably get dressed first."

And then she sort of looks me over, and her cheeks turn this sweet shade of pink. The pink is starting to travel down her neck in splotches, toward the crew neck of the big bulky sweater she's wearing.

Am I making that happen?

"Go!" she says. "We kinda need to hurry."

"Yeah, okay," I say. "Just give me a minute."

I should probably ask her to come inside, but I feel strange about it. I guess I'm wondering if anyone will see her come in, and what they will think about me inviting a girl into the house when Sally and Amanda aren't home. I really don't want to mess this up. So I turn around and walk away, leaving her in the doorway. Probably not the best decision.

"I'll just let myself in!" she calls out.

I pretend I don't hear her and head down to the basement.

I open a dresser drawer and pick out a pair of the jeans I was given. They're Levis, and they fit pretty well. I pull off my undershirt and go into the bathroom. Brush my teeth. Wash my armpits. Splash some water on my hair and start to run my fingers through it. I sometimes forget that I don't have long hair anymore. They shaved it off, back in the hellhole.

I go back to the bedroom and stare into the closet. I wish whoever gave me all these clothes had a son who wore T-shirts. I guess he was into shirts with collars, because all I have are polo shirts, which look really strange on me, and flannel button-downs. I'm not feeling sorry for myself or anything. I am grateful—*incredibly* grateful—to be looking into this closet. Because the alternative is to be standing in a bathroom with sixty guys and no walls, wearing a blue jumpsuit.

Flannel button-down, it is.

I grab my phone and text Sally.

going out with gretchen. back soon.

Then I head upstairs, taking the steps two at a time.

She's sitting on the sofa, her knees tucked up to her chest and that huge sweater covering her legs. At the sight of me, she uncurls herself and hops off the couch.

"Ready for your surprise?"

I don't reply. I have no idea what to say. Up until this point in my life, I haven't been a big fan of surprises. So, no, I'm not exactly ready for a surprise, but I am absolutely ready to go wherever Gretchen takes me.

"Don't freak out when I tell you this." She's climbing into the driver's seat of her car. "But I haven't been behind the wheel in six months."

I shrug and buckle my seat belt. "I've never been behind the wheel at all," I say. "So I guess you're still more qualified to drive this thing than I am."

"The last time I drove was right after I got assaulted," she says. "I'm pretty sure I was in shock, but I managed to get home."

"Were you beat-up bad?"

"Yeah." She chews the edge of her thumb for a second, and then she reaches down to start the car. "I tried to convince myself that it was nothing, even though I could barely see, because of the . . . the blood." She goes back to chewing her thumb, and the car idles.

I don't let myself see that image—Gretchen with blood running into her eyes. Instead, knowing she's a little nervous about the whole driving thing, I try to make small talk. "How'd you learn to drive?"

"With my dad at first, but it almost killed him." She laughs and starts to drive.

"Should I be afraid?" I pretend to shudder in fear.

"Probably," she says, deadpan. "The first time I drove with him, I thought a green light meant you could go out into the intersection and turn left. I didn't really grasp the whole 'yield' thing. My dad decided my boyfriend should take over the driving lessons—you know, to avoid a heart attack."

Boyfriend.

Ugh. I feel like I just got punched in the gut.

"It was funny. I mean, the day Adam turned eighteen, Dad handed him the car keys and wished him luck."

Adam.

And another punch, this time right under the ribs.

"He's only, like, eighteen months older than me, but he always drove me everywhere, so I didn't really need a license until he was getting ready to leave for college."

College.

And another, right up under the jaw.

"So he's away?" I force myself to ask. That last hit felt so real, I'm rubbing my face, wincing.

"Yeah, but not far. We saw each other last night, actually. He came into town and we went to dinner."

Not only does Gretchen have a boyfriend—she has a college boyfriend who drives for her and takes her out to dinner. *Awesome.*

I glance at the side of the road because I'm pretty sure my face looks like I'm in actual physical pain, and I definitely don't want Gretchen to see that. Then it hits me like another punch in the gut: we are moving too fast. Traveling too far. We aren't on neighborhood streets anymore. Instead we are on a four-lane highway, flying by fancy office buildings and huge stores. I feel the sweat begin to pool under my arms. Because I haven't told Gretchen about my twenty-mile radius.

Yeah, that's right. I'm not allowed to go more than twenty miles from Sally and Amanda's house. If I do, it's back to detention.

Mierda. Right about now this is all starting to feel like a huge mistake.

"Are you okay?" she asks. "You look like you're gonna be sick."

"I, um . . . I was just—I mean, I was just wondering where we're going, I guess." My voice shakes a little. I hope she doesn't notice.

"It's *a surprise.*"

She pulls the car onto the highway and starts hauling ass. This is getting dire.

I have to do something.

"We need to stop!" I yell. I sound scared, or maybe scary.

Gretchen looks over at me, confused. "What's wrong?" she says, biting her lower lip.

My mind searches like mad for something to say that's not going to freak her out. I do not want to be the one to give her another panic attack. *Oh Christ, what have I gotten us into?* I should have told her. I should have explained. But she had so much to deal with already. I didn't want for her to worry. I don't want to scare her. There's nothing wrong with that, is there?

"I'm feeling sick," I say. "I think we need to pull over."

"This will help." She mashes a button to roll down my window. "I used to get carsick when I was a kid, but it's better now."

A cold wind hits my face and I realize two things: this girl is not going to stop, and there is not a chance in hell I'm letting her go any farther. Without thinking, I hoist my left leg up onto the dashboard. I pull up my jeans, and shove down my sock.

"You have to stop," I say.

And then it all sort of happens in slow motion: she turns her head to look at my leg, and she sees the stupid *pinche* black box attached to my ankle, the one that I can't take off, the one that my parole officer monitors every *pinche* second of every *pinche* day, and then she looks up at my face, her eyes wide, like she's just seen a dead body or something. Her jaw drops and she lifts her foot off the gas, so the car starts to slow down.

"What are you doing?" she asks. "What *is* that?"

"I can't leave Atlanta," I say.

"Oh dear God," she says. "Oh God. Please, God, tell me that's not what I think it is."

The car is moving even slower.

"It's an ankle monitor," I say, hoping, *praying*, she's not gonna freak out.

"An ankle monitor," she says quietly. "Oh my God, you're wearing an ankle monitor."

She's gonna freak out.

And then her hands are flying from the steering wheel, her arms flailing wildly. "How could you? How could you do this to me? I trusted you! Oh God, what did you *do*?"

She starts sucking in deep breaths. The car is slowing down, and a horn honks really loud behind us. Cars are swerving around us now, and Gretchen's chest is heaving and she's pulling in air, but I can tell she thinks she's not getting any. My heart is pounding, and it hits me that if I don't do something, we might both die right here on the highway, somewhere on the outskirts of Atlanta.

I'm not ready to die. *Madre de Dios.* I am not ready. Not yet.

So I reach over and grab the steering wheel and tell her to let go, and by some miracle, she does. Slowly, I ease the car to the edge of the road. Gretchen sucks in deep breaths and I keep steering the car—driving for the first time in my *pendejo* life!

Finally the car stops.

Gretchen, that crazy girl, throws her door open, cars speeding past us at, like, a hundred kilometers an hour. I'm afraid one of them is going to slam into the door and send us spinning out onto the freeway, or even worse, she will jump into oncoming traffic, just to get away from me.

What did you do?

I hear her voice, asking me. Accusing me. Afraid of me.

I reach across her body and yank the door shut. Then I push down the lock

"What is going on?" She's screaming again. "What are you doing?"

"You can't open the door," I say, trying with everything I have to sound calm. "You might get hurt."

She reaches for her phone, which I've been holding in my lap. "I'm calling my dad," she says. "Get out. I'm calling my dad."

She's about to have a full-on panic attack. I can see it coming. She's trying to take the phone, but I put my hand over hers, touching her as gently as I can.

"Please, let me explain," I say. "You don't need to call your dad."

"Get out!" she cries.

"No." I grip her hand harder. "I'm not getting out until you let me explain."

"You can't do this to me."

"I'm not a criminal," I say. But even as I'm saying it, I'm not sure it's true. Still, I have to say something to calm her down, and even if I am a criminal—or if I *was* a criminal—this stupid thing around my ankle has nothing to do with that.

"If you don't get out, I am going to call the cops." Gretchen grabs her phone with her free hand and shakes it at me.

I let go of her and ease slowly out, trying not to startle her with any fast motions. "I'm going to stand right here, outside the car, and I'm going to explain, okay?"

Gretchen pushes a button, and I hear the click of doors locking—all of them at once.

"All I did was show up at the border without permission," I say through the window.

"What? What are you talking about?" Her face crumples.

I shove my hands into the pockets of my borrowed jeans. I'm not sure I can talk about this, but I'm going to try.

"I came up through Mexico, with my little brother, and when we got to the border, they put me in detention. It's like prison, you know?"

"But what did you *do*?"

"Nothing. I didn't do anything. I brought my brother to the border and told the guard we needed asylum, so they put me in detention. But then Amanda hired a lawyer and she got me out. But I have to wear this stupid thing."

Gretchen leans over to look at me. Her breathing is slowing down. "You're not making any sense," she says, her voice rising.

I shrug. Because, *cabrón*, she doesn't have to tell me that none of it makes any sense.

"Why should I trust you?"

She's got me on that one. I don't know why she should trust me.

"Hold on," I say. I pull out my phone and call Sally.

Sally picks up. *Finally something is going right.*

"Phoenix!" she says cheerfully. "How's it going with Gretchen?"

"Not so good," I say, talking fast. "She was trying to take me out of town, and I didn't know what to do. I showed her the ankle monitor."

"Let me talk to her."

I push my hand through the crack in the window and press the phone toward Gretchen.

And, *Gracias a Dios y a la Virgencita*, she accepts it.

CHAPTER FIFTEEN

GRETCHEN

OKAY, SO—ALL THINGS considered—I'd say I'm handling this situation fairly well. When I decided to do this nice thing for Phoenix last night, because of how great he's been all week with the kids, I made myself believe it was simple: a little drive to the country. *You can handle that, Gretchen.*

I hadn't factored in the homing device.

But after I talked to Sally, I let Phoenix back in the car, which is making me feel seriously proud, and almost normal. Maybe a little self-absorbed—since, the other night, I didn't even think to ask Phoenix *why* he was living with Sally and Amanda and trying to get permission to stay—but otherwise fairly normal.

We are sitting in the parking lot of a QuikTrip, and I'm sipping an enormous mango iced tea. We're killing time, waiting for his parole officer to call him back, to see if he can come with me to get *pupusas.*

I hadn't factored in his parole officer, either.

Oh my God, Phoenix has a parole officer. Just thinking about that sends my heart racing, but then I force myself to remember what Sally told me. Honestly, how do you have a parole officer when all you did was bring your little brother to the US—because it's not safe where you live? Sally said that Phoenix and his brother fled El Salvador because their neighborhood was dangerous, and because there were people there who wanted them dead—that if they stayed, they almost certainly would have been killed.

And how does that even happen, anyway? How do a twelve-year-old and an eighteen-year-old who aren't criminals (she promised me, again and again, that they aren't criminals) end up with death threats?

So now, here we are in the parking lot, waiting for permission to go to Dahlonega, which is a little mountain town where there are supposed to be to-die-for *pupusas*. I'm feeling bad because I assumed Phoenix did something really terrible, and I think he's feeling bad because he completely freaked me out with the ankle monitor.

"Want some Skittles?" he asks, pushing the red package toward me.

"Sure," I tell him.

I've never really understood Skittles. I mean, if you're going to eat sweets, why choose sweets that don't contain any chocolate? But I guess I want him to know I will take whatever he offers me, maybe because I feel sorry for him.

God, I feel sorry for him.

"Do you get to talk to your brother?" I ask.

"Not really," he says, putting the bag of Skittles on the dash. "Amanda and Sally bought him a phone card, but it's really expensive to call from over there, and I guess he doesn't get access to the phone."

Over there. Sally told me his brother is in Texas, in a special detention facility for children who were caught at the border without their parents. But she also told me that Phoenix and his brother weren't really caught. They swam across the river and walked right up to a border patrol officer to ask for protection.

"That's not exactly true," Phoenix says quietly.

"What?" I ask, lost in my thoughts.

"About Ari, my brother. I haven't talked to him because, uh, he doesn't talk."

"Oh," I say. "You mean he has, like, a mental disability?"

"No." He shrugs. "It's not like that." Then he looks right at me, his eyes filling up with pain, or maybe regret. "The psychologist over there, she says it's temporary. It's just from the, uh . . . from the trauma."

"Trauma?" My heart starts to thump in my chest—again. But this time, it's not because I'm afraid. Or, I'm not afraid for myself, at least. I think maybe I don't want to know these things about Phoenix. But also, I do. I want so much to know him.

"It was really hard," he says, "coming through Mexico. A bunch of bad stuff happened to us. But, I mean, we *made* it." He shifts in his seat and puts his feet against the dashboard. "We were so relieved when we finally got to the US side of the border. But then they took us and put us in this room—like a holding cell. Everyone calls it the *heladera*— the freezer. It was so cold, and my little brother, he was, like, shivering." Phoenix folds his arms across his chest, as if it is cold now, as if this car is a freezer. "We were still really wet from the river. His lips were, like, turning blue, and I was holding him, you know, trying to warm him up a little."

He hugs himself tighter and looks over at me. "You don't need to hear all this shit."

"I do, Phoenix." I touch one of his arms and gently unfold it. "Tell me."

It feels good, holding on to his arm, like if I can just keep holding on, this might all make more sense.

"We were there for a really long time, like hours and hours. Then the guard came back. He told me I had to leave, but my brother was staying there." He folds his free hand behind his head and looks up, at the roof of the car. "Ari didn't understand what was going on. They pulled him off me—not rough or anything—and then they put me in handcuffs."

"Your brother saw this?"

He's leaning back, looking up at the roof, or maybe through it. Maybe he's imagining the wide-open sky.

"Yeah, and I kept telling him everything would be okay and we would talk soon. I tried to explain that he didn't need to worry—that they were going to protect him and . . ."

The car is completely silent—because Phoenix stopped talking, and because I can't speak. *What can I possibly say?*

Phoenix turns toward me. "His eyes, Gretchen—the way he looked at me."

I study Phoenix, feeling his hurt in my own body—real physical pain, stabbing into my gut.

"I'm so sorry," I whisper. That's all I can come up with.

"Ari didn't say anything when they took me out of there. He curled up, like into a little ball, and he watched while they pulled me out of that *heladera*. But he didn't really have to say anything, because—I guess I knew."

"Knew what?"

"I don't know how to explain it. I think I knew he was kind of, like, dying inside. You know? Does that make sense?"

No. Not a single word of it.

"I can't believe they separated you," I whisper.

"Yeah." He looks away, toward the highway.

"How could they do that?"

"At least he's safe," he says. "But he still won't talk to anyone. Not even me." He grabs the bag of Skittles from the dash and pours some into his hand. "Or, maybe, especially not me. I think he hates me for bringing him here."

He studies the Skittles, and then he begins to separate them out slowly. Green on one side, red on the other.

"He doesn't hate you."

Neither of us says anything for a long time.

"I don't know," he says finally. "He sends me letters, at least. Well, pictures."

"Like, from magazines?"

"No, he draws them. They're really good."

He pops the candy into his mouth and pulls a wallet from his back pocket. He takes out a piece of paper that's been folded into it and hands it to me. "This one's of our hammock, the one outside our grandmother's house."

The hammock is hanging between two fruit trees, with mountains in the background. It's got little flowers underneath, butterflies, even a caterpillar.

"It looks just like the place, which makes me wonder about my little brother. He was only seven the last time he saw that hammock."

"It's really good." I hand it back to Phoenix. I'm trying to imagine him there—swinging in the hammock. It's not easy to picture. That landscape seems so far away from where we are right now, at a random exit off the interstate.

"Ari doesn't hate you," I say again.

Phoenix puts the drawing back into his wallet and reaches for the last of the Skittles.

"Will he be able to come and live with you?"

"I don't think so." He takes a piece of candy between his thumb and forefinger and examines it. "But he'll probably get to stay here, which is really good."

"Why not with you?"

"It's different for me." He looks over at me. "I'm an adult." He smiles a big innocent grin. "At least, they think I'm an adult. I'm not so sure."

"Yeah, I'm an adult too. *Technically*," I say. "What does that even mean?"

"To be an adult?" he asks. "I have no idea. But I guess what it means for me is that my chances of staying here are pretty bad. I'll know for sure in a couple of weeks."

He's not staying here. Those words have a strange effect on me, like they've punched a tiny little hole in my chest. I squeeze my eyes shut, trying not to overthink my reaction to the thought of him leaving. I barely know him, after all.

"What happens in a couple of weeks?"

"I go back to court. Until then, I'm free to do whatever I want, as long as I stay within twenty miles of Amanda and Sally's house."

"Wow. What freedom."

He stretches his hand out to offer me the last Skittle. It's green.

"I'm not complaining. You should see where I was before I got this thing," he says, gesturing toward the tracking device beneath his jeans.

You'd never know he was wearing it, unless you *knew*.

For better or worse, I know. That's not the sort of thing you forget. "What was it like?" I ask. "I mean, in detention."

A strange emotion flashes across his face—one I can't read. Then he turns to look at me again. He really looks. It's like he actually sees *me*. His eyes have a little crinkle around the edges, like they're smiling. And then his face actually breaks into a real smile that makes my stomach do a flip.

"Let's just say I'd rather be sharing these Skittles with you than sharing a room with sixty men dressed in blue jumpsuits."

"Sixty men? They put sixty people in the same room?"

The whole flipping-stomach thing is still happening, which makes me feel a little more awake or something, and also a little scared and confused.

"Yeah." He nods. "And there was no privacy—you couldn't even shower or, uh—Well, I mean, we had to do everything out in the wide open."

I look at Phoenix, and my mind starts to conjure the image of him standing under a hot stream of shower water. I let it, even though I know I shouldn't, since I have a devoted boyfriend, and since Phoenix is telling me all these terrible, sad things. But it feels so good to have that thudding pulse spread from the pit of my stomach—to feel *anything* that isn't fear or anxiety or the dull, hazy distance of life going on around me, without me.

Sitting here with Phoenix, sharing candy I don't even like, imagining what water would look like running through his hair, across his face, down his back and chest. God, it feels like living.

I'm pretty sure he feels it too.

Phoenix's phone rings.

"It's my parole officer," he says. "Give me a minute."

Phoenix steps out of the car and starts to talk. I sit there, still wondering how a boy like Phoenix can end up with a parole officer.

Phoenix laughs, which is not really what I expect from his conversation with a law enforcement official. Then he leans through the window of the car and covers the receiver with his hand.

"Officer Worth needs to know where you plan to take me."

"Dahlonega," I say.

"No, he needs details."

"It's a surprise."

"He doesn't do surprises."

"Ugh," I say, trying to sound dramatic. "There's a lady in Dahlonega who makes homemade *pupusas* every Saturday morning. She sells them outside her church. And she makes that kind with the little flowers. I checked."

Phoenix leans in closer, an adorable smile spreading across his whole face. Seeing that smile, it makes me breathe a little easier.

"You're taking me to another city for homemade *pupusas de loroco?*"

"Yeah," I tell him. "As long as Officer Worth gives us permission. And I think we need to hurry, because she quits selling them at noon."

"That's so amazing," he says. "I can't believe you're doing that for me."

I hear the officer's voice coming through the phone's speaker.

"Pupusas?" Phoenix speaks into the phone. "They're a food from El Salvador—like tortillas, sort of, stuffed with meat and cheese and stuff."

He listens again.

"What's the address?" Phoenix asks me. "Of the church?"

I show him my phone, where the address is programmed into the map.

He reads it aloud. "Ninety-Three Main Street. It's called Saint Matthew the Apostle."

After a moment of listening, Phoenix says, "I understand." And then, "I can do that." And then he laughs and says, "Yeah, sure, Officer

Worth. I'll bring you one. But they're only really good when they're fresh."

Phoenix looks over and gives me a thumbs-up. So Officer Worth is going to let us go on this little adventure.

Phoenix turns his back to me and I let myself study him—the curve of his neck, that place where his hairline ends. I let myself notice the way it feels to study his angles.

The parole officer must be saying something funny again, because Phoenix laughs nervously and shakes his head.

"Dude! We're going to a *church*."

Then more nervous laughter.

"We're just friends," he says quietly.

Then he listens some more and begins to nod.

"That sounds great. Thanks."

He shoves the phone into his pocket and gets back into the car. "Did you hear that? Uh, the last part?" His cheeks are flushed, and the tips of his ears have turned red. I can't really imagine what Officer Worth would say to cause Phoenix such embarrassment. Or maybe I can.

"Your parole officer thinks we are, like, on a date?"

"Yeah, well, not exactly."

"What did he say?" I ask.

He shakes his head. "It doesn't matter."

"Come on." I shove him, teasing. "Tell me."

He looks over at me and runs his hand over his short hair. "He told me not to let you take me to some cheap motel—that he knows exactly where I am at all times."

I'm pretty sure I start to blush too. But I can handle this.

"Bummer," I say, nudging his knee again. "I guess that ruins part two of my surprise."

He shakes his head, but he doesn't move my hand from his knees.

"Drive," he says, looking at the clock on the dash. "We've got forty-eight minutes until those *pupusas* disappear, and you'll lose your chance to try the best food ever invented."

And then I have this thought, that even if he might be leaving soon, Phoenix will need to be part of my life for now—like, every day. Because I know he's running away from something so terrible I can't imagine it, but when he's with me, we both are here. Right here.

CHAPTER SIXTEEN

PHOENIX

I'M EATING MY THIRD *pupusa de loroco*. The *curtido* is perfect and the *pupusas* are damn near perfect, and this crazy beautiful girl is next to me—so close that, even though we're not touching, I feel the warmth from her body. And she keeps closing her eyes, leaning her head back a little, and releasing these small, soft moans.

I guess she likes *pupusas*.

"OhmyGodohmyGod," she says. "What is this stuff called again?"

"Chicharrón."

"Okay," she tells me. "Chicharrón is my new best friend." I watch her take another bite of *pupusa* and then slowly wipe the *curtido* juice from her lip. "And this slaw stuff? What do you call it?"

"*Curtido.*"

"Is there more?"

I look into the white plastic bag that the nice *abuelita* gave me.

"There's a ton," I say. "Enough for, like, a week of binge-eating *pupusas.*"

Gretchen smiles big. "Let's do it! Let's sit here until next Sunday and stuff our faces with *pupusas!*"

We both know that's not gonna happen, but it's amazing to hear her say that she wants it. I still can't figure it all out—why she's spending her time with me, why she's doing this great thing for me. And also, if I'm being real, why we're sitting so close to each other, so much energy tugging at the space between us, when she's got a college boyfriend somewhere, who takes her out for dinner and drives his own car. We can be friends. I mean, that's fine. But what it feels like to sit this close to her isn't really a friendly kind of feeling.

Gretchen sped all the way up here on narrow, curving roads that cut through the forest. When the trees cleared, we were in this town surrounded by mountains, and the church was right in front of us. I didn't know Georgia had mountains. I guess this shouldn't surprise me. Until a few weeks ago, I couldn't even find Georgia on a map. And now, here I am, sitting alone with her on the stairs of this pretty white church in a little mountain town. I've never seen a church like this, except maybe in the movies. It's wood, painted a pure, bright white. All the windows are filled with colored glass. When the light comes through that glass, it changes entirely, making long shifting patterns on the floor. There's a tall tower in the front, and a little porch with white columns. That's where we're sitting now, on the concrete stairs. We're looking out across the street of a town with shops all lined up in rows. And behind the shops are mountains, their angles soft and gentle. The trees have these tiny new leaves on them, so they're not quite green. They almost look yellow when the sun filters through them. Or gold, maybe. They're so thin and translucent that they look fragile, like they might break if they fall to the ground before the summer heat toughens them.

When we pulled up, we saw a table propped beside a big *comal*. A bunch of mismatched plates sat piled on top of the table, next to a white plastic bucket. It reminded me so much of my *abuela's pupusa* stand back in Ilopango that it hurt to look at it. Even the flowered tablecloth looked familiar, like my grandmother might have just pulled it from under the sink in her courtyard to spread it on that table herself. But there was no one at the table, and there weren't any *pupusas* there either.

"We missed them," Gretchen said, pulling into a spot in front of the church. I looked over at her, trying to ignore the ache in my chest. Her face was twisted into a sad grimace, so I wanted to say something that would let her know it was okay—that just being here with her was enough.

"Don't worry," I told her. "It's not a big deal. Maybe we can come back."

We both knew that wasn't likely. Officer Worth made clear that this was a one-time-only thing. He told me that if I decided to leave the state of Georgia with Gretchen, or if we weren't back inside my twenty-mile radius by six, he would send the cops to chase us down.

Gretchen wasn't ready to give up on the *pupusas* yet, so she made me go inside the church with her to see if we could find someone to ask. We walked to the front of the church—through big wooden doors that creaked and squealed on their hinges. Pushing on those heavy doors, Gretchen almost plowed right into an old lady in a housedress. Turns out, that old lady was Mama Lola, the sweet *abuelita* who sells *pupusas* here every Saturday morning to raise money for the church.

Gretchen launched right in. She told Mama Lola that we came all the way from Atlanta because she read about the *pupusa* stand on some food blog. Mama Lola squinted in confusion and repeated the word *blog?* a couple of times, rolling the word around in her mouth, like she was trying to get the flavor of it.

"*En la computadora,*" I told her, because at first I thought maybe she didn't speak English, but she spoke plenty of English. Once Gretchen figured that out, she decided to go on and tell that lady my entire story, all the way down to how I'm separated from my brother. I'm not sure how much of it Mama Lola understood. Gretchen was talking really fast.

But the *abuelita* must have gotten most of it, because she took us out to her son-in-law's truck, opened the back, and loaded about thirty *pupusas* into a plastic bag, complete with little containers of red salsa and a bunch of plastic Baggies filled with *curtido*.

Gretchen tried to pay her, but she refused, saying the *pupusas* were a *regalo*—a gift. Then Gretchen gave Mama Lola a huge hug, which I think sort of shocked her. I went with a more subtle approach, shaking her hand and saying, *"Gracias, señora. Muy amable."*

Then Mama Lola's son-in-law drove her away in his truck, down that country road.

So here we are—Gretchen and Phoenix alone on the steps of an empty white church, stuffing our faces with *pupusas*, looking out at mountains that seem to go on forever. The sky is blue, the trees are bright yellow-gold, and the sun is shining, like it's trying really hard to produce some heat for us.

I push up my sleeves and let the sun warm my skin.

"I'm so completely full," Gretchen says. When I look at her, she's closing her eyes and leaning back on her elbows. She's wearing another one of those enormous sweaters with a huge, wide neck, and it slides down her shoulder. Her eyes are still closed, so I let myself look at the thin black strap of her undershirt and the pale skin of her shoulder. Her skin is so light that the sun seems to shine right through it. I can't look away.

I catch the scent of the *curtido* and I feel tired, suddenly. That smell— vinegar mixed with cabbage, and the earthy aroma of the masa—it takes me right back to my *abuela*'s *pupusa* stand down by the lake. It's like I'm standing behind the *comal* with her, a scrawny kid who wishes he were out climbing rocks with his friends, but he's helping his *abuela* instead, because he hasn't got any choice in the matter.

I was the one who scooped the *curtido* out of the bucket. Every Saturday, Abuela made me go down to the commercial district by the lake with her to help. I put on clear plastic gloves that made my hands sweaty, and I grabbed handfuls of the stuff and dumped it onto the *pupusas* after she served them on plates. I used to stand there with her for hours, hating the stench of vinegar and the feel of the gloves on my hands, looking out to the mountains and the lake, thinking about all the adventures I wished I could be on with my friends.

"I should have let her teach me how to make these things," I say quietly.

"Who?"

"My grandmother. She tried to teach me."

"You should get the recipe from her. I'll help you make them."

My head is starting to spin. "She's not around anymore," I hear myself say.

"She died?"

"Yeah, a while back."

"How?" Gretchen asks. It's an innocent question, but I can feel my whole body starting to shake.

I don't think I can answer. I guess I'm looking pretty bad, because Gretchen reaches out and puts her hand on my knee. It feels good there—warm, even through my jeans. I brush my finger lightly against hers and let myself notice how touching her, even like this, makes the blood pump faster through my veins.

"It's okay," she says, squeezing my knee. "We don't have to talk about it."

I look over at her, watching me, and I decide to talk. I can't tell her *everything*, but I want her to know *something*.

"A few years ago there were floods in my town. There was, like, a   a current, a river of mud." I close my eyes. I am whispering. "I don't really know how to explain it."

That's the truth. *How could I possibly begin to explain it?*

"A landslide." Gretchen nods. "I'm sorry, Phoenix."

She leans into me, and suddenly I don't care if Gretchen has a boyfriend. Maybe she doesn't care either. Maybe it's fine for me to want this—to want to feel her body pressed against mine. I want to sit like this for a long, long time, to study Gretchen's soft hand on my leg, to know every detail of it. Because I don't want to see any of the images that are taking shape in my head. I don't want to see my *abuela*'s gnarled old hand, showing me *como se golpea la masa con la palma de la mano.*

My grandmother showed me so many times, how to pound the masa into discs, into just the right thickness for the filling to go inside. Her palm open, her wrist moving quickly up and down. I never could do it right. *Con la prácitca,* she told me, still working the dough. *Con la práctica, se logra perfeccionar la técnica.*

We would stand in my *abuela*'s courtyard, pounding that dough, and she would tell me how proud she was of me—a boy not afraid to make *pupusas.* She said there was no reason for this to be women's work, that I could do it too. She said all I needed was practice. If only she had known that I didn't care a thing about making *pupusas.* I wanted to leave that courtyard and head for the hills. But I was a good boy back then, so I stood beside her and pounded the dough.

Until the *gangueros* started showing up at my *abuela*'s courtyard gate.

Until they demanded money, telling us that she would need to pay, if she wanted to keep her *pupusa* stand.

Until those assholes grabbed me by my feet—held me out of a window, three stories above the street, every day for weeks.

Until my grandmother and her courtyard disappeared, carried on powerful waves of mud into the lake below.

Until I abandoned her.

The corners of my eyes start to sting. I push myself up to stand, and I gather up the last of the used napkins and containers.

"I'm gonna go find a place to throw this stuff away," I say, still looking away from her.

I take my time walking around the perimeter of the church, trying to pull my shit together. I tell myself to stop thinking about the past. I tell myself to think about the blue sky, and the warm sun, and the fact that I'm hanging out with a beautiful, kind girl who brought me to the countryside to buy me *pupusas*.

I find a garbage can around back and drop our bag of trash inside. I'm worried that maybe I've been gone too long—that Gretchen will wonder what happened, or come looking for me. But when I round the corner to the front of the church, Gretchen is still there on the steps, exactly as I left her, waiting for me. Except she has her phone out, and she's texting.

"Ready?" I ask her.

"Mmmhmm," she mumbles, standing up. She looks at her phone and back at me a couple of times, like she's trying to figure something out.

"We've gotta get back to Atlanta, right?" she says.

"Yeah, unless you want for our next adventure to be getting chased down by the Dahlonega police."

"Could be fun." She shrugs. "A low-speed chase through the mountains."

"Not my kind of fun," I say. I know she wants to lighten the mood, so I'm trying to play along.

"Wanna meet up with some friends of mine Downtown?"

I hear the anxiety in her voice. I don't know if it's because she's nervous about introducing me to her friends, or because she doesn't feel comfortable going Downtown. I've seen enough to know that Gretchen doesn't like being in crowded places.

"Do you wanna go?" I ask.

She nods. "Yeah, I think I do, but it might be stupid." She starts walking toward the car. "It's my best friend, Bree, and her new boyfriend. They want to do, like, a tourist night—go Downtown and pretend we're from out of town, do all the stupid touristy stuff."

Then she smiles in a way that would make it really damn hard to say no. The truth is, even without that smile, I don't want this day with Gretchen to end.

"Let's do it," I tell her.

CHAPTER SEVENTEEN
GRETCHEN

"YOU KNOW HOW EVERYBODY'S always talking about the American Dream?" Phoenix asks me. The windows are rolled down in the car, and we're winding our way back toward Atlanta. We've been driving in silence for a while, breathing in the damp mountain air.

"Yeah, I guess." That's what I tell him, but I don't really. No one I know makes reference to the American Dream unless they're being sarcastic.

"And people are always talking about the almighty dollar—like the American Dream is all about getting a shit-ton of money and then buying a big house and a bunch of fancy cars." He's sitting in the passenger seat, his feet on the dash, his head tilted back, eyes closed. "That's not my American Dream," he says quietly. "I don't even care about money and cars and all that."

For a moment I look right at him, concentrating on what he's trying to tell me, but he doesn't look back. I return my gaze to the road.

"My American Dream's way more simple than that. I just wanna be able to go for a walk in the woods alone—get on one of those little trails in the forest and walk for hours. That would be so awesome. Or maybe head over to a friend's place after dinner to watch a football match on

TV, and not have to look behind my back every five seconds, not have to worry about whether I'll make it home alive. You know?"

No, I don't know. And I don't know what to say. I want to reach out and touch him, but instead I grip the steering wheel tighter.

We pull out of the mountains, back onto the highway, and then two high-pitched beeps break the silence—instead of my own voice, which appears to have disappeared.

"We're back inside my radius," Phoenix says, pulling up the leg of his jeans to inspect the ankle monitor.

The ankle monitor.

"Can you ever take it off?" I ask.

"Nope," he says. "Never."

When we get to my house, we don't go inside. By the time Bree and Ty pull into the driveway, it's getting dark. Phoenix and I are sitting together on the hood of my car, leaning into each other, close. Bree rolls down her window and Ty leans across to call out to us.

"Get in, y'all!" he says, smiling big.

We jump off the hood and Phoenix opens the back door of Bree's car. He touches my back lightly to let me in first. Bree is watching, studying us both carefully. I don't recognize the look on her face, which is unusual, in light of the fact that we've been friends forever. Maybe it's just curiosity. Or concern. I slide across the back seat and Phoenix gets in beside me. Ty half stands in the front passenger seat and turns around to face us completely.

"Check it out," Ty says, pointing toward the baseball cap he's wearing. "I've got on my Falcons jersey *and* my Braves cap! We're going full-on tourist tonight."

We all laugh at Ty. He's sort of a buffoon, but he can be funny sometimes. After Ty and Bree introduce themselves, Bree maneuvers thorough the neighborhood to DeKalb Avenue, and then we drive west along DeKalb toward Downtown, skirting the edge of the train tracks. We talk about all the graffiti art on the walls of the elevated train. Phoenix seems fascinated by that art, especially when we tell him that most of it was painted by volunteers, as part of a city project to beautify the area. I guess where he's from, graffiti isn't usually created as a community service initiative.

Soon we're Downtown, snaking our way through city streets, looking out the window at the high-rise buildings stacked one beside the other. Bree pulls into a parking spot and we all look up.

"Um, Gretchen," Phoenix says, "what is *that*?"

"The Atlanta Eye," Bree tells him. "Doesn't it look fun?"

An enormous Ferris wheel with enclosed cars spins slowly above us, lit up in a dozen different colors.

"Let's do this thing!" Ty says with much more enthusiasm than necessary.

We all tumble out of the car. Except Phoenix. He closes his eyes and rubs his head a few times.

"Come on!" Bree says, leaning back into the car. "The line is getting long."

Phoenix steps out of the car slowly. He looks up at the spinning lights and then clenches his jaw tight and wraps his arm around my shoulder. We start walking toward the Eye, and he keeps his arm hanging on me, which is fine. *Because that's what friends do, right?* They walk down the street, their arms casually draped across each other's shoulders. At least, that's what I'm trying to convince myself.

Bree was right. The line is long. So we decide to wait while Ty and Phoenix go and buy us some Cokes.

"What's going on?" Bree asks as soon as they walk away from us.

"What do you mean?"

"You know what I mean. What's going on with Phoenix? The air between you two is so thick, I could cut it with a butter knife."

"I don't know," I tell her. And it's true, I don't. I'm pretty sure he doesn't either.

"Well, figure it out," she says, shaking her head slowly. "Because Phoenix seems great, and all, but you have a very devoted boyfriend, Gretch."

Ty and Phoenix come back and, by the time we get to the front of the line, we've already finished our drinks. Ty buys a ticket for Bree. Bree doesn't even put up a fight. She doesn't say one thing like, *Excuse me. I think I'm capable of buying my own ticket.* Or *My, how nineteenth century of you!* Or *Look at that! A hundred years of women's struggle for independence right out the door!* She is so entirely un-Bree that she actually giggles—*giggles!*—when the salesperson offers them the VIP car with "limo-tinted windows, red leather seats, and a glass floor." It doesn't take much creativity to imagine what goes on inside those little pods as they dangle above the Atlanta skyline.

Gross.

The only upside of Bree's strange behavior is that she's so busy giggling with Ty that she forgets about me and Phoenix and the heavy air between us. Not surprisingly, Bree and Ty strategically land themselves alone in the VIP car. As soon as the doors start to slide shut, they're all over each other. They don't even wait for those doors to fully close.

As soon as their doors close, Phoenix and I are standing together, in ear-shattering silence. We walk up a short stairway to the next car. We both stand perfectly still at the edge of the walkway, staring forward, waiting for the attendant to open the doors and let us in. I'm at the edge of the platform, trying to put some space between us.

I know Phoenix feels as anxious as I do. We are about to be alone in something clearly designed as a full-on make-out pod. Of course, I'm not supposed to be thinking about this, since I am here with my *friend* Phoenix. But I am. I mean, thinking about it. I am thinking about his body, to be more specific. I am thinking about what it would feel like to taste him on my lips and feel his bare skin under my touch, to feel his hands against my hips.

Why am I letting my mind go there? Why is my body sending out all these crazy signals? Maybe it's all that mountain air we breathed on our drive back from Dahlonega. I should have kept the windows rolled up.

Our pod comes to a stop in front of us. It's swinging back and forth a little, so the doors stay closed.

"*Motherfucker,*" Phoenix says, releasing the word slowly, drawing out each syllable.

This is unexpected.

"You swear like a sailor," I tell him, trying to sound casual instead of really confused. (I am really confused.) "Where did you learn to talk like that?"

"The missionaries," he tells me, still unable to tear his eyes away from the pod we are about to climb into. "They taught me everything I know."

"Goddamned missionaries," I say, trying to make him laugh. He doesn't even smile.

The doors slide open and a woman stands on the other side, welcoming us onto the Atlanta Eye. I step into the pod and sit down on a bench. The woman looks at Phoenix, who is standing as still as a statue outside.

Oh, God. How could I have forgotten? He's afraid of heights.

"Is he gonna make it?" she asks me.

"I think so." But I'm starting to doubt it. I look over at Phoenix and realize he definitely isn't thinking about what it would feel like to have his hands all over my body. What he's thinking is, *Motherfucker.* In fact,

I'm pretty sure Phoenix is headed toward a full-on panic attack—freak-out. I know panic attacks. I can see the signs.

"Because we need to get this thing moving," the female attendant continues. She isn't being mean. She's just stating a fact.

I stand up. "I can't believe I forgot. How could I have forgotten?"

"Forgotten what?" He's looking up at the thin metal cable that connects our pod to the frame of the Ferris wheel.

"That you're afraid of heights." I start to step out of the pod. "We don't have to do this."

The attendant is watching us both, a bored look on her face. "On or off?" she asks.

"On," he says, squeezing his eyes shut. He still doesn't move, though.

"Are you sure?" I ask.

"No," he growls. "But I'm also not ready to look like an idiot in front of your friends, so I guess we're gonna ride this thing."

"We'll wait for them down here." I say, stepping out of the car. "It's not a big deal."

He grabs my arm to stop me, and then he pulls me back into the car. "It is to me." His eyes dart around frantically. "Let's get this over with."

We're standing inside the doors. The entire car feels charged with energy—and not the good kind. I do a quick search for barf bags, but there aren't any. This could be bad. I pull him onto the bench next to me, even though there is another one across from us—an empty one, designed so that under normal circumstances friends can sit across from each other, chatting and laughing and *not hooking up*. But these are not normal circumstances.

Phoenix presses himself against my side. The woman drones on about the Atlanta skyline, and all that we will see. I can tell he's not listening. His eyes are fixed on a warning sticker that's stuck to the window across from us. It's got drawings of stick figures, intended to illustrate several completely improbable ways a person could get hurt in this very secure little pod. Like, *Don't shove the doors open with your bare hands* and *Don't stick your arms and legs out of the very small window.* His jaw clenches and his back goes rigid.

"Phoenix," I say. "Look at me."

CHAPTER EIGHTEEN

PHOENIX

LOOK AT ME.

I tear my eyes away from the warning sign and look right at Gretchen. The woman whose job it is to seal us into this death pod keeps talking, saying the same load of crap she has said three times already tonight. But I don't listen to her. I focus on that little brown freckle in Gretchen's right eye, and I start begging sweet baby Jesus that I'll be able to hold myself together.

One time around, and then I'm outta here.

"The ride will last for three full revolutions. If you want to get out early"—the woman pauses and looks directly at me, her eyebrows arching—"or if for any reason you need to get out early, push the red button."

Three times. Oh Christ. Do I look as sick as I feel?

The woman points to the ceiling, where a red emergency button glows in the very center. Then she steps out of the car and the doors slide shut, but I don't watch her go—because I'm staring at that red button. It's like a goddamned beacon in the night.

Click.

And then there's a jolt, and the car starts to swing wildly, and this stupid circus ride begins to move. I mean, *what the hell?* Why is there

a big-ass fair ride in the middle of downtown Atlanta, anyway? And
more important, how did I—Phoenix Flores Flores—the number one
candy-ass sissy of all time, end up inside it?

I can't take my eyes off that red button.

The car only moves a few yards, and then it jolts to a stop again and
starts to swing. This time it swings like it's out in the middle of the Pacific fucking Ocean, and the waves are pounding it. Back and forth,
back and forth. And I'm still staring hard at that light on the ceiling.

Then the stupid ride starts to move again, and this time it doesn't
stop. We are climbing fast, but at least the death pod stops swinging like
mad. I feel Gretchen pressed up against me, and—*I'll admit it*—I sink
into her.

"You need to hold me down." I hear myself say. "The whole time.
Or else I'm going for that red button."

"Yeah," she tells me. "I can do that."

And the way she says it, it's not even like she thinks I'm insane—or
a total wuss. She says it like everything is okay, or it's going to be okay.

She grabs both of my hands in hers and holds on tight. I feel her
press our hands into my lap, which makes me look away from the
red beacon, finally. She leans in so our foreheads touch, and then we both
sit completely still, staring at our hands, wrapped around each other.

Our hands, they're amazing to look at.

Hers are smooth and white. Her skin is almost translucent. Next to
hers, my hands are bigger, and the skin is darker. They look stronger,
but they're not. She's the strong one, keeping me together.

Her body shifts.

"Don't let go," I beg.

So she doesn't.

For three revolutions we sit like that, not moving, not saying a word,
dangling over this big bright city in a glass pod. It feels like forever,
and it feels too fast.

When it's over, I pull back and look at Gretchen, her cheeks flushed pink, lips pressed together.

"It's done?" I say.

"Yeah, it's done," she says.

I don't want to let go of her hands. Not yet.

"Now can we please go have some fun?"

"Sounds good." She bites her top lip and the flush rises in her cheeks, or maybe I'm just imagining it. It's a little dark in here.

Another click and the door slides open. Bree and Ty are waiting for us, their hair all messed up. Bree's shirt is half untucked and her lipstick is smeared. They look like they just climbed out of bed.

And then I get it. It hits me all at once—why people love this crazy-ass death machine. They jump in those pods and get all up on each other. How did I not even *think* about that? Me? Alone with Gretchen? And we just went three goddamned revolutions, holding hands.

Which is probably a good thing, since she has a boyfriend and all.

"Let's ride the trolley!" Bree calls out.

She sounds so pumped about the idea that it makes me think: *Does a trolley have hookup pods too?* I'm pretty sure I've never heard the word *trolley*.

"Trolley?"

"Yeah, you know. A streetcar. It's like a train."

"And it stays on the ground?"

She smiles big. "Yes, Phoenix, a trolley stays on the ground. It's a cute little choo-choo train that rumbles along the tracks. You'll be fine."

"I'm not sure I trust you and your friends," I say to Gretchen. But I do.

We head out behind Bree and Ty. We walk along, close enough that our bodies sometimes touch, but I resist the crazy urge to take her hand, and I force my head to stop imagining what could have happened in that death pod.

If things were different.

If I were different.

We cross the street and join a big crowd of people waiting under a silver overhang.

"Where are all these people going?" I ask.

"Probably nowhere," Bree says. "It just started running. I think everyone wants to come out and ride."

"See what it's like," Ty says. "You know?"

I guess, but it seems strange that they're all lining up and swiping their credit cards at a machine, paying perfectly good money to go nowhere.

"Don't we need to get a Breeze Pass?" Gretchen asks.

"I got this," Ty says, opening his wallet and pulling out a blue card.

I don't even have a wallet. *I've got absolutely nothing.*

I nod and say, "Thanks, man."

A slick blue train pulls up, so quiet you barely hear it, except for a short high squeal as it turns the corner to come into the station. It jolts to a stop, the doors slide open, and we pile on with a bunch of other people. Ty slides into the last available seat, and Bree climbs right onto his lap. I follow Gretchen all the way to the front, where people are standing. She holds on to the center rail, and I grab an overhead bar nearby.

Three high chimes, and the doors are closing. The trolley starts to move and a woman, dressed in really fancy leather boots and a cropped jacket, starts talking to me.

"Disculple," she says. *"En dónde encontramos el tour de CNN?"* Her Spanish is as fancy as she is. If I had to guess, I'd say she's from, like, Argentina or somewhere.

"Lo siento, señora," I say. *"No soy de aquí."*

She smiles and shrugs. Her smile is nice. It makes me want to help her. I lean toward Gretchen. "Hey, Gretch," I say. "Where's the CNN tour?"

Gretchen glances up at the map on the wall of the trolley. "It's this one," she says. "You have to go inside that building and there's a kiosk." She squints a little. "Why?"

I shrug and motion toward the fancy lady. Then I turn back to her. She is looking away, so I touch her really lightly on the shoulder.

"Disculpe, señora. Mi amiga dice que se puede entrar por ese edificio." We're pulling up to the stop, and I point to a big glass entryway. *"Hay un kiosko adentro."*

The doors slide open, and the lady nods and smiles. She grabs the hand of a little girl, and they push their way out, through the crowds.

About a hundred people pile into our car, including a guy with a big-ass boom box blaring. Gretchen scoots in closer to me and says something, but I can't hear over the old-school hip-hop.

"What?" I call out.

She leans in and talks right into my ear. She is really close. Her lips are brushing up against my face, which is doing strange things to me.

"Sometimes I forget," she says. "I mean, that you're, like, a Spanish speaker."

Her cheeks have gone pink again, and she's watching my lips, like she wants to touch them. I swallow hard.

"I don't know any Spanish," she says, still looking right at my mouth, like she can't look away. "Do you *think* in Spanish?"

I'm not even sure she said it out loud. She mouthed it. She made me read her lips. I glance down, because the pink is spreading along her neck, creeping down under her shirt.

"Yeah," I sigh. *Christ,* I am sighing. "I guess it sort of, uh, well—it depends, I guess, on what I'm thinking about."

The streetcar jerks to a stop, and she loses her grip on the rail and falls into me. I have to grab her waist with my hand to hold her steady.

A sign glows outside the doors. WORLD OF COCA-COLA. The tourists keep piling on and that's so completely fine with me, because they are pushing and shoving and Gretchen is pressing against me and I am not letting go. The doors close and she moves in even closer, like she wants to fold herself into me.

And then the trolley starts going, and we're surrounded by them—a wall of American tourists folding us into each other.

The trolley jolts and Gretchen shifts, her hand flying over mine. She keeps it there and she slides my hand down a centimeter. I mean it— just the smallest bit, and the tip of my finger is on the bare skin under her shirt, right at the edge of her jeans.

We're lighting up, both of us. We are filling up with heat and light. I know she feels it too. Everything disappears: the music, the tourists, the walls of this trolley packed with people. Gone.

She turns to face me. She's so close, I can feel her breath. I watch her neck—her hair, spread across my chest.

"Are you now?" she whispers. "I mean, are you thinking in Spanish?"

I nod. I'm pretty sure I've forgotten how to speak.

"Tell me what you're thinking," she says. "I want to hear it." I close my eyes. I'm so lit up that my mouth can't form a single word. "But tell me in Spanish," she says.

I can do that.

I lean in, my lips against her hair, and I start to whisper. We ride along and she listens, taking in slow breaths. Gretchen's chest rises and falls and the place where my finger touches her skin burns with blue heat—that crazy intense heat that turns whatever it touches into pure white ash. And it's so damn beautiful, saying all the things that we could be together. So I let myself tell her. Just for now, I allow myself to believe that the aching and the wanting are okay, because I could love her, and she could love me back.

If things were different.

If I were different.

CHAPTER NINETEEN

GRETCHEN

MY PHONE LIGHTS up with Adam's face—a picture I took a year ago, forever ago. I need to pick up, to prove to myself and to Adam, and maybe even to Phoenix, that all this is perfectly normal.

By "this" I mean the fact that Phoenix and I haven't talked about that day at all—the *pupusas*, the Ferris wheel, the trolley (*Oh God, the trolley*)—but the kids and I are still hanging out with him every afternoon in the community garden. Or maybe, by "this," I mean that Phoenix and I keep finding ways to be close to each other out here, to touch a hand lightly, to brush up against a bare arm. And when the kids and I leave in the afternoon, we hold our hug for a beat too long, pressing in to inhale our combined scent—lavender and patchouli, dirt and sweat.

"Hey, Adam!" I say, brightly.

He is sitting on the bed in his dorm room. I can tell by the poster behind his head. "You sound good," he says. "What's up?"

"We just planted a tree—Luke and Anna and I."

"A tree?"

"Yeah. It was fun."

"Let me see," he says.

Phoenix is standing with a hose, watering the tree. He darts a look at me, questioning.

I shrug and turn the phone so that Adam can see. He sees the tree. He also sees Phoenix, boring an enormous hole into the tree with his cold stare. I really hope Adam can't tell—that he can't read the slouch, the look, the way Phoenix's entire body says, *I do not want to be part of this FaceTime conversation with your boyfriend.*

"Cool tree," Adam says. "Fig, right?"

"Yeah." *How does Adam know these things?*

"Who's that guy?"

"Oh, um, that's Phoenix. He's helping with the garden."

Phoenix watches me, his eyes searching.

"He's sort of in charge."

Phoenix hears me say those meaningless words.

"He's, like, really good at this stuff."

He's helping me come back alive. He's sort of amazing.

That's what I want for Phoenix to hear me say, but he doesn't, because I can't.

"Cool." Adam looks away from me, toward the door. He looks like he's ready to head through it. "Listen, *mon chou*, I know I said I was coming home this weekend, but my friend—"

His eyes dart to the corner of the room. "My friend is playing in this show—well, their band is playing . . ."

Their band. Interesting use of pronoun. "No worries," I say. "What's the band called?"

"Flower Girl—the name's ironic. They're emo, alt-rock, like Ex Hex with a little Girlpool mixed in."

I was right. "They" is a girl. And I'm not even bothered by this, at all. I'm also completely in the dark about what kind of music this girl plays, since I've never heard of Girlpool or Ex Hex.

"You definitely should go to the show, Adam," I say. "Support your friend."

"Maybe I'll come next weekend," he tells me, looking back toward the door.

"Yeah," I say. "That works."

He nods once. "Gotta get to class, *mon chou*. I love you."

I say I love you too because I do love him. But I guess I'm realizing that love is a complicated thing.

I don't remember what Adam did when he first saw me on that night back in August, after the incident. I don't even remember whether he hugged me or took my hand or kissed me. But I remember him sitting on the edge of the leather ottoman, watching in silence as the police officer grilled me. Adam listened to me describe what happened, and his eyes got so wide. And the moment that his jaw dropped, that was the exact moment when Adam began to see me differently, or maybe not to see me at all.

When I stumbled into the house, my face covered in blood, my eye bulging and already turning black, my mother was standing in the kitchen with a cup of tea. I remember that detail, the tea, because the porcelain cup fell to the ground and splintered into a million pieces, but my mom didn't even notice. She was already running toward me, calling out my father's name, again and again and again.

"Dan! Dan!"

She tried to wrap her arms around me, but I held out my hand to push her away. "Don't," I said. "I'll bleed on you."

My dad ran into the room, ignored my protests, and pulled me in close. Then I collapsed, sobbing into his chest.

He cried too when I told him. And he kept asking me, "Did he *hurt* you—did he try to *hurt* you?"

It's so weird that I kept saying no. Because, yes, he hurt me—in more ways than I could even begin to imagine at that point, but I knew what my dad was trying to ask me, and I didn't want to hear him say the word.

The police officer, though, he had no trouble asking that question, or any other question. By the time he arrived, Adam was there, too. I guess my mom called him. While my dad was holding me, my mom had been fuming and pacing and doing things. I don't even know what things. I think she was just trying to stay busy so she didn't have to face me.

After the police left, Adam stayed. He kept asking if I was okay and I kept saying I was. Which was an enormous lie. But I wanted him to feel okay, so I said it. I said it all the way to the hospital, where he held my hand tight while a bunch of nurses fussed over me and tried to put me back together.

Over the next few weeks, people came to the house to see me, and I was asked that question a lot. My aching muscles began to heal and my bruises faded from black to brown to yellow and I was asked so many questions and told so many things and none of them were right.

What did he look like? Was he black? Was he white? Was he on drugs?

Why did it matter what he looked like? These friends and well-wishers were supposed to be showing up at my house for *me*, to see how I was doing, to help me feel better. So why did everyone keep talking about *him*? I hated it when they asked about his race. I hated it so much. God, what a stupid, terrible, senseless question.

If only you hadn't been walking alone to your car. Why were you alone?

Jesus. The blame. I mean, really. They were telling me what I should have done differently, and my bruises weren't even gone yet. How was this helpful?

I always carry my keys in my fist for protection. I park under streetlights and weave to my car to avoid assault.

Advice. So many people with so much "useful" advice. Because, *yeah*, I was totally planning to go out that night and park on an empty street and walk to my car alone. I didn't leave the house for weeks, but the advice just kept coming.

I bet he was a drug dealer. He probably just wanted your credit cards so he could buy a big-screen TV at Best Buy. Maybe he was homeless and just desperate for money to eat.

So much speculation about *him*. Maybe because no one dared to speculate about *me* and whether I would come through all this—ever.

You'll go back to being your old self soon, Gretchen, and I will wait for you. I'm here, waiting. I promise not to go anywhere.

That was Adam. That's what he told me a few weeks later. And I didn't have the nerve to tell him that I was pretty sure my old self was gone for good.

After I'm finished babysitting the kids—after I've washed all the dirt from the garden off them, fed them, bathed them, and put them to bed—I get into the car and start to drive. I don't really have a plan, but I'm driving toward Athens. I need to see Adam. I think I want him to know it's okay. I want him to stop feeling like I *need* him, like he can't move on until I'm better. Because I am getting better, and because I think we both need to let ourselves move on.

When I am about twenty minutes away, I have to stop for gas. I drive past two stations, because they're not very well lit, and just the thought of getting out of my car at one of those places pulls at my chest and makes my hands tingle. But then I find a QuikTrip with enormous stadium lights and a bunch of people waiting in line at the pumps. I circle twice, trying to get up the nerve to stop and get out of the car, alone. My heart is beating a little faster than usual, but I know I can manage. I pull up behind a family—the dad is pumping gas, and the kids are in the back of the minivan, watching a movie. I swipe my credit card, and I'm looking all around me at first, hyperaware. But everything is fine. It's just a normal gas station and a bunch of typical suburban people. So I set up the nozzle and pull my phone from my pocket. I'm looking at my phone, trying to stay calm—to distract my mind from all the potential dangers it wants to conjure.

I check Adam's feed:

Studying @ Henderson's w/Rose and crew waiting on Kaukauna Kid up at 9 not to be missed if you're into experimental jazz improv.

Rose. It's a nice name. I'm guessing she's probably the Flower Girl he wants to stay in Athens for. I guess I'm about to meet her.

Henderson's is easy to find. It's right off Prince Avenue, in an old converted factory building. Redbrick with a sign hanging above the door, a gramophone record player etched into the dark wood. There are a few tables outside, but they're empty. The night is cool, and the air feels damp.

A big plate-glass window opens onto a coffeehouse/bar/live-music venue that's filled with people. Adam's type of place.

There's a bunch of street parking, but I can't bring myself to park on the street. I'm afraid it might bring back the memories. So I drive until I find a crowded parking lot. I lock my car and head inside fast, not even pausing for a second to think about what I'm doing or what I'm going to say or what might happen once I get this over with.

As soon as I go through the door, I see them: Adam and a girl, sitting next to each other at a table. A strange energy fills the space between them, and it makes me want to stop and watch. He's sort of leaned in toward her, but he isn't talking. His face looks scruffy, like he might be trying to grow a beard, and he wears Wayfarer eyeglasses, black-rimmed. They're new. The girl has on suede boots with three layers of fringe and a really short poufy skirt that has a complex flower design. Her hair is long and wavy. The way it falls creates a sort of wall, blocking out the world. Her bare knee is close to his, but not touching. They aren't touching anywhere, but it's like they are touching *everywhere*. Or at least wanting to.

I don't feel much of anything watching them, except curious about how that energy forms, how it can be so visible—so evident, even to strangers, probably. They're sitting with another girl. I recognize her— the pink-haired one from that awkward Skype conversation. I don't know how long I stand there—long enough to notice weird jazz music with a bunch of dissonance playing over the speakers, and to take in the acrid scent of roasted coffee beans, long enough to see them like that, in their own world, not doing anything at all except for inhabiting that space together.

I watch my boyfriend of two and a half years build a field of intense energy just by sitting next to this girl, and I start to wonder whether that's what people see when they watch me and Phoenix working beside each other in the garden, or sitting on the edge of a raised flower bed, sharing a bottle of water.

I know—it's so far beyond time to get this over with.

"Adam," I say, walking quickly toward him. He looks up at the same time as the girl.

"Mon chou!" He stands and throws his arms around me. We hug, and he lifts me just a bit off my feet.

"What are you doing here?" he asks, pulling back and smiling. "I can't believe you're here." He looks quickly around, still holding on to my shoulders. His touch is soft, soothing, familiar—but not electric.

"Where's your dad?"

"I came alone," I tell him.

"You drove here?"

"Yeah," I say. "I've been driving more and, you know, doing stuff on my own."

He lets go of one shoulder and turns to the girl with the wavy hair and fringed boots. "Did you hear that, Rose? She drove here, on her own."

The girl—Rose—stands up to face me. She smiles a sweet smile and says, "That's really great, Gretchen. I'm so glad you're getting better."

How much does this Flower Girl know?

Then the pink-haired girl gets up and throws her arms around me, pulling me into a tight hug. "I'm so glad you're finally well enough to come up here! We've all wanted to meet you!"

Does everyone in the entire town of Athens know I'm a mess?

"Sit down," Adam says to me. "I'm gonna get you a coffee."

He sort of pushes me into his chair and takes off for the bar. Rose and the other girl sit too.

"Your timing is perfect," the pink-haired girl says. "Kaukauna Kid comes on in, like, two minutes."

My timing is so far from perfect.

I nod and look around. They seem way younger than most of the hipsters packed into this place.

"Are you back in school?" Rose asks. "Are you applying here?"

"Oh," I say. "Uh, I don't really know yet. I might take a year off or something."

"That's cool," the pink-haired girl says. "You could travel!"

Yeah, I think. *I guess maybe I could.* I made it to Athens by myself. That's a start.

Adam comes back with a huge mug of coffee. He puts one hand on my shoulder as he sets the mug down in front of me. "Nutella Latte," he says.

"Seriously?"

"Yeah," he says. "They make the thing with real Nutella, straight from the jar. Every time I see them do it, I think of you, standing in your pantry, eating spoonfuls of the stuff."

"Thanks," I say. I take a sip. The flavor carries me home, to a place that feels safe and secluded. But I need to be here, and I need to be brave, so I put the coffee down onto the table.

Adam pulls an extra chair into the space between me and Rose, just as a group of three heads up to the stage.

A few people in the crowd call out an enthusiastic *yeah*, and the drums launch in. The beat is just a little off, but I think they mean for it to be that way. Then the bassist starts to fool around some, playing off the drummer. A woman tucks her violin under her chin and begins to move the bow across it really slowly. It lets out a series of high, mournful sighs.

"She's so amazing," Rose says, almost swooning.

Adam puts his hand on my knee. He looks over at me and smiles. I look down at his hand on my knee while the violin keeps sighing and the drumbeat intensifies. I grab on to Adam's hand.

"Can we go outside for a minute?" I ask.

"Sure, yeah." He stands up and pulls me toward the door.

I realize that it's the first time we've held hands in a long time. His fingers feel cool and soft, his touch light and airy. It's almost as if he's already slipped away.

When we get outside, I gesture to one of the empty tables.

We sit there in silence for a while, which is unusual for Adam.

A few people pass by and look at us. I think about what they see, about how they don't see our bodies inclined toward each other, because they aren't; about how they don't see that charge in the space between us, because it isn't there.

"I'm so glad you're getting better," he says. "And that you could come up here alone."

"Me too," I say. "It feels really good."

He nudges my hand, which is resting flat on the table. "I told you that you'd be back to your old self," he says brightly. "You just needed some time."

I take Adam's hand in mine and I look directly at him. "That's the thing, though," I say. "I'm not back to my old self. I'm never going to be back, Adam."

"I don't believe that." He's rubbing the top of my hand with his thumb. "You're still *you*, Gretchen."

I'm completely at a loss for how to make him see what I'm trying to tell him. I think maybe we need to start over. I need a different way to bring us into the hardest part.

"Your friends seem nice," I tell him, squeezing his hand lightly. "Are they the ones in the band you told me about?"

His eyes dart to the side, just as they did when we talked on the phone. "Rose is. She sings and plays drums."

"Like Sheila E.," I say.

He smiles and lets out a short laugh. "No, actually. Nothing like Sheila E."

I'm reminded of when I was a kid, watching *American Idol* with my parents. We loved to watch that show together—the only program my mom would let us eat dinner in front of the TV for. It was a guilty pleasure, I guess.

Needless to say, Adam is not a fan of *American Idol*.

"I wrote a song about you," he tells me. "She's gonna play it this weekend."

He wrote a song?

"I didn't know you wrote songs."

"I told you. Remember? I've been fooling around with it some in my creative writing class." He bites the inside of his lip. "My professor really loved this one, and all my classmates did too. It's called 'Instigator.'"

Instigator. My head starts to spin while my mind forms the image. Deep-red lipstick smeared across my forearm. *Why did I tell him?*

"You can't do that, Adam. You can't take that from me." My hands are shaking.

"Take what?" He looks genuinely surprised.

"My story—all that terrible stuff I told you. It's *mine*, Adam."

Adam leans toward me, shaking his head slowly from side to side. "No, Gretchen. It's not just yours. It's mine too."

I squeeze my eyes shut, trying to focus on what he's telling me. But all I can think about is that he called me Gretchen. Adam never calls me by my name.

"It's your mom's and your dad's. It's Bree's. We all went through it too."

Maybe he's right. Maybe part of it belongs to him. But I know I don't want any more of it to be Adam's. Not another moment of it.

"I love you, Adam, but it's time for us to let this go." I breathe deep, relieved to have said it, finally.

"Let *what* go?"

"I'm so sorry," I tell him. "You have been patient, and good to me, and I wish I could be what you want." I touch his hand. "We're done, Adam. We've been finished for a long time."

"So that's it? After everything, that's it?" He pulls his hand away and pushes back his chair. The metal legs scrape across the brick and we both look down.

"And I don't want you to write songs about me," I whisper. "About *us*."

Adam stands up. "Thanks for sharing your opinion, but"—his voice is getting low, angry—"it's not really your choice—who or what I write songs about."

The door opens and we turn away from each other. We both watch a few people walk out of the coffeehouse. The band is still playing, but

I don't hear the violin anymore. I watch Adam as his gaze moves to Rose through the plate-glass window. He studies her, a puzzled look on his face. I see it all, suddenly. Adam and Rose huddled together while he recounts every detail of my dissolution. And then she goes to the keyboard or the drums, or whatever, and they dive into my story, my pain, my hurt. They use it to make music together. To make something beautiful, or maybe something totally sucky, but it's mine. It's not theirs to use. It's not theirs to build a relationship out of.

"Hey, Adam?" I say. "You know how people talk about rebounding—how you're supposed to take time to heal after a breakup and stuff like that?"

"Yeah." He clenches his jaw. Once. Twice.

"I don't really think that applies to us. I mean, you're obviously ready to move on. We haven't been—"

"Don't say it." He's still looking at Rose. "I get what you're trying to tell me." He gestures toward Rose. "We haven't—"

"I know," I say. "Thanks." I guess I am grateful, but I also feel used, like maybe I was the drama that Adam and Rose and all their artsy, emo friends needed to make their own lives more vivid or more meaningful. Like Adam stayed with me, not because he was worried for me, but because he needed to suffer to make art, or some crap like that.

"I'm going back in now." His voice is cold, sharp at the edges. "Do you need me to walk you to your car?"

I shake my head once, and he turns away.

CHAPTER TWENTY

PHOENIX

SO NOW I'M THE GARDENER. The piece-of-shit gardener who waters the plants. How many ways could Gretchen have described me to her college boyfriend?

And she picked the *gardener*?

Christ, how I wish I hadn't seen his face framed by Gretchen's phone. He was looking right past me, like I was that Random Brown Person who waters the plants.

I guess that's what I am. . . .

This is how the stupid, awkward conversation went, after she hung up:

Me: "*Was that your boyfriend?*"
Her: "*Yeah. That was Adam.*"
Me: "*He seemed*"—like more of a candy-ass wuss than I am—"*nice.*"
Her: "*He is. He's been there for me, you know?*"
Me: "*Yeah.*" Oh, has he? Because when I met you, he was not there.
    You were a complete wreck, and he wasn't anywhere near you.
Her: "*He's a really good guy.*"
Me: "*Yeah.*"

Her: *"Yeah."* And then her hand flew to her forehead. *"What am I doing?" she said.*

Me: Nothing. Not a word. I'm pretty sure she wasn't asking me, and, even if she was, what could I say?

I'm losing my mind, thinking about her and that guy, and about me, the piece-of-shit gardener, watching them chat about the tree I planted. And I'm wondering what she meant by the whole "What am I doing?" thing. I figure that was just typical Gretchen, the crazy, beautiful girl who always goes on and says whatever strange idea happens to pop into her brain.

The girl who is driving me completely *insane.*

I'm walking through Downtown with Amanda, staring at my feet while all this keeps running through my head on a loop. But thinking about Gretchen might actually be a good thing, because it's keeping me from thinking about the meeting with Ms. Pérez, my kick-ass lawyer. And about going into that court after our meeting.

This is it.

I didn't tell Gretchen about court. I couldn't figure out how. Part of me didn't want to worry her, and the other part figured that, since we're killing ourselves trying to be "just friends," it would be too much, too personal for me to talk about how scared I am. At least I told Bo and Barbie. I've been spending a lot of time with them at the tattoo shop. At first I kept to myself, working my ass off every day to earn my tattoo removal. (I'm still a long way off.) But then I started to get comfortable. In Bo's shop, nobody ever judges anyone, not even for the ugly shit they decide to put on their bodies—permanently. And then one day Bo and Barbie invited me over for dinner after work. About four of their

houses could fit into Amanda and Sally's, but I keep going back whenever they ask me. It's just more comfortable over there or something.
It's, like, the couches already have a couple of stains and the wood on
the kitchen table is scratched, so I don't have to be so careful all the time,
worrying I might mess something up. Last night I told them that today
is my court date. It was good, talking with them.

Like I said, Bo and Barbie don't judge, which makes it easy.

Amanda tugs on my arm. I look up, and she's pointing across the street
at a big sculpture in the middle of a park.

"Hey," she says. "Do you know what that is?"

It's pretty cool, actually. It's, like, two stories high, and there's this
girl. She's not wearing a top, but in an artsy way, like when you see pictures of angels painted on the ceiling of a church or something. I guess
she's not a girl—she's more like a woman, but she looks young. Her
neck is long, and her hair is flowing behind her back, like there's wind
blowing, but not too much. She's leaning back a little and her arms are
reaching up, holding a bird that looks like it's about to take flight. It's
like she picked him up, all careful, and she's helping him—releasing
him—like she wants to set him free. And that bird, he's all stretched
out too. He's totally ready to fly.

"It's a Phoenix," Amanda says. "Like you."

I look over at her. "What is?"

"The bird. It's a Phoenix, rising from the ashes."

And here I went eighteen years thinking Phoenix was just a city in
Arizona.

"Atlanta burned during the civil war—right to the ground,"
Amanda says. "After the war, the people rebuilt the city. That's how it
earned its nickname, the Phoenix."

"Yeah?" I say. "That's cool."

"I guess this place is your city," Amanda says, smiling. "You were meant to be here!"

I shrug and look at my feet. A month ago I would have thought she was crazy for saying so. It was completely random that I landed in this place. But now I'm starting to wonder.

We walk for a while, not saying anything, and I'm trying not to think about going to court, or about Gretchen, or about being the stupid *pinche* gardener. So instead I think about how cool that sculpture is, that girl just lifting the bird and sending it off into the sky.

We see Sally from across the lobby as soon as we walk into the lawyer's office building. I take one look at her, and I know something's up. She's standing there, her phone up in her face, reading something. She looks like she's about to hurl the phone through the big plate-glass window.

"Wanker!" she cries out as we approach. "Feckin' wanker!"

Did Sally just drop the f-bomb? Is that how people from England say it?

I look over at Amanda, wondering if she's as shocked as I am, but she's reaching out for the phone. Sally comes and puts her arm around my shoulders, and I just stand there, not moving, while Amanda reads Sally's screen.

"Bitch," she says. "Who does she think she is?"

What the hell? What happened to the sweet churchy lesbians I've been living with for all this time?

"Threat to our community. What a load of crap." That's Amanda.

And then Sally: "Criminal gang activity. Feckin' horseshit."

Oh. This must be about me.

"What's up?" I ask.

"It's Jane, that uptight ninny."

"Who?"

"Mrs. Walsingham," Amanda says. "You know, the neighborhood watchdog? The one who gets on people's cases for not bringing in their garbage cans? She posted something on our community message board, online."

"Horseshit," Sally says again. "Pure feckin' horseshit spread around to a thousand people."

This comes as no surprise to me. That woman does kind of seem like a first-class bitch. Or a "feckin' wanker," or whatever.

"We'll take care of it," Amanda says, putting her hand on my arm and trying to sound calm. "Don't you worry about it."

Sally looks right at me, and her face relaxes. "That's right, sweetheart. Don't worry that pretty little head of yours. This is nothing. Rubbish! We'll send one e-mail and—snip, snap—all cleaned up."

She wipes her hands across each other twice. As if cleaning up messes is that easy.

And I'm like, "Yeah, okay. I'm not worried," because the sweet churchy lesbians are back, smiling at me. And anyway, how much damage can a few words on a screen do to a person? Not much. That's what I say.

"We're going to be late if we don't go on up," Amanda says.

Sally shoves her phone into her purse, and then we all head toward the elevator.

Pretty soon I start to question my whole theory about words on a screen. We're barely even sitting down when Ms. Pérez looks up from her computer, her face all serious.

"I'm going to be as direct as possible with you three," she says.

As if she usually beats around the bush? Ms. Pérez, my kick-ass lawyer, is always direct.

"In preparing for your merits hearing, we have encountered some evidence that Phoenix appears to have hidden from us."

She looks right at me.

Am I supposed to say something? I stay quiet.

"The DHS attorney responsible for your case was in contact with a Federal prosecutor. They report credible evidence of criminal gang activity."

"But, Ms. Pérez," Amanda says, "Phoenix has been honest from the start about this. They know he was in a gang—for a very short period. Right?"

"Until this point, they"—she looks right at me—"*we* were aware that Phoenix had been coerced to join a gang at the age of thirteen."

"Right," Sally says, "and that he left just a few weeks later. So what's changed?"

I didn't exactly leave. They all know that. I was too afraid of what they'd make me do if I left for real. The thing is, those guys make you do crazy, terrible shit before they'll let you leave the gang—*if* they'll let you leave. They say you have to prove your loyalty one last time, but if you suck at proving your loyalty in the first place—which I obviously did—they expect the worst from you. Like killing people. I'm not even exaggerating. I was not going down that road, so I hid out with Sister Mary Margaret and pretended I had nothing to do with them.

"There's an FBI unit in El Salvador, the TAG unit. They work with the *federales*, the federal police on gang activity—to protect witnesses, victims, family members—"

Because the federal police in El Salvador really wanna help . . . That's what I call horseshit.

"They have testimony from a man named Rogelio Cruz Benítez, El Turbino."

El Turbino. A hole opens in the floor. I grasp the armrests of my chair and hold on, trying not to free-fall, trying not to imagine his face, his skin, his screams. *Oh Christ*, the smell.

"He's alive?"

That's me talking. Why can't I keep my mouth shut?

"You recognize the name?" Ms. Pérez asks me.

I look down at the disappearing floor and nod. The little gray lines on the carpet are turning into complicated swirls.

"He offered testimony," Ms. Pérez says. She is sitting still, but her voice is moving away from me, fast.

El Turbino spoke English. I remember that. He was in a rival gang—one of the big-shot leaders deported from California. It used to be that all the big shots were from California. That's where these stupid gangs started in the first place. But then those guys were getting in trouble and getting deported. The US doesn't want them—*who would?*—so they dump those gangsters' asses in my neighborhood, broke, no job, don't even speak much Spanish. Then the gangsters find a gun—which is way too easy—and they take charge.

Maybe that's why Delgado made us go all apeshit on him. He was the one in charge. Maybe he wanted to prove we were as tough as the original gangsters, the ones from Los Angeles. Those *mareros* who had been sent back to San Salvador from Los Angeles, they were pretty much running the place. People like Delgado—the real *Salvadoreños*—they didn't like it.

Delgado is smart. He's crazy, and the meanest person I have ever known, but he's smart.

So he made us take off El Turbino's tattoo—the hard way.

You putos *are straight* chavalas. That's what El Turbino said. That's what he was spitting out, his saliva landing in little droplets on my forearm while I rubbed a rag across his arm, scrubbing away dirt and blood, just like Delgado had told me to do.

Before I'd even laid eyes on El Turbino, Delgado and his boys had beat the shit out of him. Now they wanted me to clean him up so they could see his tattoo better, every numeral inked into El Turbino's skin. But the smell of the rag Delgado had handed to me—it was so strong. I couldn't figure it all out.

"Is he okay?" I whisper, still looking at the floor of Ms. Pérez's office, still unable to focus on anything but the hole opening in my gut. "I mean, did you see photos?"

She bites her lower lip. "I wish I hadn't."

I can't believe he is alive. *How is that even possible?*

"Please, Ms. Pérez. What is going on?" Amanda asks.

"Rogelio Cruz Benítez, who also went by El Turbino, was a member of a rival gang. He was tortured by the specific *clique* that Phoenix was part of, after crossing into their territory."

Territory. Like my *colonia* is such an awesome place that we don't want to share it with anyone. How could I have been so damn stupid?

"In official testimony, he named Phoenix as one of his torturers," Ms. Pérez says.

"Our Phoenix?" Sally calls out. "No, that's not possible, Ms. Pérez."

"That's his testimony." Ms. Pérez sighs and props her elbows on the desk. It makes me feel like crap, seeing her do that. She looks exhausted, and disappointed.

In me. She's disappointed in me.

"This man was in a rival gang," Amanda says. "Right? I mean, how do they know he didn't just make it up—fabricate the entire story?"

"It has been confirmed by a member of Phoenix's gang, a witness by the name of Fredi Palacios Pérez."

Slayer. If he gave testimony, it means he got out. *How can it be that Slayer had the courage to leave, and I didn't?*

"Mr. Palacios Pérez testified in exchange for clemency on a drug-related charge, so perhaps his testimony could be called into question." She pauses and looks right at me. "But Cruz Benítez—he suffered severe burns over more than half of his body. Some were third-degree," Ms. Pérez says. "That's impossible to make up."

What I didn't know—because I was thirteen, and stupid and drunk—was this: the rag I used to clean El Turbino's tattoo had been soaked in gasoline. Slayer was the guy who lit the match.

"Well, he made a mistake," Amanda says, her eyes narrowing. "Phoenix wasn't there."

They're waiting for me to say something. *Oh Christ. What do I say?*

"I was there." I whisper it—quietly, but loud enough that they can hear it clearly. I want them to hear it. I need for them to know the truth about me.

"But, Phoenix," Sally says, "being there doesn't mean you *participated*."

I look right over at Sally, that sweet woman who welcomed me into her home, who fed me fresh fish in the middle of Georgia, who took me to a basketball game, who made me build a garden and helped me pick out all the plants, who swore like a sailor when she thought people were treating me bad. I look up at Sally, I look her right in the eye, and I say it.

"I did."

And, *oh Christ*, I wish I didn't keep looking at her, because her face just crumples up like a paper bag. And Amanda, sitting next to her, falls right forward in her seat, her hands rising to cover her face.

"I'm sorry," I say, so quiet this time that maybe they don't even hear me.

Ms. Pérez sighs. "I assume you know, Phoenix, that this is terrible for your case. There are thousands of young men seeking asylum from El Salvador right now—thousands. Only a handful will be granted it, and I can assure you that the ones who engaged in gang-related torture will not be among them."

"So it's over, then." That's Amanda, talking through her hands, where her face is buried.

Ms. Pérez nods. "We will go into that courtroom and do our best, Phoenix, but it's almost certain at this point that you won't be granted asylum."

"Okay," I say. "Thanks."

"But what about the appeal?" Amanda asks. "You told us that he probably won't win his merits hearing anyway, but that we can appeal. That maybe we can seek a change of venue and have a better chance of winning. Isn't that right?"

Ms. Pérez leans back in her chair and shakes her head slowly. "I'm sorry, Amanda. I think that, in light of this new evidence, it would likely be wasting our time, and a great deal of your money, to appeal."

"Even if we could get his case moved to a different court? To another state?"

"Yes, I'm afraid even in Illinois or California—even the most sympathetic courts—are not going to like this evidence."

"I see," Amanda says. Her eyes are getting all watery, and she looks like she's gonna cry.

"Phoenix, you need to understand"—Ms. Pérez looks over at me sitting there like an idiot, unable to speak—"that you will be given an order of deportation today. You should prepare yourself for that."

How does a person prepare to die? I mean, what, exactly, are the steps? Maybe I should start going to church with Sally and Amanda.

"Bloody hell!" Sally calls out, rising to her feet. "No! Absolutely not. He is not going to *prepare himself*!" Her hands are flailing wildly. "He was *thirteen*! He was just a baby. He *left* that gang!" She slams her palms down on Ms. Pérez's desk. "He left because he didn't want to be part of all of that. And then he risked everything to make sure his brother didn't have to join! He wanted to do the right thing! He tried *so* hard to do the right thing!"

She turns her entire body toward me. For such a small lady, she looks huge. It's like she's swelling up, filling up with I don't know what. And I don't know why she cares so much. *Why does she care?*

"Phoenix Flores Flores, you are not a torturer." She says each word slowly, carefully, looking right at me.

But I can't hold her gaze. I look down at my shoes—not my shoes, the shoes someone donated to me, some nice churchy person who thought I was worthy of his charity.

What would he think now? A torturer, walking in his shoes.

I shrug. Sally catches my shoulder in her hand and begins to shake me.

"Look at me, Phoenix!" Her voice is rising. "You are not a bloody torturer!"

Maybe she's right.

"I didn't know they were going to burn it off," I say quietly. "The tattoo—I didn't know I was—"

"Speak up," Amanda says, an edge in her voice. "We can't hear you."

But what I hear her saying is: *Torturer. I invited a torturer to live in my home, to sleep in my own son's bed.*

Sally takes my chin in her hand and makes me look directly at her. "If you don't tell Ms. Pérez, she can't help you, Phoenix. You have to keep talking. You have to explain." She squeezes my chin between her fingers. "I know you can do this."

Her face is going blurry.

"Phoenix!" she calls out.

I pull back and look down at the carpet, stripes swimming, floor falling out from underneath me, black smoke filling up my head.

I can't form another word. The smoke is rising and the flames are spreading and the smell of gasoline mixed with burning flesh is searing my nostrils. I sit, not saying a word, using every bit of will I have to keep this shit from coming down on me, but it keeps coming. It always does.

I stand up and bolt out of the office. I'm rushing down the hall, looking for somewhere to hide, but I can't see anything. Only black smoke, filling my senses.

I grab the handle of a door and throw it open. I think maybe it's a supply closet. I slam the door behind me, and that's when I buckle.

I don't even know it's happening until my knees hit the floor. And then all I can hear is the roaring in my ears. The horrible, brutal images keep on coming, one after the other.

Shivering, I fall to the ground and wrap my arms around my knees.

The smell. Oh Christ, the smell. It has been five years, but if I live ten thousand lives, I will never forget the smell.

After Slayer lit the match, they doused him in more gasoline.

I screamed, tore at their arms, tried to stop them. *"Por favor! Por favor, Blackie! Ja, Ja, Basta!"* Delgado turned to look at me, hate burning in his eyes. And that's when I knew it.

Oh, sweet Jesus, I so knew it.

It was all clarity, pure and clean and cool. It was like a stream of fresh water coursing through my soul. I was gonna run and never, ever, in ten thousand lifetimes, never come back.

Here's the thing: I almost never did. For five years I managed never to step foot in that place, never again to answer to Delgado, to do terrible, heinous, unthinkable things just because that lunatic told me to do them. Not until six months ago, when I showed up to drag Ari out of there. Because Delgado was after my brother. He said it was time to have a Flores kid back at work with them. And no matter how much Ari kicked and screamed and punched, nothing was going to stop Delgado from getting his way.

Except for me. I was going to stop Delgado if it was the last thing I ever did. So I went in for Ari, and I took him away. But not before

Delgado marked me one last time. This time it wasn't with ink. This time, he lunged at me, with a knife. For the first and last time in my entire life, I went completely badass. I grabbed the hand that held a knife to my throat and I swung my leg around to kick him. The force sent Delgado flying across that room, and I went in for Ari.

When I left that place for the second time, I wasn't running. I backed out while everyone watched. Blood poured from my neck, and my shaking hand held a gun for the first time in my life (and, *Christ*, I hope the last).

I pointed that gun at Delgado's heart, shielding Ari's scrawny little body with my own. When we got to the doorway, Delgado green-lighted us.

"*Están muertos,*" he said, still hunched on the floor. "*Luz verde.*"

He had ordered us dead. And soon, everyone who had ever pledged loyalty to that gang would know, and they would follow Delgado's orders, because *Mara siempre.*

The gang is forever.

When Ari and I rounded the corner, I threw the gun into the lake and we ran all the way to the Guatemala border.

I tried to protect my little brother, but I failed.

Oh Christ, how I failed.

Because if I had done things right, Ari would be in school right now, living his life, doing all the innocent things that twelve-year-olds do. Instead he is in Texas, where at least Delgado can't get to him. And here I am, still living, I guess. Curled up on the floor, in the supply closet of some fancy American lawyer's office, the stench of burning flesh still in my nostrils.

That's how they find me—Amanda and Sally.

Sally leads me into the bathroom. There's a man in a suit standing at the urinal, and she tells him to leave. He looks her up and down once—this tiny woman with a giant presence—and he walks right out, zipping up his pants as he goes.

She holds me up while I splash water onto my face. Then she takes me by the arm, and we walk together toward the courthouse.

"You can do this," she tells me. "You're ready."

But I'm not. I'm not ready.

Three hours later—and I'm sitting on a hard wood bench at the front of the courtroom, shivering my ass off. I'm still not ready for what that judge has to say. It doesn't matter that she's using a bunch of legal language I've never heard before and that I barely understand. Because I understand.

She's sending me back to El Salvador.

Luz verde. Green light.

I'm as good as dead.

CHAPTER TWENTY-ONE

GRETCHEN

"SO, THAT'S IT, THEN?"

"Yeah," I tell my dad. "It's over."

Dad and I are sitting at the kitchen table, talking about my night with Adam. I have my compass in one hand, and I'm smoothing a map with the other—an actual map.

"And you're okay with it?"

"I was the one who did it, Dad."

I can't remember the last time I looked at a map—like, a real paper one with lots of folds and complicated keys. Maybe never. It took forever to find this stupid thing. Anyway, I have a plan, and it requires a map.

"And Adam, how did he take it?"

"Honestly, I think he was relieved."

Dad nods slowly and looks back at his work. That's one thing about my dad. He knows when to stop prying. We work together in silence for a few minutes, until I start wrestling with the folds of the map again.

We've basically arrived at the point in my homeschooling career where I'm on my own. We sit at the table every morning for a couple of hours together, just out of habit. But I don't really need my dad anymore. And when it comes to subjects like calculus and physics, he has absolutely no idea what I'm doing. Mom and Dad are both baffled by my ability to solve complicated equations. Neither one of them is any good at math. Mom asked me once how I do it. We were at the thrift store and I was calculating discounts on a big stack of clothes we had found. She asked me how I manage to do this in my head, without a calculator or even a pencil and paper. I thought for a minute and then I told her. The solutions form in my mind—I can *see* them. It's that simple. She looked at me like I was an alien from outer space, and then we went back to searching through the racks at the thrift store.

"What's the map for?" Dad asks. "History project?"

"I finished that project," I say. "I'm actually working on something else."

I measure a distance of twenty miles with the key, and then I expand the compass to that width and place it on the table. I find the point on the map where Amanda and Sally's house would be and mark it with a red dot.

Dad stands up and looks over my shoulder. He watches as I stick the compass needle into the red dot and direct the pencil tip northeast—toward Snellville. I feel relief to see that its radius stretches across Stone Mountain Park. There are nice hiking trails there—if you know where to go to avoid the crowds.

I came up with the idea while driving home from Dahlonega, after Phoenix told me about his "American Dream." I decided to give Phoenix a map of all the places he can hike and spend time in nature, within his twenty-mile radius. I want to go with him, to take him places. I want for him to see things, experience things, with me. I hope he wants that too.

I was planning to go over to Amanda and Sally's this morning, to tell Phoenix about Adam, but he said he had somewhere to be all morning, that maybe we could hang out later. But now it's afternoon, and he still hasn't texted me back. I'm trying not to worry.

The pencil tip lands on Snellville. I start to trace the circle north and west. As the pencil moves west, I realize he won't make it to Kennesaw Mountain—that's way outside the twenty-mile radius. The protractor's arc cuts out Sweetwater Creek, too.

I sigh—that's such a beautiful park. Phoenix would love it.

"What's that sigh about?" my dad asks.

"The map is for Phoenix," I say. "I thought it might be nice for him to see all the things he can do near Sally and Amanda's house."

My dad knows about the parole, and about the ankle monitor. I told both of my parents as soon as we got back from Dahlonega. At first they seemed really nervous, but Mom called Amanda and they talked for a while. Then Mom chatted with Dad for a few minutes in their bedroom, the door closed. When they came back out, they told me how proud they were of me, how well they thought I'd handled the whole thing. Then they asked to meet Phoenix, so he came over for brunch with Sally and Amanda. He was so nervous the whole time, and really polite. When my parents insisted he call them by their first names, he looked at them like they had grown two heads. But then he nodded and said he would. He did his best, but every time he said Dan or Lisa it sounded wrong, like he was forcing out the words.

My dad sits down beside me. "You want to take him to these places?"

"Yeah," I say. "Some of them—he doesn't really have any friends, you know? And he can't drive. I'm going to ask Aunt Lauren if maybe the kids and I can take him to see some of these things."

Dad reaches out across the map and takes my hand. "I'm so proud of you, sweetheart. A couple of weeks ago, you weren't even driving yourself to Ivywood Estates, and now *this*. It's great, honey."

He squeezes my hand gently.

"And now you're gonna say, 'But—'"

"You know me too well." He gives me the Dad look—the one that goes right through my eyes and into my gut. "Lauren called me, about Phoenix."

"What?" I say. "Why?"

"There was some notice posted on the neighborhood chat, online. Something about him being dangerous."

"Dangerous?"

"The post said he has a record of involvement in gang activity."

"What?" I stand up and clutch the edge of the table. "You know that's not true, right?"

"I know that Phoenix is a good kid, and that Amanda and Sally trust him implicitly. That's all that matters to me, Gretchen, but your aunt—"

"Whatever, Dad," I tell him. "I'll explain it to her, okay?"

Dad nods and looks back at his computer screen, but I know he wants to say more. It's the squint of his left eye, the way the skin wrinkles around it. A dead giveaway every time.

"What?" I ask him. "I know there's something else you're dying to say to me."

"Karen called," he tells me. "The prosecutor?"

A question. As if I've forgotten the woman who showed me photos of a bullet-riddled body. And not just any bullet-riddled body. The body of *that boy*.

"She has a few things she'd like to discuss with us. Your mom and I can talk with her first if you'd like."

"Okay," I say. "Thanks."

We work in silence, because there's not really anything more to say, except maybe that I'm grateful to them, for dealing with Karen. I'm studying the map, double-checking the radius at several points on the circle's circumference, when I get a text from Aunt Lauren.

Won't need your help today. I've decided to come home early to take kids for haircuts.

That's a first.

Okay. See you tomorrow?

She texts back immediately.

Yes, but need to talk tonight. Want you to plan some new activities with kids. Maybe library? Ancient history museum?

In other words: not garden. Not Phoenix. I sit there, staring at the screen, trying to imagine Luke's reaction when I tell him that instead of digging in the dirt, he'll have the wonderful opportunity to walk quietly through a dusty room and look at statues.

Is this about my friend Phoenix?

As I said, let's talk tonight. But that was bad judgment, Gretchen. It's not safe for them to be with that boy. You shouldn't have taken them there. We can't let it happen again.

I feel my gut clench. I can't even form a response. I don't want to talk to Aunt Lauren. I want to talk to Phoenix.

Why isn't he texting me back?

"Gotta go," I tell my dad, pushing my chair back from the table. "I'll drive today if that's okay."

"Sure, honey. Have fun with the little terrors!"

I don't answer. He doesn't need to know I'm not on my way to work. I'm going to find "that boy."

Finding Phoenix is easy. He's in the garden, where he is almost every afternoon. But getting him to look at me is something else entirely. He's all wrong. His body is hunched over, his eyes are darting around. I can't figure it out.

"Where is everyone? No volunteers today?" I'm walking alongside him as he carries a big bag of topsoil from the shed to a raised bed.

"No shows." He hurls a bag of soil to the ground and turns to get another.

I try to help, but he won't let me.

I follow behind him, thinking he must know about the online forum and what that woman said about him. Maybe that's why he's acting so strange.

"Because of that neighborhood message board post?"

He's leaning down to pick up more topsoil. Two bags this time. He lets out a grunt when the bags hit his shoulders. His jaw clenches tight and he walks slowly, deliberately, under the weight of the soil.

"You know about that?"

I nod. "I can't believe she said that stuff about you."

"Yeah." He leans forward and lets the bags fall to the ground. Then he shoves them on top of the one he's already carried over. I feel like an idiot, following him back and forth, so I finally give up on trying to help, and sit down on top of the pile.

"It doesn't matter," he says. "Except the neighborhood bridge club was supposed to show up for a garden workday this afternoon, and no one did."

"God, that's so lame." I'm shaking my head, because this is all happening a mile from where I live. It's so *wrong*.

He takes a shovel from the shed and starts to jab it at the ground. He still hasn't looked me in the eyes. Not even once.

"I don't even know what a bridge club is." He tosses the shovel so that it lands next to the pile I'm sitting on. "All I know is that I can't plant a hundred flats of flowers and vegetables alone." His voice is low and grumbly. "And all my volunteer groups canceled."

"*All* of them?"

He nods but doesn't answer. I glance toward an enormous quantity of little pots, lined up in neat rows on the other side of the shed. When I turn back, I catch him looking at me. His expression is one I've never seen. His eyes are bloodshot and rimmed in red. He looks away quickly.

"Are you *high*?" I'm not even thinking. The words just come tumbling out of my mouth.

"Jesus, Gretchen!" he says, angry. "You think I'm out here getting high alone?"

"No, it's just—"

"No, I'm not high. And just so you know, I never have been."

"Sorry," I whisper, looking away from him. "You seem a little off or something, and I thought maybe—"

He gestures to the bags I'm sitting on. "I need those."

I get up and he grabs one from the top. He tears it open and starts to dump dirt onto an empty raised bed. We both watch in silence as the dark soil hits the ground. He shakes the last of the dirt from the bag and grabs another. Tired of feeling useless, I go to the shed and grab a hoe. I bring it back to the bed and start to spread the soil.

"Thanks," he mutters. "Where are Luke and Anna, anyway?"

"Their mom sort of freaked. She said I shouldn't have let the kids be with you."

"Really?" he asks, looking up. His face doesn't have that light in it, and he won't smile. Everything feels so off balance.

"It's just a misunderstanding," I say. "I'll clear it up."

He keeps dumping soil into the bed, and I keep pushing it around, and it feels to me like neither of us can say what we want to say. When the last bag of soil is in, Phoenix glances at me, like he wishes I weren't still around.

"Can we take a break?" I ask. "Talk, maybe?"

He points over to three spindly bushes. "I've gotta get those in the ground."

"What are they?" I ask.

"Dunno. Amanda bought them. Some kind of berries I've never seen."

"I'll help."

It turns out, they're blackberries. I hold the branches steady while Phoenix fills the holes around them with dirt. By the time we've finished the third one, I can't take the silence any longer.

"Adam and I broke up." I blurt it out.

He stops shoveling and looks up at me. "What?"

"Last night I went to Athens and we ended it."

He studies my face for a split second and then starts to shovel again. "I'm sorry."

Not the response I was expecting—or maybe hoping for.

"I'm not," I tell him.

"You can let it go now." He nods once.

"Huh?" I don't get what he's saying.

"The vine. You can let go."

I release the bush, and Phoenix starts to pound the dirt with his shovel, packing the dirt around these bushes or vines or whatever they are. They don't even have any leaves on them. They're just these weird-shaped sticks, all lined up in a row.

"So, that's it?" I ask him. My heart is starting to beat fast in my chest.

"What?" he asks.

"That's all you want to say about Adam?" I feel cold, suddenly. I cross my arms and hug my chest tight.

Phoenix looks away from me, across the garden and toward the street. It's like he's ready to bolt out of this conversation as fast as he can.

"Let's sit," he says.

We walk over to a stack of two-by-fours and sit down at opposite ends.

"There's something I need to know—I mean, a question I need for you to answer. It's been bugging me—" He's staring down at his hands.

"Sure," I say. "Anything."

"What did he look like?"

"Who?"

"You know who," he says.

Of course, he's right. I know who he's talking about. *That boy.*

"It doesn't matter," I tell him.

"It does to me."

I turn to face him, but he doesn't look up. He keeps studying his hands.

"You never even said—" I watch his face, his sharp jaw, clenched teeth. "I mean, was he black or white or . . ."

I press my lips together and look away from him. I don't understand what he's doing.

Phoenix finally faces me. "He looked like me, didn't he?"

"He was Latino, if that's what you mean," I say. Now it's my turn to study my hands.

"And he looked like me." The words come out sharp, like shards of glass. "Just say it, Gretchen."

"I guess he sort of did at first, but . . ."

At first I thought so, I want to say. *His hair was the same color as yours, and he was lean and strong. But you're much taller, and you're you. He looked nothing like you. He was nothing like you.* But I don't say any of that. Why can't I say any of that?

"I was wrong," I tell him.

"Are you sure?" he asks. His eyes meet mine, under thick black lashes and dark eyebrows. The angles of his jaw are so perfect, strong and gentle at the same time.

"Yes, I'm sure."

He wasn't beautiful, I want to say. *You're beautiful. Your eyes are brown, but also gold. They shine, they glimmer. And your skin. I can't help touching it. It's so smooth, except for those calosses on your hands. I love the way they feel against my skin. And your color: it's light, but rich and deep, and it makes me want to climb inside you to see what substance God filled you with, to give you that sheen. It's like nothing I've ever seen. You're like nothing I've ever seen.*

But I don't say any of that, either.

"I think maybe—" He's talking to me, but he can't look at me. He closes his eyes and bites his lip. "I think we shouldn't hang out, Gretchen."

"What?" My heart is beating fast inside my chest, making its way up into my throat. "Why?"

"We shouldn't be spending so much time together. I can't give you what you need, Gretchen. I'm not *him*."

I feel heat rush to my face. *What have I done?*

"No," I say. "No! Jesus, Phoenix. Of course you're not *him*. What are you talking about?"

"I think you need help."

"But *you're* helping me. I'm so much better." I hate the way it sounds. I sound so needy. I can't believe I'm saying it, but it's true.

"Yeah, um—"

Oh God. He thinks I'm crazy. And maybe he's right. There's plenty of evidence. But I need him, and not because he looks like the person who hurt me. That is insane. He doesn't. Not anymore. He probably never did.

"I think you need, like, professional help or something." He's mumbling. He opens his eyes and looks into mine. I see it there. He wants to be close to me. It is killing him to say this.

Why is he saying all of this?

I stand up and walk over to him. Then I speak, loud and firm. "Listen," I say. "I've had professional help. It completely sucked. I hated it and I am never going back if I can help it. That's not what I need."

His eyes are closed again. He's leaning away from me.

"Phoenix, look at me."

He opens his eyes.

"I need you," I say. "And you need me too."

He stands up and starts to back away from me. "You don't need me, Gretchen. I'm not who you think I am. I can't be what you need. And maybe I do need you, but I definitely don't deserve you."

"You're not making any sense."

"You're into me because of that guy who died, which is messed up." He says it so slowly. "I'm sorry, but that really *is* messed up." He keeps trying to move away, but I close the distance between us.

"You're wrong," I tell him. "This may be the only thing in my life right now that's *not* a mess."

He stops and studies my face. And for just a second he smiles—the real smile, the one that opens up the whole world. "I gotta go," he says.

"Wait," I say. "I want to give you something." I dig inside my bag and grab the map I've been working on, with the twenty-mile circumference and the color-coded tabs. By the time I pull the map out, though, he's already running, fast.

"Phoenix, wait!"

He doesn't look back.

CHAPTER TWENTY-TWO
PHOENIX

IT'S BEEN TWENTY HOURS since that judge pretty much green-lighted me, and sixteen hours since I ran away from Gretchen in the garden. I haven't slept. I haven't eaten. I'm hungry, but after what Amanda and Sally heard about me yesterday—I don't even want to face them. So I've been hiding out in the basement.

I wish I could talk to Ari. I think maybe that would help—just to hear my little brother speak. I wish I could tell him that he's gonna be fine, that he's gonna stay here, and he'll go to one of these big-ass American middle schools with the flag flying out front, and he'll study the presidents and play on the soccer team—maybe the baseball team too, and that after school he will walk home with his buddies, and they'll go to, like, McDonald's and stuff. They'll go get a milk shake and some French fries. Maybe Ari will get fat; maybe he'll stop being a scrawny little bastard and he'll pack on the pounds. He'll be a *real* American. Maybe he'll be in one of those pep bands, like we saw at the basketball game. He'll be so buff that he'll play trombone, or maybe he'll wanna bang on the drums instead.

Christ, maybe he'll even have a new family or something. Who knows? Maybe he'll have a bunch of little brothers and sisters, and they'll all look up to him. Maybe they'll live in a brick house with trees out front and, like, a fence around it, and they'll have a dog—and not a scrappy little stray that wanders around, searching for garbage. They'll have a good-looking dog that lives inside the house. They'll call it Ruff or Buster. And Ari will be the one who has to feed it every day—little cans of food that they buy special at the supermarket just for that dog. Two dollars for each can, but it won't even matter, because Ari will have plenty of food, plenty of everything.

But I can't talk to my pissant little brother, because he refuses to speak.

God, I need to get out of here. I need to stop thinking about all of this—about Ari and Gretchen. *Oh Christ. Gretchen.*

I really fucked it up this time.

I'm not an idiot. I know I handled things all wrong yesterday. But I'm not gonna let myself think too much about it, because the thing is, I've let too many people down already. I'm not adding Gretchen to that list.

After hanging out alone in the basement all day, I'm pretty much crazy with worry and regret. So I decide to head over to Bo and Barbie's. I figure they're the only people inside this twenty-mile radius who don't have a reason to be pissed off at, disappointed with, or just plain afraid of me. When I get to the shop, Bo tells me we've gotta make a stop to visit the Colonel on the way home. At first I haven't got a clue what he's talking about, but then he pulls into the KFC drive-through and I understand.

When we get to the house, Barbie pulls out some paper plates and we dig in. I'm gonna be honest, Amanda and Sally's dinners are way better than the food Bo and Barbie feed me. But I'm not complaining. It's great to be here, actually. Sitting in plastic chairs around their kitchen table, licking chicken grease off our fingers, washing it down with a cold beer. TV's on in the background, playing some bad reality show that no one even cares about, and the kids are in bed now, but before, they were running around like maniacs, screaming at each other about who the hell even knows. They're cute kids. Both of them have hair so light that it's almost white, and the little one, the girl, has those fat little cheeks and dimples. I had to ask Barbie how to say that tonight. *Dimples*. It's a cool word, actually. The kind of word that sounds like what it means.

Anyway, all the noise is good. I mean, it can be so *quiet* at Sally and Amanda's place.

"You want some more mashed potatoes, baby?"

I don't really know why, but Barbie always calls me baby. Maybe she forgets my name. She picks up a Styrofoam container and reaches toward me.

"Sure," I say. Honestly, I don't, but I'm not gonna be rude about it. I scoop some white stuff onto my paper plate and Bo hands me this brown juice to pour on top.

"Gravy," he says.

We've got a bunch of KFCs in San Salvador. For some reason, they always build them near the Walmart. We've got a couple of those, too. When I was working for Sister Mary Margaret, Ari and I used to meet up outside of Walmart for me to give him money. It was safe, because of all the security guards. That place was swarming with security guards carrying big-ass guns. And the KFC, too. Nobody's going near the KFC unless you got a wad of cash in your fist and you're headed straight for the counter to order up some food.

That place is *expensive* in El Salvador—like a dollar and a half for a Coca-Cola.

So, yeah, I've never tried KFC until tonight. It isn't bad or anything. It's kinda making my stomach hurt a little, though. Probably all that grease. But, *madre de Diós*, the beer tastes good. It's been, like, six months since I've had a cold beer. When Barbie offered me a second can,

I went ahead and took it. I know from movies and from some of the missionary groups that kids in America love to get drunk off beer. They have wild parties and drink straight from the keg. Over in El Salvador, though, we mostly just chill with a beer. When it's crazy hot outside and the air is so steamy you can see it, a beer's about the best thing to cool you off.

We start talking about stuff. I don't really know why, but it's pretty easy to talk to Bo and Barbie. I tell them about Gretchen, and how much I like being around her, but I think she might need more help than I know how to give her. I tell them that I messed up, and I said a bunch of things I wish I hadn't said. They listen, but they don't say much until I say it doesn't matter, because I'm gonna be deported soon anyway. That's when Bo's fist lands on the table.

"You can't talk like that, El Salvador."

Bo sometimes calls me El Salvador. Maybe he forgot my name too.

"I'm just being honest with myself," I say. I'm thinking about why I couldn't be honest with Gretchen—why I couldn't tell her *that*, instead of saying all the hurtful things I did.

"You've gotta fight for it, boy. You have a little brother to look out for."

We talk about Ari for a while. They ask me a bunch of questions about what he looks like and what kinds of things he likes to do. I explain that Ari's not talking because of what happened to him.

"Y'all come through the desert?" Bo asked.

"Yeah, but it wasn't bad. Nothing compared to coming up through Mexico."

"You walked all the way from El Salvador?"

"Nah, we walked some, but we caught rides, mostly on trains."

"Oh, baby!" Barbie says. "Were you and your brother riding up on top of those freight trains like I seen on TV?"

I nod. "Some of the time. It scared the crap out of me the first time we had to go up there, but I got used to it pretty quick."

What I didn't get used to were the bodies—the ones we passed by, torn apart. And when the *pinche* bandits came to steal from all those poor idiots, and Ari and I had to flash gang signs to keep them from taking the clothes right off our backs. It kept us safe, but I mean it when I say that seeing Ari flash those gang signs made me puke, right over the side of the train. No joke.

"How long did it take you, baby?"

"Too long—like a couple of months. We ran into some assholes that made us work for a while before we could keep going."

I thought slavery was a thing of the past—until Mexico. A bunch of thugs gathered us up and made us work for nothing. Could've been worse, though. All they made us do was harvest their crops. Pretty little flowers. I don't even wanna know what that stuff was. Probably to make heroin. They didn't bother us, though. As long as we did our work. The girls—they had it bad. When Ari and I busted out of there, we made sure to take a couple of those girls with us. We lost them getting on the train a week later. They were from Honduras, sweet kids from the country. And the stuff Ari saw down there . . .

Christ, I hope those girls made it out alive.

"You all right, Phoenix?" Bo asks.

"Yeah," I say, nodding slowly. "Just thinking and—you know—wondering if I did the right thing, putting my little brother through all that shit that happened in Mexico."

"I'll tell you what, Phoenix," Bo says. "I'm thirty-two years old, and I made enough mistakes in my first twenty-five years to last about a hundred lifetimes. Ain't that right, Barbie?'

"That's right, sugar."

"But if I've learned one thing, I've learned this: No lookin' back.

It's not gonna do nobody any good, boy. You just do the right thing *now*."

If only I knew what the right thing was. If only I weren't such a candy-ass wuss.

"And don't punish yourself, baby." Barbie says. "The world's gonna do that for you. You ain't gotta add to it."

I nod. She's got a point, I guess—about the world punishing us enough.

"I know they're probably sending you back," she says. "And Bo told me it's probably gonna be real bad for you over there."

I nod again, not really wanting to think about what *real bad* means.

"Phoenix, baby, I just wanna tell you that while you're here, you ought to just go on and let yourself live, you know?"

I guess she does remember my name.

"And don't you worry about the past, sugar. What's done is done."

"Thanks," I say. "I won't—I mean, I'll try. And thanks so much for dinner."

"You come on back over on Sunday and I'll make you a pot roast," Barbie tells me. "I make it up good, don't I, honey?"

"Yes, you do." Bo leans in and gives Barbie a big kiss right on the lips.

"And you can bring that girl, if you want—what's her name?"

"Gretchen." It hurts to say her name.

"Go on and tell her you're sorry, baby. And then bring her over here to meet us."

Barbie stands up and wraps her arms around Bo, as far as she can get them, and she squeezes tight. I'm starting to have a feeling that it might be time for me to leave, with them getting all up into each other. I carry my paper plate to the trash can.

"I'm gonna take you home," Bo says.

"Nah, man. You've done enough already," I tell him. "I'm good with the bus."

"You try and ride the bus this time of night, you'll be waitin' till mornin'."

He has a point. The bus system around here isn't exactly efficient. It's better than San Salvador, though. Over there, nobody can even ride the bus after dark. That's when the *maras* take over. You gotta have a death wish to get on a bus after six.

"Plus, I need to treat my volunteers with respect, you know?"

Barbie comes up and gives me a big hug. Then Bo and I get into his little car, and he drives me back to Ivywood Estates, without us hardly saying a word to each other.

I explain how to get to the house, and he pulls up in front of it and lets out a long, low whistle.

"Nice digs," he says. "That lady couple must be loaded."

"You mean rich?" I ask. "Yeah, I'm pretty sure they are."

"You gonna report for duty tomorrow?"

"Absolutely," I say. "I've gotta do some work in the garden in the morning, but I can come out to the shop after lunch. What do you need me to do?"

"I'm gonna get some shelves from the Home Depot. You can set them up over on the empty wall across from the sink, for me to display my photos. It'll be like my own art studio, you know?"

"No need to buy shelves, man," I say. "That shit's expensive. Just get me some wood and some paint. I'll make you some nice floating shelves. You got a sander and a jigsaw?"

"Nope. But I can borrow them from my buddy."

"Do that," I say, opening the car door. "And I'll get to work on that art studio."

I get out of the car and watch Bo drive away. I head toward the door, but before I open it, I decide to sit on the front porch for a while. It's a nice night, not too cold. I sit there on the steps for a long time, and I'm thinking about the shelves I wanna build, and what shape I'm gonna make the brackets on each end. I think maybe I don't want to go back into Sally and Amanda's house. I'm not ready to face Sally and Amanda yet. Maybe I'm thinking that if I just wait out here a little longer, they'll be in bed when I go inside.

But then I'm thinking about Gretchen, and the mess I made with her. I pull out my phone and text her.

Can I have a do-over?

Her reply comes back immediately.

Only if I can too.

Before I can lose my nerve, I text:

Meet me at the garden in five?

Okay.

CHAPTER TWENTY-THREE
GRETCHEN

THE PLACE WITHOUT A SOUL is like a ghost town this late at night. There's not a single car on the streets. I guess they're all tucked into their three-car-garages until morning.

When I pull up to the garden, Phoenix is sitting under the fig tree, legs stretched out in front of him. The headlights of my car sweep across his face, and he lifts his arm to cover his eyes. He's wearing a sweat shirt, the hood pulled over his head. I cut the lights and sit there, watching as he hops to his feet and starts to walk toward me. He pushes the hood from his head and studies me carefully.

I step out of the car, and a siren goes off, far away. Phoenix looks in the direction of the sound. I move closer to him. I want to touch him, to feel him—solid and real. I think he wants to touch me too.

"I'm sorry," he says, still looking away. "I shouldn't have—"

Another siren starts up. I put my hand on his cheek and turn his face toward mine. His chin feels rough under my fingers, like sandpaper. But the soft skin of his neck is under my thumb, and I can't help but stroke it lightly.

"You don't need to apologize. We get a do-over, remember?"

He nods. My face is so near that I can feel his breath on my cheek.

We stand like that, and we listen to the ambulance or fire truck or what-ever, the sound fading.

"Me first." I say. "When I told you that Adam and I broke up, I should have said this: it was for a lot of reasons, but one of them was you."

He rests his hand lightly on my waist and leans in toward my ear. "My turn," he says. "When I said I didn't want to be with you, I was lying."

I move my hand around to the back of his neck, letting my fingers slide through his short hair. I've watched that place on his neck so many times, always wondering how it would feel to touch him here. I try to lean in closer, but his hand pushes softly against my waist.

"I feel like the whole neighborhood is watching." He glances quickly around and then looks toward the shed. "They probably think I'm gonna attack you or something."

Heat rises to my cheeks—not the good kind. And not because I'm thinking about *that boy*, but because I hate that people might see Phoenix in that way. "You shouldn't care what these stupid misplaced subur-banites think."

He shrugs. "I have no idea what those words mean," he says, "but I *do* care. I guess I feel like I owe it to Amanda and Sally to—"

"What? Behave yourself?"

He looks down at the ground. "Yeah, something like that."

Oh God. It kills me that he feels that way, that he has to feel that way. But I can't change it—not now, at least.

"Okay, let's go in there," I say, gesturing toward the shed.

The shed is new, and it has this incredible clean smell of freshly shaved plywood mixed with soil. As soon as we walk in, the room fills with that inexplicable gravity that always pulls me toward him. I feel it tugging us together, in this space that's barely big enough for two people. I lean against the wall of the shed, trying to steady myself. Shovels hang on a row of nails across from me, arranged in perfect order, from small to large. Several green hoses are stacked neatly in the corner. Seeing them reminds me of all the afternoons I've spent here with Phoenix and the kids, of the times I watched him coil those hoses, so careful, pushing up his sleeves to wrap the end around one shoulder. And how I watched his arms, his bare skin. He knew I was watching, and he let me.

In the garden, Phoenix always seems somehow more himself—more relaxed than anywhere else I've been with him. But he's not relaxed tonight. He's something else. I don't really know this part of Phoenix. I think he's been careful not to let me sense it, except on the trolley (*Oh, God. The trolley*). I want to know this part of him—so much.

He stands by the door, like he can't gather the courage to come any closer to me.

"Are you planning to stay out there forever?" I ask, teasing.

I know he's nervous, because I am too.

He shakes his head, pulls the door shut, and unzips his sweatshirt. He takes it off and spreads it on the floor of the shed, using it to cover bits of soil and mulch.

"For you," he says. "I mean, if you want to sit."

I sit down on his jacket and draw my knees into my chest. He's standing by the door in a plain V-neck T-shirt and jeans, shifting from one foot to the other, as far away from me as he can possibly be in this small space.

The whole room is buzzing with it—the urge, the energy, our wanting to be closer.

"Oh," I say, jumping back to my feet. "I need to get something from the car. It's for you."

I was so distracted, watching him there under the fig tree, that I forgot to bring his map. I reach around him and grab the doorknob. I'm so close that I can see the veins on his neck. And for the first time I notice the edge of a dark scar, just above his collarbone. I have this overwhelming urge to touch it, with my finger—or maybe even my lips.

My heart is pounding and my hands shake. He looks down at them, wrapped around the doorknob, and sees me tremble.

"Will you come with me?" I ask. My voice is trembling too.

He steps away from me. "Oh Christ, Gretchen. I'm so sorry." He's shaking his head. "I should never have asked you to come out alone at night. I wasn't thinking—"

"I'm not scared," I tell him. "It's not that."

And I'm not—not even a little bit. He's misreading me. I drag my teeth over my lower lip and close my eyes, knowing that he's studying my face, seeing what I really feel now.

"Oh," he whispers. "Good—I mean, good that you're not scared."

I grasp the knob tightly and turn. When the door opens, I feel grateful for the cool air and open space. Clearly, Phoenix wants to take things slow, which would be fine, except that my body seems to have different plans.

He walks beside me to the car. I pull the map from the glove compartment and lead him back to the shed. Once inside, he closes the door and we sit across from each other, careful not to touch. I spread the map out on the floor between us and trace the red circle with my finger.

"It's your circumference," I tell him. "I marked the twenty-mile radius of where you can travel." I take his hand and put it on one of the places I've marked. "There are woods here, and trails." Touching his hand is almost too much—like all that energy pulsing through this little shed has converged on this one place, where my skin meets his.

"You did this for me?" He's not looking at the map anymore. He's looking at me.

"For us," I tell him, meeting his gaze. "I want to take you to these places."

He smiles. "Tell me about them." Then he moves my hand over the Sope Creek Trail.

"That one's on the Chattahoochee."

"The what-a-what-chee?" He laughs. "What's a Chata-w-woochie?"

"It's a river," I tell him. "It's a Native American name, I think. Probably Cherokee."

"And it's nice?"

"Yeah, the river is really pretty, unless there are a bunch of drunk rednecks floating down it on inner tubes and singing Lynyrd Skynyrd songs."

He laughs again. God, I love hearing him laugh. "You really know how to sell a place."

I tell him about Stone Mountain Park, and the long hiking trail around the base of the mountain, the one most people don't know about, about the waterfall at the old mill, and the covered bridge. I try to convince him that he'll love the botanical garden—my favorite tourist attraction in Atlanta. When I describe rooms filled with orchids and a garden of cacti, he's skeptical, but I convince him to give it a chance.

"When do we start?" he asks.

"Tomorrow?" I say. I would start this very moment, truth be told. I would leave this shed with him and go to every place inside this red circle, not even stopping to sleep.

"Tomorrow's no good," he says. "I have a thousand plants to get into the ground and zero volunteers, thanks to that nosy neighbor and her chat post."

"Okay," I tell him. "Then the next day."

"We might not have much time," he says. "I should have told you—"

"Told me what?" I ask. I'm not sure I want to know.

"My asylum case was denied yesterday—I got a deport order."

I feel the blood drain from my face—I feel it rushing down toward my toes, creating the sensation that the floor of the shed is opening up and I will drop through the earth.

"You're leaving?" I hear myself ask. "For sure?"

"I don't know." He's running his finger along the edge of the red circle. "They want me to appeal, but it's really expensive, and I don't have any money."

"Who wants you to appeal?" I'm grasping onto him, gripping his forearm. I think maybe I'm trying to hold him down, keep him here.

"Sally and Amanda, and my lawyer, too. But—"

"Then you'll appeal," I break in, squeezing his arm tightly between my fingers. "And we'll use the time we have."

He lifts his hand from the map, and I let go of his arm. He touches my face. It's such a relief, feeling his hand against me. We both shift onto our knees, the paper map crinkling below us. Our bodies are close, finally. He runs his hand along my cheek, my neck behind my ear, and then pulls his fingers through my hair.

"You're so amazing," he says, breathing into my ear.

"You're so beautiful," I whisper.

And, *God*, he is. His amber eyes are shining and his skin is glowing from the inside. I study his lips, his throat, the place above his collarbone where the skin is darker.

"A scar?" I ask.

He shrugs. "Doesn't matter," he says.

I run my finger along the scar, pushing his shirt aside, and he pulls in a deep breath. I can feel his chest rising.

"Wait," he says, squeezing his eyes shut. "It *does* matter, Gretchen. There's more that you should know."

"I want to know everything," I tell him. "But right now what I want more than anything is for you to open your eyes and kiss me."

"I can do that," he says.

He tugs lightly on my hair, bringing my face to meet his. He leans in to kiss me, the touch of his lips soft at first. He keeps looking at me. I watch him, too. And then we close our eyes and tumble back onto the map, falling into each other, searching with our hands and our mouths, wanting to feel still and safe and whole.

CHAPTER TWENTY-FOUR

PHOENIX

I SLEPT LIKE A BABY, or maybe I slept like the dead. *Honest to Christ*, I haven't slept that well in years. I wake up, sun already high in the sky. Gretchen's map is folded on the bed beside me. It's a little wrinkled, and torn in one of the corners, but *damn*, it feels good to remember why—to think about kissing her last night on the floor of that shed.

I unfold the map and look at it for a while, running my fingers across the words she wrote, trying to remember what she told me about all the places she marked. I'm feeling so good that I decide to face it—the thing I've been putting off for way too long.

I grab a big envelope from the desk. Inside it is a bunch of papers I need to read before Ari's case goes in front of a judge. I had to write a letter explaining how we were "abandoned" by our mom, telling the judge all the reasons they shouldn't send that kid back to El Salvador. So now it's here—this account of our pathetic lives, in black and white for random strangers to read. Ari's lawyer wants me to read through it one more time, just to be sure all the "facts" about our lives are "accurate."

I don't even notice when Gretchen walks in. I probably look stupid, sitting there in my undershirt, surrounded by stacks of paper. But I don't even care, because I'm so damn happy to see her leaning up against the doorframe, in faded cut-off shorts and a light-blue tank top, her hair pulled back into a ponytail.

I push a stack of papers out of the way and slide off the bed.

"Whatcha doin'?" she asks.

"Kissing you," I say, walking over to her.

And then I do. I take her hand and pull her into me and I kiss her softly.

After a while she steps back. "I have a surprise for you."

"I'm not really into surprises."

"You'll like this one," she tells me. "I promise." She starts to head up the stairs and then turns back to tell me, "It's in the garden."

We walk out of the house, holding hands. I don't know if it happened overnight, or if I just didn't notice before, but the trees aren't bare anymore; they have little flowers starting to come out all along their branches. Some are white and fluffy, others have tight, purplish-pink buds, and there are even a few enormous trees with big light-pink flowers growing from the tip of each branch. They remind me of trees in a comic book, or one of those rhyming books for little kids. I'm so busy staring at all the trees and breathing in the sweet air that I barely even notice the big-ass SUV that's slowing down beside us.

Gretchen hops back a little and her body stiffens. It's almost like someone has jumped out of a closet to scare her, the way she's freezing up.

"What's up?" I ask.

Eyes wide, she looks over at the SUV. Then she shakes her head twice and smiles. "Nothing," she says. "The noise just startled me."

The driver is leaning into her passenger-side window, watching us. It's that nosy lady. The one Sally called a "feckin' wanker" the other day. I look away, fast.

"That's her, isn't it?" Gretchen whispers through closed teeth.

I barely nod. I'm inspecting the sidewalk instead.

Gretchen leans in and kisses me, right on the lips. Then she turns to wave a little too vigorously at the lady driving the SUV. The woman waves back, halfheartedly, with a strange look on her face. I think maybe it's disgust. But truth be told, I don't give a shit what that woman thinks. I'm too happy.

Jesus, I didn't even know I could be happy like this.

We turn a corner, and the garden comes into view. There are, like, twenty kids standing around, eating doughnuts and drinking coffee from paper cups.

"Who are all those people?"

"Bree's friends," she says. "And Ty's. He helped us get the word out."

"How did you convince them all to come hang out with a 'dangerous criminal'?"

"Krispy Kreme doughnuts"—she points toward a stack of green and white boxes on the ground—"and coffee."

I stop and pull her into a hug. "Thanks," I whisper into her ear.

Four hours later Ty and I are crouched down next to the hose, taking turns drinking from it. I'm feeling pretty damn good about the progress all these American high school kids have made. They work way faster than most of the missionaries. And they're better at following directions than the dads of all those girls in green dresses. We've planted all but three flats of vegetables, and I'm starting to tug the hose toward the newly planted herb garden when my phone rings. I look down at the screen. I recognize the 210 area code—Texas.

I drop the hose and gesture toward the phone. "I have to take this."

Ty nods and grabs the end of the hose.

"Bueno?"

"Good afternoon, Phoenix. This is Jill de Leon from the CARA Project in San Antonio. I'm representing your brother, Ari?"

"Yes, ma'am. I remember."

"I'm so sorry to bother you with this on a Sunday afternoon, but, as you know, Ari's hearing in Texas juvenile court will be this Wednesday."

"I've been reading through the papers I got in the mail," I tell her. "If that's why you're calling."

I'm watching Bree and Ty leaning against each other, holding on to that water hose.

"Thank you, Phoenix," she says. "That's great. But I'm not calling about that. I'm calling about your brother. . . ."

The water moves in a long arc toward the bed of herbs, catching the sunlight.

"Is he okay?" I ask.

"I'm sorry, but—"

Ty slowly moves the hose up and down, transforming that arc of water into a long S. Bree's hand enters the stream, sending drops of water across her arm, across the front of Ty's shirt.

"Your brother still isn't speaking with us—with *anyone*."

"Oh," I say.

Ty turns the hose toward Bree. She squeals and tries to run away, but the water follows her, soaking her through. She's running straight toward Gretchen, who looks up from the tomato cages she's tying together with thick brown twine.

"I am very concerned. . . ." The lawyer's voice is all serious, which is making my heart beat fast. "Without his testimony, it will be difficult to demonstrate abandonment."

"Oh," I say again. *What is she trying to tell me?*

"To make a strong case, we will also need for him to explain to the juvenile court judge why he can't return."

"To El Salvador?"

Ty has turned the hose toward Gretchen. A stream of water hits her face, runs down her chest. She throws her hands out, trying to block the flow, but it doesn't help, so she starts running, straight toward Ty.

"Yes," Ms. de Leon says. "We're beginning to feel a bit desperate here," she tells me. "Do you understand, Phoenix?"

Yes, I understand. I understand desperate.

I'm backing up, slowly moving away from the scene, almost unaware I'm doing it.

"Can you try again—to speak with your brother? Can you explain the gravity of this situation to him?"

My back presses against the wall of the shed. Feeling a little dizzy, I watch as Gretchen and Bree tackle Ty, wrestling him to the ground. Gretchen wrenches the hose from his hand. Bree is holding him down while Gretchen steps back and drenches him.

"Phoenix? Are you there?"

"Yes, ma'am," I say, my voice wobbly. "I'm here."

"Will you try?"

Will I try? I am trying. I left, didn't I? I dragged him all the way through Mexico. I hauled him onto the tops of moving trains. I snuck him out of a work camp. I led him through a desert. I got him across the border. I took him to that guard. I told them all that I know. I wrote it all down for them, for chrissake. Or, almost all of it.

"I don't know what else I can do."

I'm giving up.

Gretchen looks toward me. She's laughing, her face all radiant, her shirt clinging to her body, slick with water. She takes one look at the giving-up me, watching the coming-alive her.

I hate myself for giving up.

The hose drops. Her smile drops. Her hand flies back, gesturing for Bree and Ty to stop whatever they're doing. My body is curling into a tight ball, and Gretchen is heading toward me, fast.

She knows what's about to happen.

CHAPTER TWENTY-FIVE

GRETCHEN

THIS IS THE KIND of night when a girl needs her best friend, preferably without a plus one. I try not to let on how disappointed I am when I walk through the kitchen door at Bree's to see her and Ty wrapped around each other on the family room sofa, watching basketball.

Basketball. Good Lord.

Clearly, Bree's in love. And that's fine. It's good, even. She and Ty are sweet together, and with the exception of the occasional absurd comment (usually prefaced by "Dude!"), Ty's personality has grown on me. But I need Bree—*my* Bree, the one I don't have to share.

Bree jumps up from the sofa and rushes over to me, across the marble floor of her parents' rarely used designer kitchen.

"Oh my God, Gretch! Is he okay?" She throws her arms around me.

I have no idea how to answer that.

Two hours ago, when I left Phoenix in the basement of Amanda and Sally's, at least he was talking again. He had unwound himself from the ball he collapsed into by the shed, the one he stayed in—not saying a word—for far too long. It was strange to see him like that. I've known for a while that Phoenix has been through far more than I can imagine, but he's always been so solid, so reliable. I never thought I'd be the one telling *him* to breathe deeply, asking him to lean against me.

I tried getting him to use some of the many techniques I've learned over the past few months—measured breathing, visualizing light. He didn't even respond to my voice, until I told him to close his eyes and imagine a safe place. That's when he finally spoke. He turned his head to face me and he whispered, "I'm already here."

Why hadn't I ever thought of that? I remembered all the random places I've tried to imagine myself into—beaches and mountains and fields of tulips. All along, I should have been looking for somewhere closer to home. Somewhere real.

I took his hand and made him stand up. By then we were alone in the garden. The two of us went over to the fig tree and stretched out under it, holding hands, feeling the sun on our faces, the ground cool and damp below us. We looked up at the leaves, just starting to unfold, and he told me about his brother. He said it was all for nothing. That's what he kept telling me again and again.

And I felt so selfish, because I wanted to tell him that it wasn't for nothing, that he was here—in the most random of places—for a reason. But Phoenix didn't come here for *me*. He came for his brother, and it was killing him to think that, after everything they had been through, together and apart, this was the end. All because Ari wouldn't speak—or couldn't.

Listening to Phoenix, I got an idea—a good one. All I needed to do was convince my parents to let me do it.

When I showed up at home this afternoon, they didn't even let me past the kitchen table. At first I thought maybe they had heard about Phoenix, and how he'd broken down at the garden. But the concern on both of their faces wasn't about Phoenix. It was about *that boy*. They had talked with Karen, the friendly "major crimes" prosecutor.

"The prosecutor called with good news."

That's what my mom said when I sat down beside her. And the whole time, while my dad was telling me about their conversation with Karen,

I kept wondering: Which part of this is "good news"? And then, after I had listened intently to it all, I told them, "Thank you for letting me know." I also told them that I needed to go to Texas, to help Phoenix and his brother, Ari.

Here's how that conversation went:

Dad: *"Are you sure you're ready? That's a big step, sweetheart."*
Mom: *"She's ready, Dan."*

And so, with my mother's pronouncement, it was decided. I am better. I am ready.

I think they're right. Honestly, I do, and I want so much to be able to help—finally to do something useful for Phoenix and his brother. I just wish I could *feel* like my parents were right. Instead I feel jittery and off-kilter. I need Bree. Maybe it's selfish that I'm even thinking about what I need, considering all I know about Phoenix and Ari. But I need her.

Bree's still holding tight to me, and I'm saying nothing, because I don't even know where to start.

"Food," she says. "What you need is a big plate of Thai."

Okay. Maybe I need food, too. I haven't eaten since that half doughnut and three cups of coffee in the garden this morning. Maybe if I eat, my stomach will stop doing somersaults.

Bree releases me from her grip and opens the stainless-steel refrigerator. Inside, white takeout boxes neatly line the clean, glass shelves. You can tell a lot about a family by looking into their refrigerator. Bree's fridge says: upper-middle class, too busy to cook, lovers of all foods Asian.

"Massaman? Panang?" She crouches to look at the bottom shelf. "Or sushi. We've got veggie sushi. No fish."

She pushes a few trays aside. "Oh, Pho! That's exactly what you need, Gretch. Vietnamese comfort food."

"Massaman for me," Ty calls out. I cringe, waiting for Bree to unleash a torrent of fury, to explain in no uncertain terms that *she does not exist to serve him.* But she doesn't say a word. Instead she pulls out several containers and starts to arrange food on plates. She takes a big glass bowl from the cabinet for me. I pull up a stool and watch in silence as she pours broth into it, heats it, and then adds noodles, greens, thin slices of meat. She pushes the bowl toward me and I slump over it, taking in the smell—cilantro, curry leaves, warm chicken broth. *Sooo good.*

Bree was right. This is exactly what I need. How does she always know?

"So tell me—everything."

I don't even know where to start.

"My parents talked to the prosecutor. She found other witnesses." I tell Bree, between slurps of rice noodles.

"So they know who killed him?" She's sitting across from me, popping rolls of sushi into her mouth.

"He was in a gang—well, I knew that already. The tattoos and all . . ." Ty turns around on the couch, suddenly interested. "And the man in the car, the one who shot him, he was in a different gang, but he wanted to get out. His girlfriend was in the car too. She was pregnant, and they were planning to get married."

"I'm not following," Bree says.

Ty mutes the TV. "I know about this," he says, sounding anxious. I didn't know Ty could be anxious.

Bree looks at him, skeptical. "You know about gangs? Really, Ty."

"I saw it on a documentary." He shrugs.

Then Ty comes into the kitchen and pulls up a stool next to Bree. "They call it 'calming' or something—when somebody wants to get out of a gang. He has to do some crazy shit—like a last chance to prove his loyalty, and then they'll let him go."

"Seriously?" Bree asks, looking at me.

"Yeah," I say. "It's like that. The boy who robbed me, he was at a gas station. . . ."

Buying Doritos. That's what the prosecutor told my parents. He was getting a bag of Doritos, in the wrong place at the wrong time.

"There were a bunch of other guys in the car, with the man who wanted to get out of the gang, and his girlfriend was with them too. Or fiancée, I guess." I watch Ty dig into his massaman curry, already warmed and waiting for him. He mutters a thanks to Bree, and then I continue. "While they were filling up, a couple of those guys went inside and saw him buying Doritos. I guess they knew he was in another gang by his shirt or something."

"And so they chased him down and made the guy kill him, just like that?" Ty asks, having already shoved half a plateful of curry into his mouth.

"Yeah, I guess *that boy* got a head start, but he left his wallet at the gas station, or something." I stop talking and breathe in deeply, trying to let the broth and the curry and the smell of the spices bring me back here—take me away from that empty street. But the soup is getting cold, and the smell isn't as strong as it was. "The prosecutor thinks he jumped me because he needed money—he was cutting through back streets to the bus station. She thinks he was trying to get away."

"And that man just shot him for no reason?" Bree asks. "That's messed up."

"The boy who attacked me, he didn't even have a gun, or a knife, or anything," I whisper. "He was seventeen."

"Younger than we are." Bree sighs. "God, that's insane."

Ty has just shoved another enormous mouthful of massaman curry into his mouth, but it doesn't stop him from talking. "On that show I watched, they said that if you were, like, a 'bad' gang member"—he stops to swallow and then takes a deep gulp of water—"if you weren't really active in the gang, they made you do even worse stuff to get out," Ty says. "I bet that man who wanted to get married was like that—like, not a 'good' gang member."

"That's what my parents said too," I tell them, wondering why Ty was paying so much attention to this documentary. "That he never really did much for them while he was part of the gang, and so they made him do this random thing, just to make him need their protection or feel more connected to them or something."

"What happened to the man?" Bree asks. "Did they catch him?"

"Yeah," I say. "He's in jail for life. And the girlfriend, the one who was in the car, she's testifying against the other people in the car—the ones who made him do it, in some big Federal trial."

That part was the "good news." They don't need me to testify, because the girl with the red-dyed hair saw it all too, and she came forward.

"Like I said: that's just messed up," Bree says, carrying Ty's plate to the microwave to dish out and warm up a second plate of curry. "That anyone could be stupid enough to join one of those gangs—to do all of that crazy stuff, just to be part of a group."

Ty has been quiet for a while, listening. When he finally speaks, he seems upset. "You don't know anything about it," Ty says to Bree. "I mean, who knows what makes them join those gangs, what kinds of pressure they might be under or, I don't know—"

"I'm with Bree," I say. "I don't care how hard your life is. There's absolutely no excuse to do all those terrible things, just to be part of some group."

Bree stands up and walks around behind me. She wraps her arms around me and rests her chin on my shoulder. "Well, anyway, now you know," she says, her voice gentle again.

Yes, now I know. For better or worse, I know. And now Phoenix needs me, so it's time to move on.

When Ty has cleaned his second plate of curry, he gets up and puts it into the dishwasher. Then he wanders back to the basketball game, leaving Bree and me as alone as we'll be in this new plus-one life of hers.

"Hey, Bree," I say.

"Yeah, honey?" She's still leaning against me.

"Do you think I'm better?"

She pulls back and looks at me. "I think you're getting there."

"Do you think I'd be okay traveling, you know, in airports and on planes and stuff?"

"Sure, yeah. Absolutely. Why?"

"I think I'm going to Texas on Tuesday, to help Phoenix with his brother."

Bree steps back. "*This* Tuesday? Like, in two days?"

"Yeah," I say. "Is that crazy, Bree? Am I crazy to think I can do this?"

"No," she says forcefully. "It's brave." She shakes her head slowly. "You're brave, Gretchen. You always have been."

CHAPTER TWENTY-SIX

PHOENIX

"YOU HAVE TO APPEAL, Phoenix. Do you understand what I'm telling you?"

It's been two days since I fell apart in front of a bunch of strangers in the garden. I've been sitting on my bed in Sally and Amanda's basement, talking to Sister Mary Margaret for an hour—which is about fifty-five minutes longer than we've ever talked on the phone. I'm not going to think about what an idiot I made of myself out there in the garden, because the truth is, it doesn't even matter. I'm probably never going to see any of those people again—plus, I've got more important things to worry about.

It's not like Sister Mary Margaret and I have been sitting around shooting the shit for an hour. We're working on how I can help Ari, running through the facts together. Ari's lawyer out in Texas said that if I get even one fact wrong—a date that's a day or two off, the color of a shirt—it could ruin his case, which is so completely nuts. I feel like I'm back in *colegio*, studying for a really hard test. I'm also worrying the whole time about how much this call is gonna cost.

It took me a long time to get up the nerve to tell Sister Mary Margaret what happened in court a few days ago—with *me*. But she needs to know, and I need to stop talking her ear off before I make her go broke, paying for this call.

"There's nothing I can do about it," I say. "The judge ordered me deported."

"You cannot come back here, Phoenix," she says, her voice firm and scolding, like she's one of those school-teacher-with-a-ruler nuns, instead of laid-back Sister Mary Margaret.

"Where am I supposed to go?" I ask her.

"Anywhere but here," she says. "I haven't wanted to worry you, Phoenix, but that Delgado boy has been coming around the construction site, chatting it up with the missionaries."

Delgado. I can see him acting all *suave* with those American girls, making them think he's the good guy.

"He's asking about you and Ari, telling me how much he's 'missed you,' and how he and his boys are planning to spend lots of time around here, waiting for you to get back."

I feel like I'm gonna puke.

"And he said I didn't need to worry, because if you're thinking you might not come back to Ilopango, they'll just meet you at the plane and escort you back themselves."

Or maybe I'm gonna dry heave. Good thing I didn't eat breakfast.

"How long do you have to decide?" she asks me. "Whether or not to appeal the judge's decision?"

"Thirty days, but it doesn't matter, Sister. They know about what happened that night."

"What night? You mean, the night with *El Turbino*—the night you ran away from them?"

I mutter a quiet yeah.

"Damn," she says. And then: "Damn it all to hell!"

Neither of us says anything. We just sit, the phones to our ears, listening to our breaths come in and out.

"Appeal," she says. "You have to do it. If nothing else, it will buy you some time." She sighs deeply. "Maybe Delgado and his boys will get bored and decide to go off and harass someone else."

"Who's gonna buy me that time, though?" I ask her. "That shit's expensive! I can't ask Sally and Amanda to pay even more money, after all they've done."

"Watch your language!" she commands. "I hope you're not using that foul language with your hosts."

Do as I say, not as I do. It's Sister Mary Margaret's favorite expression for a reason. She curses like a sailor, but she always threatened to wash our mouths out with soap if we said even one bad word.

"Relax, Sister," I tell her. "No need for soap. I'm squeaky-clean."

And I guess it feels good to know I really *am* squeaky-clean. I mean, I've got this amazing, beautiful girl who is really into me, and all we've done is kiss, which is sort of killing me, and I know it's killing her, too. But *damn*, it's all so complicated. I worry about Gretchen all the time— not just because it sometimes seems like she's right at the edge of a meltdown. I'm trying to figure out why she wants to be with me, of all people, and I know I'm gonna do something to mess it all up. It's just a matter of time.

Amanda calls down the stairs, "Phoenix! We need to head out!"

I shove my toothbrush into the duffel bag Amanda gave me. "I gotta go, Sister."

"You'll do great, Phoenix," she says. "And about your appeal, just give it some time," she tells me. "We'll figure something out."

I tell her I will, not because I think she'll come up with some miracle solution. It's just that I can't say no to Sister Mary Margaret.

I hang up, shove my phone into the pocket of the duffel bag, and head upstairs.

———

It feels really weird to haul ass out of town in the backseat of Amanda's car, without having to worry about whether the stupid ankle monitor is going to start going off. I have Gretchen to thank for that—for all of it.

After everyone else left the garden a couple of days ago, we were sitting together under the fig tree. I had just told her about Ari, and about how it was all for shit because he wasn't going to talk to the judge, and if he didn't talk, his lawyer couldn't prove he had a right to stay here. I was telling her this, absentmindedly tracing shapes in the dirt—lines and swirls, nothing special. And that's when she blurted it out: "He can *draw* it."

"Draw what?" I kept dragging my finger slowly across the surface of the dirt.

"The story—what happened."

I looked up at her. "Do you think that would work?"

"Sure. He's an amazing artist."

I told her I wasn't sure that anyone could get him to draw those images—that he wasn't going to want to remember them, much less *draw* them. But Gretchen said she had a friend who could help. She said she used to go to these classes. They were called art therapy, and a bunch of kids in there were really messed up. Their parents had died and stuff. But the woman who taught them used these special techniques to help the kids draw their memories, even if they couldn't talk about them.

It seemed like maybe it was worth a try, to get him to draw stuff, but I still couldn't figure out how a judge would know what he was looking at—what Ari was trying to say with the pictures.

Gretchen told me the solution to *that* problem was simple. She said I knew every part of the story, so I could tell the judge what Ari's pictures meant.

At first we thought that maybe there could be a way to Skype me into the courtroom, or use some sort of teleconference system. But when

Ari's lawyer called my parole officer and explained the situation, Officer Worth gave me permission to visit Ari and go to the hearing as a witness.

I always knew Officer Worth was a stand-up guy.

Gretchen got in touch with the woman who ran those art groups, and she offered to help. That lady wasn't gonna go all the way to Texas for my little brother, but she said she would come up with a plan for Gretchen to use, and that she could talk Gretchen through it. She said she knew Gretchen could do it. I've spent enough time around Gretchen and kids to know that lady is right. Gretchen can do just about anything with kids. But the completely, amazingly, insane thing is that she *wants* to do it. She wants to go to Texas and help me. And so do Amanda and Sally. They both said they "wouldn't even dream" of not being there to support me and Ari. And they also said they'd pay for the whole thing, which I'm trying not to think too much about. I'm pretty sure I could work an entire lifetime and never come up with the money to pay Amanda and Sally back for what they've done.

So there's only one thing standing in the way of making this plan work: convincing myself to get on a plane.

When Gretchen said we'd need to fly, my first reaction was simple: "No fucking way."

"Stop being such a baby," Gretchen told me. "Planes are safer than cars!"

"Let's test that theory by *driving* to San Antonio," I suggested.

"San Antonio is a thousand miles away. There's not enough time."

I told her I'd do it, or at least I'd try. So, I'm still wearing the stupid *pinche* ankle monitor, but I can fly to Texas and be there for three days. If I can keep from losing my shit on the plane.

I'd say the chances are about fifty-fifty.

———

Damn, this airport is insane. I've never seen so many people in one place. And the parking lot, it's like rows of cars in every direction, as far as I can see. Sally had to take a picture of some sign next to Amanda's car, just so that she'd remember where she parked it when we get back. We walked about two kilometers to get inside the place, and then we stood in this really long line so that we could basically strip down in front of thousands of strangers. We took off our jackets, tugged off our shoes and belts, emptied everything from our pockets. Then we put it all on this conveyor thing, like at the Walmart checkout. We had to go one by one into this big-ass glass tube and hold our arms up, like we'd been chased down by the *federales* and one of them had a gun pointed at us. The tube swirled around us—I guess to see if we were packing heat, or had a bomb strapped to our thigh or something.

Everybody in line was just doing all this shit, like it was perfectly normal. They all knew exactly what to do—how to get those big plastic tubs from the stack and put their computers inside them, when to take off their shoes. I did whatever Sally and Amanda told me to do, and I kept looking around for Gretchen, because I figured this whole thing had to be completely freaking her out.

She texted me earlier and said she would meet us at the "gate," whatever that is. Amanda and Sally don't seem worried that we're not seeing her. Amanda said this is the busiest airport in the United States, so it's not like we'll run into her before we get to the gate. I'm really hoping Gretchen's dad is here with her, or that maybe there's like a special line somewhere else for people who can't handle crowds, and she's in that one.

It turns out that the "gate" is just a big open space with a bunch of seats lined up, but no Gretchen. Not yet, at least. There's a lady in a blue pantsuit standing at this counter by a door—I guess the door goes out to the airplane, because everyone is crowded around it, like they're all excited to be getting on an airplane, like they just can't wait to climb inside that big hunk of metal and go hurtling through the sky in it. I'm way too nervous to sit down, which is fine, since there aren't any free seats anyway. Amanda and Sally plop down on the floor by a big window, and I pace back and forth, trying not to think about how much I want to puke, and looking for Gretchen. She's still not here, and she hasn't texted or anything. I'm starting to wonder if she's gonna bail on us.

Christ, I wish I could bail.

The lady in the blue suit says something into a microphone, and then Sally and Amanda stand and start gathering up their stuff.

"Let's go ahead and board, love," Sally says to me.

"I'm sure Gretchen will be here soon," Amanda assures me.

"And we want to get you settled," Sally says, all sweet and gentle.

I let Sally take me by the elbow. I want to wait for Gretchen, but I don't really know what the hell I'm doing, and I need to let them take control. Because, here's the thing: if I take control, I'm going to start hauling ass toward the packed-out shuttle that brought us out to this place, and I'm going to push my way into it and then curl up into a ball on that bench in the back corner, close my eyes, and ride around in circles for an hour or two. I'll listen to the soothing voice coming through the speakers, telling all those people they've arrived at their terminal; I'll hear the doors open and close, and the people and suitcases and bags coming on and off, and I'll let all those sounds wash over me, and not move. Then maybe Gretchen will sit down beside me, and she'll put her hand on my arm, and it will feel cool and smooth, and she'll tell me that it's fine for us to stay in that shuttle, that we can ride around in circles, holding on to each other for as long as we want, that we don't have to get off, we don't have to go anywhere.

But I do have to go somewhere. Even if Gretchen doesn't show, I have to get on this plane and try one last time to do the right thing. So I clench my jaw tightly and let Sally lead me through that door and down a narrow hallway, lined up behind a bunch of people who I guess also have somewhere they need to go.

CHAPTER TWENTY-SEVEN

GRETCHEN

I PUT ON MAKEUP this morning before I left—mascara, blush, a thin line of brown eyeliner, and even lipstick.

Bare Again.

That's the name of the color I'm wearing. I felt like I needed to ease back into wearing makeup, so I chose an almost nude tone. When I came out of my room, grasping tight to my duffel bag, my mom commented on the color.

"You look so *beautiful*," she said. "I love that lipstick on you."

She looked me up and down—took in the jeans and high boots, the cute little sweater and the big dangly earrings. It was the first time in months she had acknowledged how I looked. I think maybe I did all this for her. I wanted for her to see that I was okay, that I was ready.

I'm not ready.

"This is the final boarding call for Delta Flight 2132 with direct service to San Antonio. All passengers must be on board at this time."

I am not on board. I am in a bathroom stall in Terminal A, holding on to the cold metal walls and breathing.

In. Out. In. Out.

Oh my God, what was I thinking? I am so not ready for this. I forgot how many people there are in this place—so many people, everywhere.

Except for this bathroom stall, which is why I have been here for too long, trying to recover from the security line, and the shuttle, and the man who came running at me when I was standing perfectly still on the escalator, holding tight to the moving handrail. That man ran right past me. Of course he did. He was wearing a suit—a businessman, probably on his way to Takoma to sell insurance or something.

"Final call for Flight 2132 to San Antonio, departing from gate A26. The doors are now closing."

I squeeze my eyes tight and try to think of something that will propel me from this bathroom stall. And it comes to me: Bree, shaking her head slowly from side to side, telling me I'm brave.

You're brave, Gretchen. You always have been.

"No!" I grab my bag from the hook and burst out of the bathroom stall. Everyone in line is staring at me, because—apparently—I didn't just say no in my head.

"I'm going to miss my plane!" I call out, pushing past the women in line to get out to the terminal. I'm running as fast as I can toward Gate A26, and when I get close enough, I motion to a woman in a dark blue pantsuit, "Wait! I'm here."

She gestures with her hand, slowly up and down, up and down. "Calm down, sweetheart; you're fine. We haven't closed the doors yet."

And the beauty is, the gate area is completely empty. No one is standing in line; no one is jostling to get on board first. The only person left at the gate is a nice woman in an ugly blue suit, cooing at me with soothing words.

I hand her my rumpled boarding pass. "I'm meeting some friends," I say. "They need me."

"Come on," she says, putting her arm around my shoulders. "I'll walk you down to find them."

We walk together down the empty boarding ramp, and as soon as the airplane door comes into sight, I see them—Phoenix, Sally, and Amanda, standing in the doorway, talking with the pilot.

When I see Phoenix, I know.

I'll be fine.

He turns toward us. He smiles and I breathe. I feel the breath coming, filling me with energy and strength.

"Sorry I'm late," I whisper, sliding my hand into his.

Phoenix's hand feels damp, wrapped around mine. It's shaking—not too much, but enough that I want to hold on to him more tightly. I lean in a little, pressing my side against his. I can tell he's sweating, because the scent of spring fresh deodorant is coming off him, strong. The smell makes me think of those air-freshener ads with pictures of daisy fields waving in the breeze. It also makes me miss the real scent of Phoenix. The musky, spicy, warm one.

Phoenix, Sally, and I are standing at the door of the cockpit.

"What are we doing here?" I whisper to Amanda.

"Introducing ourselves to the pilot," she says. "Sally thought maybe if Phoenix *met* the pilot, he'd feel a little more trusting—a little less nervous about the whole thing."

"Hello, sir." Phoenix lets go of my hand so that he can shake the man's hand. "It's nice to meet you."

"It's a pleasure, son," the pilot says. He's tall, with salt-and-pepper hair. He's wearing a blue polyester suit and a bright red tie. He looks just like a pilot should—responsible, confident, calm. "Your friend tells me that you're a bit nervous flying?"

The pilot looks toward Sally, who is looking at Phoenix, who is biting his lip and squeezing his eyes shut.

"Yes, sir. That's right," he tells the pilot. "I guess it's like a . . ."

He looks at me, his eyes searching. I think he's having trouble finding the right word.

"Phobia," I say. I wrap my hand around his again and squeeze.

"Well, you're in good hands on my plane, son. I've been at this for twenty-three years—longer than you've been alive, I imagine. I assure you, there's not a thing to worry about."

Not a thing to worry about. *I wish.*

"You two are in the back," Amanda says. "Sorry—last-minute purchase. You know how that goes."

"We'll be here in the exit row if you need us," Sally says, studying both of our faces carefully. I think maybe she's trying to determine which one of us will come unmoored first. I tug on Phoenix's hand and we head to the back of the plane. It's a small plane, and our side of the aisle only has two seats. I slide into the window seat, and Phoenix sits down beside me, silent. We start to buckle our seat belts.

It feels good to be nestled here between the window and Phoenix, away from all those people. Phoenix, though, he's not doing so well. He's sweating a lot, shaking a little, and barely able to speak. He's also tugging a little too vigorously on his seat belt strap. In other circumstances, with a different person, I would make some joke about how, if this plane goes down, that seat belt will do absolutely nothing to keep us from meeting our demise. But it's Phoenix, and he's close to losing it, and I'm wondering for the thousandth time today whether all of this was a good idea.

He wipes his forehead with his hand and then starts fidgeting with the air vents. "I wish there was, like, a window we could open, or something," he grumbles.

Which reminds me to pull down the shade. Phoenix does *not* need to see liftoff.

The jets fire up, and a loud noise overtakes the plane. Phoenix actually jumps a little, straining against his already-too-tight seat belt. His hands fly to the headrest of the seat in front of him.

"I can't do this."

I put my hand on his leg.

"Oh, Jesus, Gretchen. I need to get off." He's gripping the headrest so tightly that his knuckles have turned white.

Then the safety video comes on, and he turns to look at it. I need to do something to distract him. If he sees the part when those yellow emergency air masks drop down from the ceiling, this will all be over.

I make a split-second decision.

"Hey," I say, leaning into him. "I just want you to know that, under normal circumstances, I am *so* not into PDA."

But desperate times call for desperate measures.

I loosen the strap of my seat belt, put one hand on Phoenix's leg, hold the back of his neck with the other, and lean in to kiss him.

He pulls back. "Uh, Gretch——"

"Just kiss me," I say. "It's for your own good."

"We can't——"

I wrap my hands around his face and make him look directly at me. "Yes, we can, actually."

So we do.

The engines are starting to roar and the plane lurches forward. It's gaining speed, vibrating, and Phoenix's arm is reaching around to pull me closer. We're in the back row, so it doesn't really matter. I guess the people across from us could watch if they wanted to, but I don't even care. All I care about is feeling him next to me, his hand on my cheek, my neck, my back. We touch softly, kiss slowly, like we have all the time in the world.

When the pilot's voice comes on to tell us we've reached our cruising altitude of thirty thousand feet, he pulls away and looks at me. "That's it?" he asks. "We're in the air?"

"Yeah," I tell him, smiling wide. "It's smooth sailing now."

"Damn." He tugs on his lower lip. "That was a lot easier than the first time."

"If only you had known back then—you could have just made out with the person sitting next to you."

Phoenix laughs. He's rubbing my leg gently. "Wouldn't have worked with anyone but you. And then there's the whole problem of the handcuffs." He lifts both hands and crosses them at the wrist.

"What? You were handcuffed?"

I don't remember him saying anything about handcuffs, but it feels so long ago—the day we met in the Place Without a Soul, back when the garden was just a few stacks of two-by-fours and a lot of red clay.

"Sorry I didn't tell you," he says. "It's not really something you tell a stranger—you know? That you were being transported from one prison to another in a plane full of handcuffed guys."

"Don't call it prison," I tell him. "It's detention."

Phoenix shrugs and smiles. "I'm pretty sure that distinction is lost on most people—including all those guys in prison jumpsuits and handcuffs."

"But they aren't criminals. *You're* not criminals."

Phoenix's eyes dart away from me, and when they come back to meet mine, something is different about them. They're not as bright. It's like the lights inside of them have dimmed.

"Some of us are"—he looks up at the air vents—"criminals, I mean."

Phoenix starts to fiddle with the vent above his seat again. Then he reaches over to mine.

"Can I?" he asks.

I nod and he turns it so that more cold air blasts into his face.

The flight attendant arrives to ask us if we'd like drinks. Phoenix and I both ask for ice water. Phoenix gulps his water down while I try to find something for us to watch on the little screens built into the seats. There aren't any good movies, so I go with an old crime drama. Any-

thing to keep his mind off the fact that we are cruising at thirty thousand feet above sea level.

When the credits start rolling, he suddenly blurts out: "There's stuff you
need to know." He's looking at the back of the seat in front of him, but
it's clear he's talking to me. "It's just that, uh, if you are coming to court
with us, you're gonna hear a bunch of—it's just—there's some stuff
I think I need to tell you first."

I study his face—his jaw clenching and unclenching. I guess the TV
show hadn't distracted him as much as I thought.

"Okay, Phoenix. If you need to tell me, then tell me."

He still won't look at me. "I need to explain why my asylum case
was denied—why I got a deport order."

"Didn't you say that everyone's case is denied—or almost everyone's?" I ask.

"Most people from El Salvador, yeah." He's running his finger along
the rim of his cup. "But sometimes there's a chance on appeal, and it
looks like I'm not going to have that chance."

I don't want to hear this.

"Amanda and Sally are offering to pay for the appeal, and all I can
think of is: *Why me?* There are so many guys in that place. And some
of them are assholes, sure. But some of them, Gretchen? They're really
good people. They've never done anything wrong in their entire lives.
They're killing themselves to stay out of trouble. And then there's
me—"

"What are you trying to say, Phoenix?"

"I've done some stupid shit, Gretchen. I guess it was a long time ago,
and I was a dumb, scared kid, but I *did* it. And I think maybe I don't
deserve all this, you know?"

I lean in to rest my head on his shoulder. "Whatever you did," I whisper, "would you do it again?"

"Never," he says into my hair.

"Then leave it behind; don't let that stuff from your past tell you who you are."

He pulls back and looks at me. "But I think you should know——"

I reach around his neck and pull him in. "You think I should know what? How much you're looking forward to a bumpy landing, so that I'll kiss you again to distract you?"

"Yeah," he murmurs. "Well, that too."

The captain comes on to tell the flight attendants to prepare for final descent. I whisper and chat with him about nothing, trying to keep him focused on our conversation. It's going pretty well until the end, when the plane starts to swerve a little, left to right.

Phoenix grabs the armrests and lets out a deep groan.

I tell him that it's totally normal, that everything's fine, and he nods while grasping my hand and squeezing the life out of it. The wheels touch down, and the plane jolts from side to side and then bounces back into the air.

"*Puta madre,*" he calls out. I don't know what it means, but I can tell by the way he says it that it's bad. So can everyone in the rows in front of us. I see their heads swerving to see who's calling out in the backseat during a perfectly routine landing.

The breaks engage and we both lurch forward. The plane jerks and jolts down the runway, turns, and then it comes to a complete stop.

"It's over," I say.

The cabin fills with the clicks and thumps of seat belts coming unfastened and overhead bins opening. It's impossible not to notice that everyone in front of us stands up and immediately peers back to get a glimpse at the crazy person in row forty.

Phoenix crouches forward, trying to avoid the stares. "*Coño,*" he murmurs. "I am such an idiot." He looks like he's in one of those videos we used to watch in school—what to do in case of a tornado.

"Hey, Phoenix," I say brightly, leaning down so I'm crouched next to him. "A cute boy once gave me some great advice when I was in a similar situation."

He turns his head to show me his raised eyebrows. "A cute boy?"

I wrap my arm around his shoulders. "Yeah. Wanna hear it?"

He shakes his head slowly. "Not really, but I have a feeling you're gonna tell me anyway."

That makes me smile. I lean in close to him and whisper in his ear: "Fuck 'em. They don't know what you know."

And it's true. None of these people know what we know.

CHAPTER TWENTY-EIGHT

PHOENIX

WE'RE WALKING ACROSS a big patch of dying grass, toward the shelter where Ari is staying. It's a huge concrete building—up on stilts, with a covered patio underneath. No one is out on the patio, except for a couple of security guards standing around on the grass and lounging on benches in the shade.

They're hanging out, not acting particularly threatening or anything. I stop before we get to the door and look up at all of those thin slits of window that look like they need washing. No one is looking out of the windows, either. Maybe because they're so small, and so high up.

It's an ugly building, but at least there's no barbed wire—there aren't even fences.

An airplane is taking off somewhere nearby, which I guess makes sense, since this place is supposed to be an air force base. Sally told me it used to be a barracks for people in the air force, but now it's a temporary shelter for the kids coming across the border. She said there are almost a thousand kids here, from Central America. I'm sort of wondering how we're gonna find Ari, with so many kids staying here.

Sally walks up to one of the security guards and asks him where we can find the main entrance. He smiles and points us toward a metal door. It looks exactly like all the other metal doors lining this building.

"Reception's just through there, ma'am."

Reception—like this is a fancy American hotel, or something.

It's kind of a relief to walk into that door and hear kids' voices—and music, really loud Tejano music, which is strange. I smile, feeling sure that this place is nothing like that hellhole I was sent to. Or maybe hoping.

A receptionist checks us in. She speaks with us in English, but she looks likes she speaks Spanish, too—she's probably Tejano, like the music. She tells us that Ari's group is in indoor recreation time, and asks if we'd like to join him in the lounge.

The lounge. Yeah, this place is a little different from the hellhole. The only thing there that remotely resembled a lounge was the cluster of plastic tables next to our bunk beds. It wasn't exactly relaxing to hang out at those tables, since the benches were attached, and since there were always guys taking a dump right next to them. That place had no walls; the sleeping area, sitting areas, showers, toilets—they all were right up next to one another, which was really messed up. No walls—that was only one of the many really messed up things about being in detention.

We wait for a few minutes, sitting side by side in molded plastic chairs. Gretchen and Sally are quiet. I think they know me well enough to know that I've got nothing to say right now. Or that I need to save whatever I've got for what's about to happen. Right now I'm using all my energy to push that image out of my head—the way Ari's eyes looked when I left him in the *heladera*—that freezing cold room near the border, where they kept him when they took me away, handcuffed. That was the last time I saw him, the last time he spoke to me. I guess maybe it was the last time he spoke at all.

I'm thinking about how cold it was in that room, and how Ari was shivering like crazy. Thank God it's warm in this place, not like in that hotel where we are staying. When you walk into that lobby, the cold air blasts into you. They must keep the air conditioning at, like, fifteen degrees Celsius. When we dropped our bags in the room, I found that little box to turn off the air conditioner. Then I tried to open the windows, but they don't even open.

A different lady comes up to us and introduces herself. She's talking to Sally and Gretchen, but I'm having trouble concentrating on the conversation. I think maybe she's asking them where we came from, and how our trip was, and stuff like that. She leads us through another metal door and up a flight of stairs. We go through a big set of swinging doors and then we're in what I guess is the "lounge." Long strings of Mexican paper flags are draped across the ceiling and there's a piñata hanging in the corner—the kind with a burro wearing a sombrero. With the Tejano music blaring, I'm starting to wonder whether we're back in Mexico, or maybe I'm wondering why the hell they would want to remind all these poor kids of that place, since I'm guessing that most of them don't have really fond memories.

I know Ari doesn't.

A bunch of kids are sitting around on couches, and a few are crowded around a pushcart, where an old Mexican guy in a baseball cap is passing out free *paletas*. A few of them look over at us when we come in, and a couple of the kids are checking Gretchen out. I grab her hand and pull her in toward me a little. I'm scanning the room, looking for my little brother, but I don't see him anywhere.

Some guy is standing at the front of the room, talking on a microphone, like this is a big blowout birthday party or something. I guess he's an employee.

"*Y ahora, damas y caballeros,*" he says, "*comencemos con la piñata!*"

He's grinning really wide, and his voice is all animated. But I don't see any *damas* or *caballeros* in here, just a bunch of shell-shocked kids trying to figure out why the hell this guy is asking them to play piñata games.

"Do you see him?" Gretchen whispers.

I shake my head.

"He may have stayed in his dorm room," says the lady who brought us in here. "They're allowed to do that if they're not feeling up to this."

Up to what? A party? *Christ*, this place is strange.

"We'll go and see," she says. Then she gestures toward the Mexican guy and his *paleta* pushcart. "Would you like to take him a Popsicle?"

"Yeah, I guess," I say, shrugging. "Sure, yeah. Thanks."

The four of us walk over to get a *paleta*, and the kids move out of the way to give us room. There are only three flavors: guava, coconut, or cookies and cream. I pick cookies and cream.

"Gracias," I tell the old man.

He nods and looks at me with sad eyes. *"Que Dios te bendiga,"* he says.

"Would you all like one?" the lady asks. She's trying to be nice, welcoming, but it's all so messed up. I'm not sure what to say.

"No, thanks," Gretchen says.

"We'll save them for the kids," Amanda tells her.

I've got the Popsicle dangling from my hand while we walk through an empty hallway. We come up to another metal door. The lady opens it and ushers us through.

"*There* he is," she says brightly.

I look across a long row of black cots, all of them empty but one. At the end of that row is my little brother, stretched out under a thin white blanket, legs crossed at the ankles, reading a comic book.

I breathe in deep, put a smile on my face, and step in.

"¡Oye, bicho!"

I'm walking toward him with purpose, before I lose my nerve. He looks over at me, eyes peering across the comic book.

He looks tired. And skinny—his cheeks are sort of sunken in.

He sits up in bed, puts the comic book down, swings his legs slowly to the side.

"What's up, you little pissant?" I say in Spanish. I sit down beside him and nudge him in the shoulder. "What are you readin'?"

His scrawny little arms wrap around me, and he rests his forehead on my shoulder.

He's so still.

I don't know what to do. I don't know how to talk to him, how to hold him.

I grab his bony shoulder, squeeze a little, and pull away from him. "I brought you something," I tell him. "A *paleta*."

He takes the Popsicle from me and studies it, turning it over in his hands. He doesn't smile.

"Yeah." I keep my arm wrapped around his shoulders. "It was free. You didn't expect, like, a real present did you?"

He looks at me, right in the eyes. I wish I knew what that look was trying to tell me, but I haven't got a clue.

"Because I'm flat broke," I say.

He shrugs and looks away, toward Gretchen, Amanda, and Sally. I watch him, looking at them. I don't really want to see their faces right now.

Because my stupid fucking heart is breaking open again, and I can't handle watching them watch it happen. Not even Gretchen. Maybe especially not Gretchen.

Since I'm talking to Ari in Spanish, I know only one of them has a clue that I'm talking about pointless shit like Popsicles and comic books, and not about what really matters, like—

Damn. I miss this kid.

"You should eat that, *flaco*," I tell him. "I mean, you're getting a little skinny."

He starts to fool with the wrapper, but his hands are shaking and he can't get it open. I take the Popsicle and use my teeth to rip the top. I pull it out and hand it to him.

Gretchen steps up to the bed.

"Hola." She reaches her hand out toward him. *"Me llamo Gretchen."*

I have no idea where she learned to introduce herself in Spanish. I didn't teach her. He stands up to shake her hand and she pulls him into a hug. She holds him there, against her body.

He pats her awkwardly and then looks over at me. Finally I can read his expression: *Who is this pretty American girl and why is she hugging me?*

"My friend," I tell him in Spanish.

His eyebrows arch. Now he's saying: *bullshit*. I'm getting good at this.

"Yeah, okay. My girlfriend, sort of."

Sally and Amanda introduce themselves, also folding him into a hug. He accepts the hugs awkwardly and then sits back down onto the cot. I sit next to him. Gretchen, Sally, and the caseworker take a seat across from us, on some other kid's cot—some kid who's not so messed up that he stays in bed all day, I guess.

"Ari," the caseworker says, in Spanish, "don't you want to tell your brother about what you've been doing here with us?"

Pause.

"About the English classes?"

Nothing.

"Movie nights?"

Nada.

"The other kids you've met?"

Silence.

"All those great drawings you've been working on?"

He shrugs and reaches under his bed to pull out a tall stack of papers, loose-leaf sheets sloppily piled on top of one another. He places the stack on my lap.

I start shuffling absently through them—a stocky little iguana, a few dolphins jumping out of the surf.

"They're good," I say.

A field of corn, a sunset over the mountains.

"I like the clouds in this one," I say. Because I guess I'm not really sure what to say.

I shuffle that one to the bottom of the stack and look at the next. It's my bike.

I must be staring at it for a super-long time, or making some really strange face or something, because I feel Gretchen's hand resting gently on my knee, and she's leaning in toward me and whispering, "Let me see the drawings, Phoenix. Go outside; take a break."

I hand her the stack of papers and stand up.

"Be right back," I say to Ari in Spanish, heading toward that big gray door. "I gotta take a leak."

The door clicks shut behind me, and I'm in the hall, alone. I reach out with both hands to hold myself up against the concrete block wall. My eyes close and my head leans in. I feel the wall, rough against my forehead. I try to think about my breath, struggling to fill my chest. That's what Gretchen told me to do the other day—to feel the air moving in and out of my lungs.

But I can't. All I can think about is that bike.

It was a lowrider. Green. A long black seat and big tall handlebars— my most prized possession. My only possession, really. It took me a couple of years to earn enough money for it, doing odd jobs at the res- taurants down by the lake. I was so proud of that damn bike. I rode it all around the neighborhood, Ari perched on the handlebars. I taught myself a bunch of tricks on that thing too.

I thought I was a real badass.

I wasn't much older than Ari is now, the first time Delgado stepped in front of that bike. I don't remember where I was going. I slammed on the breaks and he grabbed the chrome handlebars, one with each hand.

"What's up, kid?"

"Nothin'."

"You going down to help your grandma later?"

"Yeah."

"Sellin' *pupusas?*"

"Yeah."

"She sells a lot of those things, doesn't she?"

I nod.

"Best in town, am I right?"

"Yeah," I say.

"Tell her not to forget to save a little somethin' for me, all right?"

"Yeah, okay."

"I'll be by later, with my boys."

At first I thought he meant *pupusas*—that he wanted my grandmother to save some of her *pupusas*, because they were so good. But Delgado and his boys didn't want *pupusas*. They wanted her money, and they weren't going to stop harassing her until they got it. The problem was, my *abuela* was never gonna cave. I knew her well enough to know that she wouldn't give a single cent to Delgado. She pretty much thought he was the spawn of the devil. (Turns out, she was right.)

A few days later I stood there watching them circle her. She spat in Delgado's face that day. He and his boys left, but the next afternoon, they attacked me and took my bike. I guess even though they were assholes, and mean as shit, they weren't about beating up old ladies, so they beat me up instead. After that, it was every day. Delgado rode up on my bike when I was coming out of school. He followed me, zigzagging behind me, until I turned the corner. And then Blackie picked me up, hauled me up to the roof of this abandoned building, kicking and screaming, and held me out over the ledge.

"You ready to help us out, bitch? Or maybe we'll see what your grandma thinks about the view from up here?"

Three weeks out over that ledge. That's all it took for my candy-ass sissy self to agree to work for them. It wasn't all that bad when they jumped me in. A few long seconds of getting the shit kicked out of me—that was the easy part. The hard part was figuring out what to tell my *abuela* when I got home that night, my face and arms still crusted in blood. She pretended to believe whatever stupid story I made up, but she knew better. Ari kept asking if it hurt, and I kept telling him it looked way worse than it felt. Honestly, back then, I thought it *did* all look worse than it was—the whole *member of an international criminal gang* thing. It wasn't really what I expected, what I feared. I didn't *feel* dangerous. I felt like a thirteen-year-old kid. Going to school, living my life.

Delgado gave my bike back, and he quit harassing my *abuela*. All I had to do was go down to the tourist district by the lake every afternoon after school and distract those people. I'd ride around in front of the ladies sitting at outdoor cafes, popping wheelies, balancing on my handlebars. Simple shit, really, but crazy enough to make them quit paying attention for long enough to get their purses stolen. Delgado and his guys took that money and sent it to all the homies in prison. The real badasses.

Technically, I didn't even have to steal, and my grandmother could keep selling her *pupusas*.

Win-win, right?

Sister Mary Margaret used to bring her missionary groups down there, to this one *soda* that had really good *batidos*. They stood outside, sipping on their pineapple and mango *batidos*, always in those matching T-shirts with the crosses and the Bible verses, and they watched me perform my tricks—like I was a circus monkey, or something. Delgado and his boys didn't steal from those people. They were too afraid of Sister Mary Margaret. But when the Americans tried to give me money for my tricks, Delgado made me take it, and then I had to hand it all over to him, for the homies.

Sister Mary Margaret started calling me over, asking me to tell the *americanos* a little about myself. They loved that I knew how to talk to them in English. Those people always asked me where I learned it, like it was some big miracle that a *Salvadoreño* street kid knew how to speak their language. Delgado and his boys saw me talking to those tourists, but they didn't bother me about it much. Sometimes they made fun of me—saying I was so hard up that I wanted to get it on with a seventy-year-old nun, and shit like that.

They wanted to believe they ran our town, but they knew that without Sister Mary Margaret and her missionaries, without the money they pumped into this place, without her connections to the government, Ilopango would have gone to hell even faster than it did.

The rains helped with that.

It was raining like crazy the night they got me drunk—the seventh straight day of pouring rain. The roads were starting to get washed out, so I decided not to go home. I didn't want my bike floating off—it was my livelihood. A bunch of guys were hanging around Delgado's that night. They thought it was hilarious, killing time by making the new kid get all wasted. I was scrawny, like Ari. It didn't take much. I passed out on the ground and woke up the next afternoon, the skin burning on my stomach, where they'd put that stupid fucking tattoo—the gnarled hand with two spiky fingers pointing up toward my heart. I hated that tattoo from the first moment I saw it. I sat there and inspected it, red and swollen, while they dragged El Turbino in. I guess that was what woke me up: El Turbino yelling at them in English to let him the hell go. Soaking wet. They all were.

He was filthy, covered in mud and blood. When Delgado gave me that old rag and told me to shine up his tattoo, I really thought they wanted me to clean it so they could see it better. But that was not what they wanted.

By the time I put it together: the acrid smell of gas and the rag in my hand, it was too late. Slayer already had the first match lit.

After it happened—after I realized that nothing I said or did would stop them—I took off on foot. I thought about that bike. I wanted to grab it, but the water was running fast on the dirt road in front of Delgado's place—like a river—and I knew riding my bike would slow me down. It was pouring rain, and nobody was out on the streets. I ran toward home, not looking back. I knew I didn't matter enough to those guys for them to come chasing after me, but I kept running anyway, sucking rainwater into my mouth and nostrils, struggling to wash away the stench, the burn.

I turned the corner and there it was: a huge pile of boulders, water flowing fast over them. A bunch of rocks piled up, right where my grandmother's house was supposed to be. I stumbled back, and fell.

"Phoenix?"

A hand on my back. I lift my forehead from the concrete wall and turn to look. It's Sally, rubbing a slow circle.

"Come see, Phoenix."

My hands drop from the wall and I stand straight. She takes my elbow and pulls me gently toward the door, toward Ari.

"He's working with Gretchen. They're drawing together."

I let her lead me to the narrow window that's cut into the door. Gretchen and Ari are sitting on the floor, cross-legged, a stack of clean white paper between them. Ari has a pen in his hand, and he's leaning over a sheet of paper, smiling.

They're making art together.

"Let's go join them," Sally tells me. "It will help."

"Yeah, okay." I swallow hard and rub my eyes. She pushes the door open and I follow her in.

I'm looking at Ari and Gretchen, but I'm seeing my grandmother's funeral. It was really small. Just me and Ari, and a few neighbors. Sister Mary Margaret came too. As it turned out, Ari had been with Sister Mary Margaret, at the church. They knew the landslide might come, so they made a shelter there. My *abuela* sent Ari to that shelter, but she stayed behind, waiting for me to get home.

Christ, I regret so many things.

I sit down between Gretchen and Ari. Ari looks over at me and grins, and then he goes back to work. He's drawing a picture of the place we used to meet, after I finished my work with the missionaries. It's good. He may be a scrawny little pissant with a nasty temper, but he's a great artist.

Watching him, I know: *I'll never, ever regret that I kept him away from Delgado and his boys.*

He hands me a piece of paper and gestures toward a pack of colored pencils. I look at Gretchen and she smiles and nods. "Go ahead," she says quietly. "It will help him if you draw some memories too."

I pick a blue pencil and wait, the point hovering over a blank page, because I don't even know where to start. So I decide not to draw a memory. I form a sort of prayer instead.

Madre de Dios, *help me to keep him away from them.*

CHAPTER TWENTY-NINE
GRETCHEN

PHOENIX AND I SIT DOWN together in the front row and watch Ari take the stand.

Oh, God. How are they going to get through this?

IN THE JUVENILE COURT OF BEXAR COUNTY
STATE OF TEXAS

IN THE INTEREST OF:
"AFF": DOCKET NO.: 633542
A MINOR CHILD UNDER THE
AGE OF 17 YEARS:

TRANSCRIPT OF HEARING
APRIL 16, 2015

BEXAR COUNTY COURTHOUSE
SAN ANTONIO, TEXAS
HONORABLE ROBERT GALLAGHER, PRESIDING

APPEARANCES:

FOR THE PETITIONER: JILL DE LEON, Esq.

GUARDIAN AD LITEM: LEE TAYLOR, Esq.

ALSO PRESENT: "AFF," Juvenile

　　　　Phoenix Flores Flores

　　　　Estella Moon, Interpreter

LOIS P. GILBERT

Official Court Reporter—Division III

Bexar Juvenile Court

P-R-O-C-E-E-D-I-N-G-S

MS. DE LEON: Good morning, Your Honor. This is a private deprivation hearing for file 633542 in the interest of "AFF," a minor child under eighteen years of age.

Present in the court today are myself, Ms. Jill de Leon, representing the Office of Refugee Resettlement; "AFF," the minor child; witness Phoenix Flores Flores, the minor child's brother; and Guardian Ad Litem Lee Taylor, representing the minor child.

(Whereupon the Spanish Interpreter was sworn.)

THE COURT: Okay, call your first witness.

(Whereupon the witness took the stand.)

MS. DE LEON: "AFF," please raise your right hand.

WHEREUPON,

"AFF,"

was called as a witness and, having been first duly sworn, was examined and testified as follows:

DIRECT EXAMINATION:

BY MS. DE LEON:

Q. "AFF," please state your full, true, and correct name for the record.

(Pause.)

Q. "AFF," we need for you to please state your full, true, and correct name for the record.

(Pause.)

THE COURT: Attorneys, approach the bench.

(Whereupon MS. DE LEON and MS. TAYLOR approached the bench.)

THE COURT: What's going on here? Does this boy not know how to say his name?

MS. TAYLOR: Your Honor, the child has been nonverbal since he entered the United States. He has full mental capacity, but is unable to speak.

MS. DE LEON: The psychologist assigned to his case by the Department of Family and Protective Services believes this is linked to trauma. He is capable of communicating, Your Honor. But not with words.

THE COURT: Then how exactly do you expect for us to proceed here?

MS. TAYLOR: Drawings, Your Honor. In our experience, the child has been able to communicate in the form of pictures.

He has prepared some drawings, which we would like to submit as evidence.

THE COURT: Pictures? Are you telling me that this child is not going to testify verbally? That we're going to admit pictures?

MS. TAYLOR: Yes, Your Honor. That is our hope.

THE COURT: Well, how do you expect me to interpret these pictures? Do you have an expert witness?

MS. DE LEON: I will call a second witness, Your Honor. We believe that he will be able to interpret these drawings.

THE COURT: I'm sorry, counselors, but if that's all you have, I'm going to have to dismiss this case.

(Pause.)

MS. TAYLOR: Your Honor, we have another witness to the abuse and neglect, but with all due respect, I believe that the juvenile should have a right to testify in any manner that he is able. This is no different from a case in which a child is severely disabled. The weight you give the testimony, of course, is your own choice, but it is this young man's very life that we are asking the court to make a decision on, and we want for him to be able to communicate with the court.

THE COURT: By drawing pictures?

MS. TAYLOR: Yes, Your Honor.

THE COURT: I don't see how this possibly can be effective, but proceed.

MS. DE LEON: Thank you very much, Your Honor.

(Whereupon direct examination continued.)

Q: With whom did you live, "AFF," in El Salvador before you came to the United States?

(Pause.)

MS. DE LEON: Your Honor, I have marked the picture that
the witness has drawn in response to this question as Exhibit
A, and I would move to admit Exhibit A.

THE COURT: Any objection?

MS. TAYLOR: No, Your Honor.

THE COURT: Proceed.

Q: Who was able to financially provide for you in El Salvador
before you came to the United States?

(Pause.)

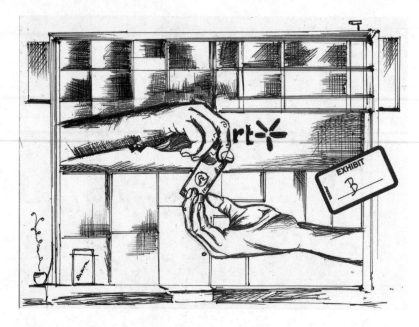

MS. DE LEON: Your Honor, I have marked the picture that the witness has drawn as Exhibit B, and I would move to admit Exhibit B.

THE COURT: Any objection?

MS. TAYLOR: No, Your Honor.

THE COURT: Proceed.

Q: What brought you to the United States from El Salvador?

(Pause.)

MS. DE LEON: Your Honor, I have marked the picture that the witness has drawn as Exhibit C, and I would move to admit Exhibit C.

THE COURT: Any objection?

MS. TAYLOR: No, Your Honor.

THE COURT: Proceed.

Q: How did you travel from El Salvador to the United States? How did you physically get from El Salvador to the United States?

(Pause.)

MS. DE LEON: Your Honor, I have marked the picture that the witness has drawn as Exhibit D, and I would move to admit Exhibit D.

THE COURT: Any objection?

MS. TAYLOR: No, Your Honor.

THE COURT: Proceed.

Q: Is it dangerous to travel from El Salvador to the United States? Were you ever afraid?

(Pause.)

MS. DE LEON: Your Honor, I have marked the picture that the witness has drawn as Exhibit E, and I would move to admit Exhibit E.

THE COURT: Any objection?

MS. TAYLOR: No, Your Honor.

THE COURT: Proceed.

Q: What do you believe will happen to you if you return to El Salvador?

(Pause.)

MS. DE LEON: Your Honor, I have marked the picture that the witness has drawn as Exhibit F, and I would move to admit Exhibit F.

THE COURT: Any objection?

MS. TAYLOR: No, Your Honor.

THE COURT: Proceed.

Q: And what do you want to do with your life in the United States if you're able to stay in the country?

(Pause.)

MS. DE LEON: Your Honor, I have marked the picture that the witness has drawn as Exhibit G, and I would move to admit Exhibit G.

THE COURT: Any objection?

MS. TAYLOR: No, Your Honor.

THE COURT: Proceed.

MS. DE LEON: These are all the questions I have for this witness, your honor.

THE COURT: Ms. Taylor?

MS. TAYLOR: Your Honor, may I approach the witness?

THE COURT: Yes.

MS. TAYLOR: Ari, I'm showing you what's been marked as Exhibit C. This is a drawing of a neck, with a knife against it. Are you in this picture?

THE COURT: Ms. Taylor, he cannot speak verbally, and the court cannot record his head movements. There is no way to record this as evidence.

MS. TAYLOR: May I have a moment to consult with a witness?

THE COURT: Yes.

MS. TAYLOR: Ari, is there someone in this courtroom who is in the picture that has been marked as Exhibit C, and if so, can you point to that person?

MS. TAYLOR: Your honor, I would like for the record to reflect that the juvenile has pointed to his brother, Phoenix Flores Flores, who will be the next witness.

THE COURT: Let the record reflect.

MS. TAYLOR: I don't have any additional questions, Your Honor.

THE COURT: Okay, you can step down. Call your next witness, Ms. de Leon.

(Whereupon the witness took the stand.)

MS. DE LEON: Will you please raise your right hand?

THE WITNESS: (complying.)

WHEREUPON, Phoenix Flores Flores was called as a witness, and having been first duly sworn, was examined and testified as follows:

DIRECT EXAMINATION:

BY MS. DE LEON:

Q. Will you please state your full, true, and correct name for the record?

A. Phoenix Flores Flores.

MS. DE LEON: Your Honor, the witness will not need an interpreter. He speaks English fluently.

THE COURT: Where did you learn to speak English, Mr. Flores?

WITNESS: In El Salvador, sir. I worked with missionaries.

THE COURT: Missionaries?

WITNESS: Yes, sir. American missionary groups came to San Salvador, to build things. I helped them. And I was able to go to bilingual schools.

THE COURT: You speak perfect English. Did you go to college in El Salvador?

WITNESS: Yes, sir. I started university, but then we had to leave because of my brother, because of the trouble. I'd like to go back to university, but I'm not sure I'll be able to.

THE COURT: Okay, proceed with your questioning, Ms. de Leon.

Q. Mr. Flores Flores, where do you presently reside?

A. At 3422 Ivywood Circle in Atlanta, Georgia.

Q. Is that your permanent residence?

A. No, ma'am.

Q. And what is the address of your permanent residence?

A. I don't have a permanent residence. I mean, not right now. My brother and I are from Ilopango, in the region of San Salvador, El Salvador.

Q. And when did you leave your home?

A. On September sixteenth of last year.

Q. Why did you and your brother decide to leave Ilopango?

A. My brother was being recruited to join a gang and he resisted.

Q. Can you explain what you mean by resisted?

A. They stopped my brother on the way home from school every day, and they harassed him when he said he would not join them.

Q. When did this start?

A. I'm not sure exactly. I was living at the university. I believe it was in August of last year.

THE COURT: Isn't this hearsay?

MS. DE LEON: We can strike it.

Q. Mr. Flores Flores, did you ever observe your brother being harassed?

A. Yes. I returned to Ilopango because a friend told me that my brother had been beat up. I worried that the gang had jumped him in. Do you know what that is?

Q. Can you explain for the court please?

A. It's how new members are brought into a particular group of a gang. They circle around the new member and they beat him up.

Q. And did this happen to your brother?

A. No, he resisted them. Which is a good thing, because I would have killed him myself if he let them jump him in.

MS. DE LEON: I believe Mr. Flores is using a figure of speech, Your Honor. I'd like to ask that you strike that last comment from the record.

THE COURT: Mr. Flores, would you kill your brother?

A. No, sir. I meant that I would be very mad at him.

THE COURT: I understand. Strike it.

Q. Mr. Flores, how do you know that these people are members of a gang?

A. Everyone knows. But they have tattoos that mark them as members of a gang. Each gang uses a different tattoo.

Q. And why did you decide to leave Ilopango, Mr. Flores, after this incident?

A. Because I took my brother away from them, and then the leader of the gang made an announcement. It's called a green light. He said that my brother and I should be killed.

Q. Did you hear this announcement, Mr. Flores?

A. Yes, ma'am.

Q. Did your brother hear this announcement?

A. Yes, ma'am.

Q. And when did this happen, Mr. Flores?

A. On September sixteenth of last year.

Q. Was this the day that you left to come to the United States?

A. Yes, ma'am.

Q. And when did you and your brother arrive in the United States, Mr. Flores?

A. Four months later, on January twelfth of this year.

Q. Where were you during those four months?

A. We traveled through Guatemala. We were there for about three days. The rest of the time we were in Mexico.

Q. Did you decide to live in Mexico?

A. No, ma'am. It was a very difficult trip.

Q. Okay, thank you. If your brother were to return to El Salvador, would he have family members there who could take care of him?

A. I don't know.

Q. Can you explain, please?

A. My brother and I do not have any family members living currently in El Salvador who can take care of him. He will not be safe if he returns to El Salvador. If I go back to El Salvador, it will not be safe for my brother to be with me.

MS. DE LEON: Your honor, I am handing the witness what has previously been marked and submitted as Exhibit A.

Mr. Flores, do you recognize anything that has been depicted in Exhibit A?

A. Yes, ma'am.

Q. Can you describe what you see?

A. This is our grandmother's neighborhood in Ilopango. We lived with her until my brother was seven. There were floods, and the house was destroyed in a mudslide. Our grandmother was killed.

MS. DE LEON: Your honor, I am handing the witness what
has previously been marked and submitted as Exhibit B.
Mr. Flores, do you recognize anything that has been depicted
in Exhibit B?

A. Yes, ma'am. Should I explain it?

Q. Yes, please explain what you see.

A. I had to leave Ilopango to work in the city. As I explained, I
worked with the missionaries. I met my brother every week
and gave him money. We met outside of the Walmart in the
commercial district because it was safe.

THE COURT: Excuse me, son? Did you say you met at the
Walmart because it was safe?

A. Yes, sir. The American stores have a lot of security guards,
so they are safer than our town.

THE COURT: Son, is this your hand in Exhibit B?

A. Yes, I believe so. I am giving money to my brother in the
picture. We met at Walmart because it wasn't safe for me to
go to our town, because of the gangs. So I met him there and
gave him money.

Q. Where did your brother live after the death of your grandmother, when you were working in a different town?

A. With my grandmother's friends. He moved around some,
but he always had what he needed because I gave him
money.

Q. So were the friends able to provide for him financially?

A. No, ma'am. But they gave him a safe place to sleep. And I
sent them money so that they could feed him.

Q. How many friends did your brother live with, from the time
that your grandmother died until the time you left El Salvador?

A. Three different friends.

Q. Where are your parents, Mr. Flores?

A. I don't know. We don't know who our fathers are, and our mother left after Ari was born.

Q. Where did she go?

A. To Phoenix, Arizona. She worked as a live-in nanny. But then she disappeared.

Q. When did she disappear?

A. Ten years ago. I was eight years old when she stopped sending money to my grandmother.

MS. DE LEON: Your honor, I am handing the witness what has previously been marked and submitted as Exhibit C. Mr. Flores, do you recognize anything that has been depicted in Exhibit C?

A. Yes, ma'am.

Q. Can you describe what you see?

A. As I said, the members of a gang in our neighborhood threatened to kill me and Ari after he said he wouldn't join. This is a picture of one of them, holding a knife to my neck.

THE COURT: Your neck? Did this actually happen?

A. Yes, sir. And then we ran. I have the scar, sir, I mean, if you would like to see it.

(Pause.)

THE COURT: Let the record reflect that the witness has revealed a scar on the lower right side of his neck.

MS. DE LEON: Your Honor, I am handing the witness what has previously been marked and submitted as Exhibit D. Mr. Flores, do you recognize anything that has been depicted in Exhibit D.

A. Yes, ma'am. I think so.

Q. Can you describe what you see?

A. I think that's supposed to be *la Bestia*. It's the train we rode on top of most of the way through Mexico. I mean, the drawing doesn't look exactly the same as *la Bestia*. The engine is different, and there's not a cross on it or anything, but I think that's why Ari drew a train. And the cross, I guess it's because, uh—

(Pause.)

Q. Because?

A. People died on that train. I mean, uh, we saw it.

Q. You saw people fall off of the train and die?

A. Yes, ma'am.

Q. Why did it take you so long to travel through Mexico by train?

A. We were kidnapped.

Q. Where were you kidnapped?

A. I'm not sure exactly where we were. Bandits took us from the train and made us work for them. We were like slaves.

Q. What kind of work did you do?

A. We picked flowers.

THE COURT: Excuse me. Did you say you picked flowers?

A. Yes, sir. I think maybe they were for drugs. We had to pick them all day and some of the night, even in the dark. There were a bunch of us, from Central America.

Q. Did you get paid for this work?

A. No, ma'am.

Q. Why did you stay?

A. Because they had guns, and they used them. There were guards who watched us all the time. One night, after almost three months, they got very drunk, or maybe high on drugs, and we ran away. Then we walked and caught rides to the border. We were afraid to get back on the train.

Q. Did they give you drugs? Is that why you stayed for such a long time?

A. No, ma'am. We stayed because of the guns. I don't use drugs. And my little brother is only twelve. Even if he wanted to use drugs, I would never let him.

Q. Did you and your brother sell drugs?

A. No, ma'am. We never saw any drugs. All we saw were the little red flowers we picked. That's all.

MS. DE LEON: Your Honor, I am handing the witness what has previously been marked and submitted as Exhibit E. Mr. Flores, do you recognize anything that has been depicted in Exhibit E?

A. Yes, ma'am.

Q. Can you describe what you see?

(Pause.)

Q. Mr. Flores, can you describe what you see in Exhibit E?

A. No, ma'am. I'd prefer not to describe it, please.

Q. Can you tell us anything about Exhibit E, Mr. Flores?

(Pause.)

Q. Mr. Flores, can you tell us anything about Exhibit E?

A. I'm not sure it's relevant, ma'am.

Q. We will let the court decide that, Mr. Flores. Please tell us what you see in Exhibit E.

A. It's a picture of a room where my brother went, with two

girls. We worked with them picking flowers. They were from Honduras. They were young. He watched them—

(Pause.)

Q. He watched them do what, exactly?
A. He hid there because, uh, the men came and he watched them, uh, he watched the men (pause) hurt our friends, and when we ran away from that place, we took those girls with us.
Q. Mr. Flores, I know this is difficult, but when you say "hurt," do you mean sexually assault?

(Pause.)

THE COURT: Mr. Flores, do you need a recess? Bailiff, get Mr. Flores some water.

(Pause.)

THE COURT: Can you proceed?

(Pause.)

THE COURT: Mr. Flores, can you proceed?
A. Yes.
THE COURT: Ms. de Leon, please restate your question.
Q. Mr. Flores, when you say your brother saw the girls get "hurt," do you mean he saw them being sexually assaulted?
A. Yes.
Q. Were you also a witness to this?

A. No. (Pause.) I came into the room when it was done. Their clothes were torn off. Graciela was bleeding so much.

Q. The girl from Honduras, her name was Graciela, Mr. Flores?

A. Yes. The other girl is named América. They are from Honduras. (Pause.) I'm sorry. You know that already.

Q. And your brother was there?

A. Yes, ma'am. He was in the corner behind that chest when I came into the room. I mean, the one in the picture. He was, uh, he was trying to hide. He was scared, I mean, so scared, and the girls, I mean, uh (pause).

Q. Where are those girls now, Mr. Flores?

A. I don't know. We lost them when we got to the border. Can we stop? I would like to stop, please.

MS. DE LEON: We are almost finished, Mr. Flores. Can you continue?

(Pause.)

MS. DE LEON: Mr. Flores. Are you able to continue?

A. Yes, I can continue.

MS. DE LEON: Your honor, I am handing the witness what has previously been marked and submitted as Exhibit F. Mr. Flores, do you recognize anything that has been depicted in Exhibit F?

A. Yes, ma'am.

Q. Can you describe what you see?

A. This is a graveyard in Ilopango.

Q. And why do you believe that your brother drew this graveyard?

A. Because my brother believes we will die if we go back to El Salvador.

Q. Do you believe that, Mr. Flores?

A. Yes, ma'am. I do.

MS. DE LEON: Your Honor, I am handing the witness what has previously been marked and submitted as Exhibit G. Mr. Flores, do you recognize anything that has been depicted in Exhibit G?

A. Yes, ma'am.

Q. Can you describe what you see?

A. I believe this is Ari. He's swimming in the ocean. He likes to ride the waves. And I think there is a school behind that big wave. I think he's saying that if he stays here, he would want to be able to go to school and swim in the ocean. He would like that.

MS. DE LEON: Thank you, Mr. Flores, I have no further questions.

THE COURT: Ms. Taylor?

MS. TAYLOR: I don't have any additional questions, Your Honor.

THE COURT: Mr. Flores, how old are you?

WITNESS: I'm eighteen, sir.

THE COURT: You are an adult, so why are you not seeking custody of your brother?

WITNESS: I can't, Your Honor.

THE COURT: Because you're an illegal?

WITNESS: No, sir, I am not an illegal. I am an asylum seeker, but my asylum claim was denied, and I have an order of deportation.

THE COURT: Is there nothing that can be done, Ms. de Leon?

MS. DE LEON: His only avenue is appeal, but he knows his chances of being granted asylum on appeal are very slim. He wants to ensure that Ari is safe here in the United States before he is made to leave.

THE COURT: I'm sorry to hear that, Mr. Flores.

WITNESS: Thank you, sir. So am I.

THE COURT: You can step down, son.

WITNESS: Thank you, sir.

THE COURT: Anything else?

MS. DE LEON: No, Your Honor.

MS. TAYLOR: No, Your Honor.

THE COURT: This proceeding has been unusual, but I think you've presented sufficient evidence. I'm going to find that the juvenile is a deprived and abandoned child. Please prepare an order for my signature.

MS. DE LEON: Thank you, Your Honor.

MS. TAYLOR: Thank you so much, Your Honor.

THE COURT: All right. All right, then. Good luck.

MS. DE LEON: Thank you.

THE COURT: Good luck, Mr. Flores.

WITNESS: Thank you, sir. And thank you for helping my little brother.

(Proceedings concluded.)

CHAPTER THIRTY

PHOENIX

SHE IS SO BEAUTIFUL.

I know I'm probably not supposed to be thinking about this right
now, but I am. It's sort of all I can think about. Maybe because I can't
deal with all the other stuff anymore. And I don't have to.

It's done.

She props her elbow on the table, at the edge of her half-empty plate
of pasta. She leans forward and runs her fingers through her hair, then
catches a handful of it, tugging gently. She's looking at Sally, talking
about I-don't-know-what, and I'm watching the curve of her neck,
the angle of her jaw, her skin.

I need to touch her. I need to feel her, firm and soft against me.

I lean back a little in my chair and stretch out, below the table, until
I feel it—my leg pressed against hers.

There. Better now.

She glances over at me and smiles. She doesn't move her leg. She
lets me touch her in this way—so simple and innocent, like a mistake,
like a misplaced body part that should be quickly readjusted. But it's not
a mistake, and I'm sure she knows it. Because she's Gretchen, holding
me here with her touch. Her presence—real and steady—is maybe the
only thing keeping me in this place.

It's definitely not the food that's keeping me here.

Apple-something. That's the name of this restaurant. I can't remember exactly. The food kinda sucks. It's expensive, too. Thirteen dollars for a bowl of macaroni with a little strip of chicken on top. I tried to order fries and a cup of soup, but Sally wouldn't let me.

She said, "You must be hungry after all that, love."

I didn't want to go into *all that*. So I ordered the macaroni—the cheapest meal in the entree section. It tasted like nothing, but I ate every bite of it. I guess I *was* hungry, or not wanting to waste more of Sally and Amanda's money. Maybe both.

We're celebrating. The judge said he would tell Immigration that Ari needs to stay, and that he doesn't have a parent who can take care of him. Ari's lawyer told us that with the judge's order, he's almost certain to get the special permission to stay in the U.S. And Ms. Rosales—the social worker—she found a foster home in California that's ready to take him, which is awesome.

He wasn't a bad guy, that judge. I don't think he meant any harm with the "illegal" question. He didn't know any better. Ms. Rosales said those domestic court judges don't know much of anything about immigration laws. But the kids have to go through the domestic courts before they can get special immigrant status, to show that they don't have parents to take care of them.

The judge came up to me after the whole thing was over and patted me on the back. "Son, you did a good thing today," he said.

And maybe I did, today. Maybe it would be okay for me to let today be what it is—not to worry about what's next, or to obsess about all the stupid stuff I did to get us here.

"Does that sound okay to you, Phoenix?"

Sally, Amanda, and Gretchen are all looking at me examining my fork.

"Sorry." I look up. "I didn't hear what you said."

Gretchen's elbow falls from the table. She reaches under and puts her hand on my knee.

"Tomorrow morning we can meet in the lobby at seven," Sally tells me.

I drop the fork and let my hand find Gretchen's. Our fingers intertwine, resting on my leg.

"I'll drop you at the shelter so you can visit with Ari for a few minutes," Amanda says, "while we have breakfast at the hotel. If you'll get your bag ready tonight"—she takes a little plastic folder from the table and puts a credit card inside it—"we can get it from your room—I have the extra key. We will pick you up after breakfast and head straight to the airport."

"Yeah," I say. "That sounds good." It doesn't sound good, though. Nothing having to do with planes sounds good to me, and saying good-bye to my brother, for who knows how long? That doesn't sound all that good either.

Gretchen's phone vibrates, doing a little dance on the table.

"My dad," she says, looking over at it. "I should get this."

She lets go of my hand and stands up. Pushing her chair back, she lifts the phone to her ear. "Hi, Dad." Her voice sounds healthy, strong. I know he will notice that too. She walks away from us, toward the glass doors that lead outside.

I watch her, feeling the absence of her body against mine. I feel my hand limp against my leg. I feel the empty space.

Sally and Amanda are talking about what happened in the court, and about how well I did up there, and I'm sort of listening and nodding, but mostly I'm watching Gretchen through the window, and it's messed up, I know, but my heart feels like it's gonna explode, watching her. It feels like I felt when I left Ari alone in that *heladera*. I guess I sort of know that it will all be over soon, and I don't want it to end. I want to stay here with her, and with Sally and Amanda.

Christ, I don't want for this to end.

Gretchen comes back to the table and lets me wrap her hand in mine, and they're all still talking, waiting to get the check.

"I didn't know your brother's name was Arizona," Amanda says to me. "I always thought Ari was an odd name for a little boy from El Salvador."

I guess I look a little confused, because Sally breaks in with an explanation. "Ari's a name that's more common for Jewish men here in the U.S.," she says. "And we knew that you and your brother weren't Jewish."

"Phoenix, Arizona," Gretchen says. "Didn't you say that's where your mom went to work after you were born?"

The thing is, I don't really want to talk about all this. I don't want to talk at all, to tell the truth. I'm tired of talking. But Gretchen and Amanda and Sally—these people sitting around a table with me in some random restaurant in some random town in Texas because they *care* about me—I want to be known by them. I don't even know if it makes any sense, but that's what I want. I want them to know me. So I lean back in my chair and I tell them.

"My mom left for Phoenix when I was a baby, and she stayed there until I was five. A lot of people in my town had to do that—go work in the US. There weren't any jobs in Ilopango—at least not jobs that paid enough to support kids. So every family had somebody who went to the US to make money."

"She knew she was going to Phoenix?" Amanda asks. "That's why she named you for the city?"

"I guess," I say. "She used to always say that she wanted to remember me every time she saw a street sign, or whatever. So she decided to call me Phoenix. She came back for a while, when I was five—to live with me and my grandmother. She said that she missed me, that she was tired of taking care of other people's kids. She wanted to be with me, to watch me grow up."

"Why didn't she stay?" Gretchen asks.

"She was hanging out with a guy—I remember him. He was nice, not a troublemaker or anything. He used to bring me little presents, toy cars and candy and stuff. But he didn't have a job either. When my mom got pregnant with Ari, there wasn't anybody to pay for us kids. My grandmother was making *pupusas*, but that didn't cover everything, I guess. So after my mom had Ari, she left us with my grandmother and went back to work in Phoenix—for a different family. That guy went too. I guess maybe he was Ari's dad."

"And she called your brother Arizona," Sally said, "so she would see his name everywhere too."

I shrug. "I guess her plan to remember us didn't work out all that well. We haven't heard a thing from her since Ari was three."

"Do you think she's still here?" Gretchen asks me.

"I don't know. All I know is that Ms. Rosales, the social worker, said they had to run a bunch of ads in the papers all over Arizona to make sure that Ari didn't have family that wanted to be with him, and nobody's claiming him, so . . ."

"Maybe she moved to another state?" Amanda says.

"Maybe." I run my hand through my hair. "Doesn't matter. We don't need her anymore."

A half hour later we're in the hotel elevator. Sally is hugging me, and Gretchen is standing next to her, looking down at her hands. I think she's waiting for me to tell her what I want—which should be pretty damn simple, but it's not.

The door slides open.

"Tomorrow at seven?" Sally asks.

"I'll meet you in the lobby," I tell her.

She nods, holding the door open.

"You did a great thing today, Phoenix," Amanda says.

"Thanks."

Gretchen looks up from her hands, right at me. Then she leans over and kisses me on the cheek.

"Good night," she whispers. "I hope you get some rest."

I feel the warm place where her lips touched me. I watch her hug her chest and follow Sally and Amanda out of the elevator. I'm leaning against the rail, grasping it with both hands. The door slides shut while I stand there like an idiot, letting her go.

My hands launch me from the wall of the elevator. I'm throwing my body between the closing doors.

"Gretchen!" I call out, probably too loud.

She turns to look at me, her eyes bright.

"Wanna hang out—like, get some Skittles from the vending machine or something?"

My heart is pounding in my chest, and Gretchen is smiling and not clutching her chest anymore.

"Yeah." She turns around, heading straight for me.

"I'll see you in the morning," she tells Sally and Amanda.

They both nod and smile and the doors of the elevator close and then she's standing close to me again.

"I don't really want to be alone," I tell her, my voice gravelly.

She leans into me. *Christ*, she feels so amazing, pressed against me.

"And I don't want to get Skittles," she whispers. "I don't even like Skittles."

"You don't?" I'm laughing. *Madre de Dios*, I'm laughing. It feels so good that I throw my arms around her and squeeze her tight. "What about all those Skittles we shared at the gas station, when you took me to get *pupusas*?"

"That was a mercy share." She puts both hands on my chest, pretending to push me away. She doesn't want to push me away, though. I may be an idiot, but I know that much.

"Oh, so you feel sorry for me?" I whisper in her ear. "That's what this is all about?"

"Yes," she says, "I feel *so* sorry for you that I'm going to let you take me to your hotel room so we can raid the minibar."

"The minibar? You wanna get drunk?"

"No." She laughs. "I want to eat peanut M&M's and Hershey bars and maybe some Pringles, too. But no Skittles. You can have those."

"Sounds perfect," I tell her.

When we get to my room, I dig the key card out of my pocket and lead her inside.

Soon we're both sprawled out on the floor. Our shoes are off, and we're surrounded by empty candy and junk food wrappers, laughing our asses off because Gretchen's telling me this crazy story about how her dad had to send a checkout lady into the bathroom of the Whole Foods to rescue her from a panic attack, and I'm describing all the insane shit they sell at Whole Foods, and how much they're ripping people off—I mean, a hunk of cheese for eighteen dollars? Who the hell needs an eighteen-dollar piece of cheese? Is it, like, laced with sterling silver or something? And it feels so damn good, to be doubled over laughing, even if my stomach is a little sick from all the Skittles and chips. It's one of those times—when being able to really laugh is like letting this enormous floodgate open up inside of you, and it's making all the bad stuff rush away, pushing it all out, and leaving nothing but the fresh air you're sucking in between laughs. It's like it's making me clean again, making me new, to be doubled over on this floor and uncontrollably laughing, Gretchen stretched out on the carpet next to me, clutching her gut because she's laughing so damn hard too.

She stops and sits up, suddenly serious. "You can't leave me," she says.

And just like that, we're climbing over all those empty wrappers, clamoring for each other. My lips find hers and my hands weave through her hair and I feel her, searching, and I'm searching too. Wanting to pull her in, to bring her in so close that she can't ever be far away.

She loosens the tie that Amanda bought, and tugs it off. She unbuttons my shirt, and I let her. I struggle to get the cuffs unbuttoned, and then shrug it off. I'm in my undershirt, and she reaches out to touch my scar. I feel the strange tingle of her finger running across it. Then I take her hand away from the scar and kiss it.

I move her hand to my chest, so that she can feel my heart beating under it. We stand up together, moving to the steady rhythm of my heartbeat.

She pulls her sweater off, over her head. I watch it fall to the ground and then I look at her. Her body is so beautiful, so perfect that I want to cry.

Oh, Christ, I think I'm gonna cry.

I take her by the hands. She kisses me again, sitting on the edge of the bed. Her lips are on my jaw, my neck, my collarbone. I'm filling up with heat and light and the smell of her, clean and bright. And I want her so much, but that's not all it is—that's not even the beginning of it.

She looks at me, directly in the eyes, and I try to focus on that brown spot in her right eye, because my vision is starting to blur and my heart is about to explode. She pulls me on top of her, gently, slowly.

I push her hair back from her face and kiss her, feeling our bodies pressed against each other, feeling her hair against my hands and her lips against mine and then I feel her face, wet with tears. But they're not her tears; I think maybe they're mine.

"You're crying," she whispers.

I nod, but I don't pull back from her. I let the silent tears keep falling onto her face, and she doesn't flinch or move away from them.

I don't have to say it, because I know that she knows.

I can't leave her.

I pull away and wipe my tears from her face. "Can we maybe just—"

"Whatever you need," she whispers.

I roll off her and take her hand. I pull her up onto the bed and we crawl under the covers together.

"I need—I want so much to be close to you, but—"

"We can wait," she says. "There's still time, Phoenix. We have time."

Under the covers, we take off most of our clothes, because we need to feel the other's skin. I fold myself around her, and I pull up my undershirt so I can feel her back warm against my chest. I wrap my arm across her, and our hands intertwine above her waist. I bury my face in her hair, and the tears keep coming, silent. I'm crying myself to sleep, but it's okay, because Gretchen's letting me hold on to her, and every time I take in a breath, I'm taking more of her into me. And I know she isn't judging me—no matter how weak, no matter how beaten down I am, she will let me hold her like this. And maybe, one day soon, there will be more.

But for now this is what we are.

I wake up, disoriented. It's dark, and my undershirt is bunched up around my chest. The air feels cold against my bare skin. The covers are thrown off the bed, and Gretchen's not near me anymore. I sit up on the edge of the bed, searching for her. I can't see her, but I hear a soft whimper, like a small animal caught in a trap. My eyes adjust to the light streaming through the open bathroom door and I find her, curled into a tight ball in the corner of the room, staring at me like she's seen a ghost.

I stand up and rush toward her, but she holds her hand out, gesturing for me to stay away. Her eyes are wide, and she's pointing at my abdomen.

"You lied to me," she whispers. "I trusted you and you lied to me."

I look down and see it, the stupid fucking tattoo I've been so desperate to get rid of.

"It's okay, Gretchen. It's not what you think it is—"

"I know what it is." She's pressing her back against the wall, like she's trying to push through it. "That tattoo, it's *his* tattoo." She's shivering, wrapping her arms tight around her bare legs.

"I don't understand." I'm kneeling in front of her. "I don't get what you're saying."

"That boy . . . his chest . . . the bullet holes." She's crying. "That hand, those terrible fingers. I know how you get that hand."

I reach out, not even thinking, just wanting to still her shivering arms. But before I can touch her forearm, she flings it violently.

"Don't touch me! You lied." She repeats it, again and again. "You lied. You lied to me. How could you lie to me? I trusted you. . . ."

I'm frozen, kneeling in front of her, unable to come up with anything to say to her. "I didn't—"

"There's only one way to get that tattoo!" She thrusts one leg out of the tiny ball she's in and kicks me. "Liar! Get away from me!"

"No, Gretchen." I'm trying to keep my voice calm. "I can't do that. Please, just let me—"

"Go away! Leave me alone!"

Her teeth are chattering and she's sucking in breath, rocking back and forth, back and forth.

You did this to her.

"Please, let me—" I reach out again. It's like I can't stop reaching toward her, trying to make it okay. But it's not; she's not.

She thrusts one hand out to stop me. She gets quieter, and her eyes squeeze shut so she doesn't have to see me. "Go," she says, turning toward the wall. "I can't look at you."

She's curling up into a tight ball, sobbing. Her body heaves.

You did this to her.

"Stay here," I beg her, standing up. "Please stay, Gretch. I'll get help."

She doesn't look at me. She keeps rocking back and forth, sucking in air. I take off. I throw the door open, run down the hall to the emergency stairwell. I take the stairs two at a time to the fourth floor, trying not to think about the fact that I'm in my boxer shorts—or the boxers some stranger gave me. It doesn't even matter. When I get to Sally and Amanda's door, I beat on it, hard.

"Sally! Wake up! Oh Christ, Sally. Please!"

My hands and my head are all beating against the door. "It's Gretchen! She's—oh God, she's—"

The door flies open. "Where is she?"

I take Sally's hand and we run back up the stairs. She doesn't ask any more questions. When we get to the room, the door is still open, and Gretchen's cries are pouring into the hallway.

You did this to her.

"Let me," Sally says, heading through the door. "You stay here."

I stumble back into the hall until my back hits the wall. I feel my body sliding down into a crouch.

I hear Sally's voice, soothing, calming. I hear them moving around the room together.

The door opens and they walk out, Gretchen wrapped in Sally's arms. She's holding her shoes in her hand, and her face is pressed against Sally's head. She doesn't look at me when they walk by. They stand and wait for the elevator, and she still doesn't look at me. She can't even look at me.

I love her. And I did this to her.

CHAPTER THIRTY-ONE

GRETCHEN

I WAKE UP in Sally and Amanda's room, freezing. I pull the covers up to my neck and stare at the ceiling, stippled white. What I see, though, is that horrible gnarled hand—the fingers curled inward, the long, sharp fingernails. I see the photograph from Karen's computer screen—tiny black bullet holes spattered across it. And then I see that very same hand tattooed onto Phoenix's perfect, smooth chest.

I want so much to forget these images, to leave them behind. I sit up and look toward the window. The curtains are closed, blocking out all but a small sliver of light. I have no idea what time it is. But I do know this: I messed up. Again.

Oh God. I messed up.

I get up and pull my jeans on. Sally and Amanda are still sleeping, so I know it must be early. I go into the bathroom and splash hot water on my face, squeeze some of their toothpaste onto my finger and run it over my teeth. I rinse the toothpaste and pull my hair into a ponytail. Then I go to the chest of drawers and pick up the key to Phoenix's room, the one he gave Sally last night so she could get his bags and pack them in the rental car.

I leave as quietly as I can, not wanting to wake them. I take the elevator to his floor, remembering the feel of him holding me against his chest, and the soft assurances I gave him—we have time. *We don't have to hurry.*

I know Phoenix. He will tell me how he got that tattoo, and it will make sense. Or, if it doesn't make sense, it will be okay, because he's Phoenix. I will go into his room and lie down beside him. I will ask him to tell me what he needs to say, what he tried to tell me so many times. I was the one who said it didn't matter. And it doesn't, or it shouldn't, but I need to understand. I need to let him tell me. I don't care how long it takes. I don't care if we miss our plane. We'll rent a car and drive home, together.

The elevator doors slide open, into an empty hallway. I grasp the key card, feeling the edges dig into my hand. I walk slowly, passing by a long row of doors, all exactly the same. When I get to his door, I slide the card in.

The green light flashes twice.

I open the door quietly, not wanting to startle him. Gray morning light filters through the room—the curtains are wide open. I see the bed, neatly made. I see a stack of clothing carefully folded on the edge of the bed. His phone rests on top, and there is a small piece of paper. I walk over to the bed. I touch the fabric of the suit, the one that Amanda bought him for court. I read the note.

> Sally and Amanda—
> Thank you for everything. I will never be able to repay you, but I will try. I can't accept your offer to help me appeal my deportation. I hope you will find someone else to help. I hope he will be able to stay. I'm very sorry I let you down.
> Gretchen—I didn't want to hurt you. I should have told you. I'm so sorry I hurt you.
> Phoenix

I sit at the edge of the bed and then pick up the white button-down he wore in court. I lift it to my face, taking in his scent. Then I look toward the bathroom door, holding out hope that maybe he's still here in this hotel room with me.

Don't let him be gone.

But the door is wide open. He's gone.

CHAPTER THIRTY-TWO

PHOENIX

I OPEN MY EYES to gray sky. The grass is wet against my back, but it doesn't matter. I grab the edge of the chain-link fence and pull myself up, looking thorough the diamond-shaped holes, onto the air force base. Across a field of brown grass, I see rows of airplane landing strips. I'm trying to find Ari's shelter from here, but it's too far away.

I hope he's sound asleep on that metal cot. I hope he'll wake up feeling happy today. I hope maybe he'll talk—tell someone how good he feels. I hope it will be me.

My hand moves to my ankle, to that stupid black box. I need to come up with a plan. My time is running out. I have been here all night, trying to think of what to do—how I can work it out to spend some time with Ari, maybe stay with him for a while before I'm sent back. I know I'm supposed to be the one who Ari needs, but the truth is that I need *him* now. I need for Ari to help me forget Gretchen—her touch, the sound of her voice, the way it felt to be trusted that much.

Gretchen trusted me. She should never have trusted me.

Maybe I should run. Maybe I should find a knife or some box cutters or something and cut this stupid black box off me. Maybe I should leave it here at the edge of this field and take off running toward Arizona or

California. I could hide out for a while, until the government forgets about me, and then I'll go find Ari.

I wonder if the government ever forgets.

A high-pitched noise pierces the air. I stand up and look toward it. The sound settles into a loud hum, and a plane pulls out onto the runway—then another, and another. Three small jets—their dark gray outlines stark against the early morning sky. They move slowly toward me, in perfect formation.

I watch them gain speed, getting louder and louder. The sound fills my ears and pulses through my head. After a few seconds it feels like my head's going to explode with that sound, or maybe with all the crap running through it. It's like the noise of the engines is making my own thoughts scream.

You screwed it all up again, Phoenix. What are you going to do now?

The front wheels lift off in perfect unison, and all three jets climb into the air, still coming right toward me. When they pass over me, it's like they knock me down with their force. I fall onto my back and look up. My ears are still ringing and my gut vibrates with their force of sound and motion. When I breathe in, the stench of those planes burns my nostrils. The smell takes me back to Ilopango, reminding me of the fuel my grandmother used in the stove when it got cold and she was out of *parafina*. I shiver, feeling the wet ground and the memories of those rare winter nights back home.

What are you going to do now, Phoenix?

These jets may be small, but they are crazy loud, tearing through my eardrums while they split apart the sky above me, long streams of smoke trailing behind them. They all turn at once, heading directly up—not at an angle, but on a direct path away from the earth. The planes move with purpose, pushing upward to create a straight line from the place where I am, collapsed on the ground, to some exact point in the sky above me. But the smoke won't let the line form. Those streams of smoke start off straight, but then they have their own plans. They lift and dance, cross in and out and around one another.

What are you going to do? Where will you go?

They're quieter now, farther away from me. One plane peels away from the other two, and then—honest to Christ—it launches into a free fall. The others keep moving directly up, toward that invisible point, while that one plane comes hurtling toward the ground. But the others fall out too—the second, and then the third. They're all tumbling toward the ground, tugged down by the weight of gravity.

And I'm thinking, *puta madre*, these planes are going to crash into the earth around me; they're going to explode in huge balls of flame and black smoke.

I need to get out of here. I need to run.

But I don't move, and they don't fall. Instead they begin to dance, one after the other, almost as fluid as the smoke that trails behind them. They curve and flip, twist and lift. Weave in and out and around one another. Those three planes are beautiful to watch, and terrifying.

I lie on the ground and let them dance above me, until the sun is hot and bright in the sky. Then I stand up, wipe the dry grass from my back, and head toward the gate. I need to convince one of those guards to let me use their phone, because I think I know what to do.

I need to call Officer Worth.

CHAPTER THIRTY-THREE
GRETCHEN

WHEN I GOT BACK from Texas, I walked. For four straight days I woke up every morning and chose one of the places I had marked on Phoenix's map. And then I drove myself there, got out of the car, and walked until the sun started to go down.

At the end of my fourth day hiking through the woods alone, I got back into my car and drove to Janet's studio. I told her that I wanted to join her group—the one that she had invited me to participate in months ago, the one with war veterans and refugees.

That very evening I sat around a folding table with amputees and survivors of genocide, and when Janet told me to draw, I picked up a pencil and I drew. But I wasn't really making art. At least, most people wouldn't call it art. I hunched over a blank sheet of paper with a dull pencil and worked out a complicated system of equations, hoping to find a solution. The answer was easy to find—systems of equations are simple algebra, after all—but it didn't *work*. Every night, I went and sat at that table, and every night I devised a new system of equations. I stared at the answers and realized that they didn't contain a solution. No matter how complicated I allowed my systems to be—no matter how many variables they included—I couldn't form a solution.

For days Janet peered patiently over my shoulder, smiling gently, allowing me to carve deep black lines into the paper, and then to vigorously erase them. Then one night, when the rest of the group had left, she sat down next to me and asked if maybe I'd like to talk about those equations, to explain the solutions I was struggling to form.

As it turns out, Janet isn't just an art therapist. She's a therapist-therapist, the kind whose work my mom calls horseshit. It's not horseshit, though. I know that now, because Janet is *my* therapist, and she's helping me to understand that even though I don't have an amputated leg or the scars to prove that I survived a horrendous mass killing, I am a trauma survivor. She says that all my relationships will be different than they were before, but they can be good again, and that what's most important for me now is to be able to have healthy relationships that are characterized by trust.

I talk with Janet every day, and I sit around that table every night with Sam and Abroon, Mike and Absmil, with Aamino, and Fartuun—the beautiful Somali woman who always brings sambusas to share. Holding tight to that routine, it only takes me a couple of weeks to devise the right system of equations, and to solve it.

When I see that solution—1 1/3, 5 2/3—a pair of numbers that must seem meaningless to anyone else, I know I need to visit Sally and Amanda.

It's late, but I go to their house anyway. Sally answers the door, in her pajamas. She reaches up on her tiptoes and folds me into a huge hug. Amanda shows up beside her, and the three of us stand together, hugging one another tightly in the doorway.

When we finally pull away, Amanda says, "He won't change his mind." She's looking at me, her eyes heartbroken. "We've tried everything to convince him—"

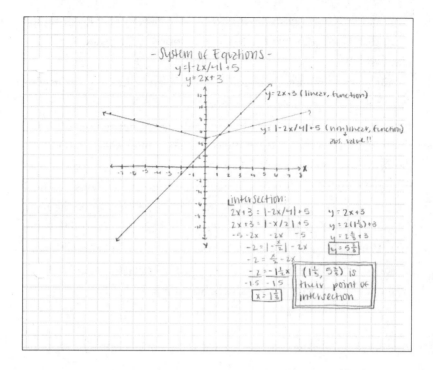

"Hon!" Sally scolds. "The poor dear hasn't even come inside yet."

Amanda takes my arm and leads me to the sofa. "She wouldn't let me call you," Amanda says. "She told me you needed some space, time to work things out."

"No," I say as we head toward the living room. "I don't need any more time. That's why I'm here. I want to help."

They make me a cup of chamomile tea and we curl up together on their sofa. They tell me that the clock is ticking. Phoenix only has five days. If he doesn't agree to let Ms. Pérez appeal the immigration court's decision to the Board of Immigration Appeals—if he doesn't let her file some document called a "stay of removal"—he'll be deported. The problem is, he won't let Ms. Pérez do it. Sally and Amanda keep begging him, and he keeps saying he'll never win on appeal. He keeps telling them that he doesn't want to waste any more of Sally and Amanda's money.

I'm sipping my tea, listening to all this, and thinking about what Janet told me about trust and relationships. I'm trying to work out who Phoenix might trust. Who could convince him that appealing is the right thing to do, even if he loses in the end? I don't think that person is me, but I still may be able to help. Maybe what he needs is evidence, concrete information, sort of his own solution to a system of equations. Maybe I could find some bit of information that will make him believe he has a stronger case than he thinks he does. He's always worrying about money, never wanting it wasted on him. But if he could believe it's not a waste—that the investment would be worth it, that *he's* worth it . . .

"Do you still have Phoenix's phone?" I ask.

"Yes," Amanda says. "We've kept everything for him, just in case. . . ."

"Can I see it?"

The next morning is a Saturday. I go over to Bree's house early, with coffee and Krispy Kreme doughnuts. I'm banking on the fact that Ty won't be there at nine thirty a.m. on a Saturday, and feeling only a little bit guilty about the relief that washes over me when she comes to the door to let me in—alone.

I've been up since six, thinking. I went out and got the doughnuts from the shop on Ponce where they make them fresh. They're still warm—gooey and melty—when Bree and I sit down at the bar in her kitchen to dig in. We're on our second doughnut, studying Phoenix's phone to see what we can find in there. He only has two numbers saved—besides mine, Sally's, and Amanda's. Bree convinces me to call the first one—a 770 area code, which means it's local. Well, sort of local. It's in the suburbs.

I take a swig of coffee and push the call button.

"Phoenix, you asshole. Where the hell have you been?" That's what the guy says when he picks up, and then: "You left me hangin', dude. I'm flailin' over here—haven't got a fuckin' clue how to finish this kitchen, and my Barbie and the kids are waitin' on me."

"Um, this isn't Phoenix," I say. "He's gone."

Bree's kitchen door flies open, and Ty walks in without even knocking. She stands up and heads over to kiss him on the lips. I wave at him and put my finger to my lips, to keep him from making one of his obnoxiously loud comments while I'm trying to figure out who this person is, yelling at me from the other end of the line.

"Gone where?" the gruff voice on the phone says. "Tell me that kid's not back in El Salvador."

I wipe my sticky hands on my jeans and then hold the phone tight against my ear. "Not yet," I hear myself say. I feel a little dizzy. "He's in California. With his brother."

"Well, I know about that. . . . Who *is* this?"

"Gretchen. I'm a friend of—"

"Oh, I know who you are."

"You do?" I close my eyes and lean against the counter. When I open them, Bree is standing next to me, mouthing, *Who is it?* Ty's standing behind her, his arms wrapped around her waist.

"I know all about you," the voice says. "But Phoenix never told you about me, did he?"

Silence. I bite my lip.

"I guess there are a lot of things Phoenix never told me," I say.

"Come on over to the shop," he says. "I'll text you the address. I can tell you what I know."

I hang up and let the phone slide onto the counter. Then I go over to the sink and wash the gooey doughnut glaze from my hands.

"It's a friend of Phoenix's, I guess. He said we could come visit him."

Bree takes the last doughnut from the box and feeds it to Ty.

Ugh.

A text comes in, and Bree and I both lean in to see the message. The guy on the phone sent me his address. It's a place called Georgia Boyz, in Acworth.

"Oh no, no, no. I love you, Gretch. You know I do, and I'm proud of you for doing this, but I will not be taking you to *Georgia Boyz*!"

I look up from the phone, right at Bree. "I need you, Bree."

"To go to a place called Georgia Boyz? In Acworth? Not a snowball's chance in hell I'm going to that place. It's probably wallpapered with Confederate flags."

"What are you talking about?" I ask her.

"I'm talking about the fact that black girls from Decatur don't go to Acworth to visit biker tattoo parlors called Georgia Boyz. That's what I'm talking about." She's got her hand on her hip, which means she's *serious*.

Ty laughs. "My girl's got a point."

His girl?

Okay, *his girl* may have a point. But I need her. So I try a new tactic. "You're prejudging."

"Yes, Gretchen." She nods, hand still on her hip. "Yes, I am. It's a little thing we colored people call self-preservation."

"Colored people?" I say. "Really? Okay, then. Phoenix is 'colored' too, right?" I tell them. "And this guy appears to have been his only friend in Atlanta, besides us."

"Nope," Bree says. "Not happening. Plus, I have a Model UN

meeting in a half hour." She turns away from me and starts to walk out of the room. "Can't miss it. Sorry! Gotta get ready."

Ty grabs a napkin to wipe his mouth and then stands in front of me, looking dumb and shaking his head. "My baby's already *in* Wellesley," he says. "I keep telling her it's senioritis time, but that girl won't listen to me."

I bury my face in my hands. I have to do this, but I don't think I'm ready to do it alone.

Ty shoves me gently with his elbow. "Hey," he says. "I'm free."

I let out a sigh and bury my face deeper into my arms.

"C'mon." He's dangling his keys over my head. "Let's do this thing!"

When Ty pulls into Georgia Boyz, a heavyset white woman rushes out to greet us warmly. She has dyed-red hair and brightly colored tattoos on every inch of her body, except for her face. She's so nice to both of us, wrapping us in big hugs. She has a pretty face—a kind face. It makes me glad she didn't decide to tattoo it, too.

"Look at you!" she says, stepping back to examine me. "You're such a lovely thing!" Then she turns to Ty. "And you're a good friend to bring her out here to us. I've been dyin' to meet this little lady."

She takes my hand, and she tugs us both through the bright blue door, under the (somewhat offensive) sign with a half-naked woman painted onto it. Ty's quiet, smiling that big, genuine smile of his—the one that says he's wide open to the world. It usually bugs me, that smile. But right now I'm feeling grateful to see it.

"I'm Barbie," the tattooed woman tells us, pushing us into two of the molded plastic seats lined up by a desk at the front of the shop. "And this here's Bo, my knight in shining armor."

"That's what I'm talkin' about," Ty says, nodding at Bo.

I feel like laughing out loud. I don't know whether it's because Ty just said he thinks it's cool to be a "knight in shining armor," or because this nice woman has the unfortunate name of Barbie—or maybe it's because she called a chubby guy with too many facial piercings her savior. They're cute together, though. I mean, they look like they really love each other. You can tell that, sometimes.

"I'm so sorry I couldn't have y'all over to the house for a bite to eat," Barbie says. "It's just that my man here is painting the kitchen cabinets for me." She leans over to kiss him on the cheek.

"It smells awful over there," Bo says. "Phoenix said I had to use oil-based paint, or it would all come right back off. But I don't know what the hell I'm doing."

"You're doin' just fine, baby." Barbie pulls a pack of Oreos out of the desk and offers them to Ty, then to me.

Ty takes a big handful and grins wide. I can tell that he likes this couple. I think I do too.

"My kitchen's gonna look so pretty," Barbie says. "He helped me pick out the color."

"You mean Phoenix?" I ask quietly, taking a cookie.

"Well, yes, sweetheart." Barbie sits down next to me and sets the cookies onto the floor.

"That kid knows damn near everything there is to know," Bo tells me. "I mean, about fixing places up and building and shit like that."

I guess that's another thing I didn't know about Phoenix. I thought he just knew gardens.

"How's our Phoenix doin'?" Barbie puts her hand gently on my knee.

I appear unable to produce an answer, because I don't know. *Oh God. I wish I knew.* I haven't spoken to Phoenix—not since I screamed at him and called him a liar. I want to talk to him, but I don't think he wants to talk to me. He told Sally and Amanda it would be better if we didn't talk, and I think maybe he was right. Not because I was mad at him, but because I needed to pull myself together, to work on getting better. The last thing Phoenix needs right now is to deal with my messes, my issues, my stupid drama.

Ty jumps in to say something. He's good at that—breaking awkward silences. "He got really lucky. His ICE officer—you know what that is?"

"Phoenix explained it all to us," Barbie replies.

"Anyway, he arranged it so that Phoenix could go out to California, to be with his brother until he gets deported."

I didn't realize Ty had been paying so much attention to all this. I'm sort of impressed.

"That's what he told us," Barbie says. "He calls sometimes."

Phoenix calls Barbie but doesn't call me. That feels sort of like a punch in the gut. But it's my fault—I know that now.

"Did Phoenix tell you that never happens. Like, *never?*" Ty asks. "I guess it was because his brother had some problems. And they thought Phoenix could help."

"Ari?" Barbie asks. "That's his brother's name, right? He's talkin' again?"

"Yeah," I say quietly. "I saw Amanda and Sally yesterday—do you know who they are?"

"Yes, honey. We know," Barbie says gently.

"They told me he's much better now. He's in a foster home out there."

"So, our Phoenix is living the life out there in Cali," Bo says.

"Not for long," Ty says. "If he doesn't agree to appeal by the end of the week, he'll be sent back to El Salvador, like, soon."

I told Bree all this last night, after I got home from Sally and Amanda's. Needless to say, it's surprising that she's shared it all with Ty, and that he paid enough attention to get the facts straight.

"Well, that's just downright crazy." Barbie stands up and starts to pace. "He didn't tell us that! He can't do that!"

"That boy's gonna get himself killed if he goes back. You know that, right?"

Yes, I know.

"I'm going out there," I whisper, looking down at my hands. "To see if I can get him to appeal."

It's the first time I've said it—to myself or to anyone. I don't know if it will work, but I need to try.

"That's awesome," Ty says, and at the same time, Barbie sighs.

"Oh, baby," she tells me, "that's a good idea. He'll listen to you. I know he will."

I wish I were so sure. He won't even talk to me. But he doesn't have to talk. That's what I keep telling myself. He just has to listen, and I need something to tell him—some piece of information, some argument that will convince him.

"Phoenix doesn't think he has a chance," I tell them. "And he doesn't want to waste the money. Sally and Amanda would have to pay for it, and I guess he's sort of having a hard time with that."

"Stubborn kid." Bo shakes his head. "Wouldn't let me take off that damn tattoo, either. Not until he earned it doing odd jobs around this place."

I look up at Bo. "He wanted you to take it off?"

"Hell, yeah. That's why he came in here in the first place. He hated that thing with a passion—brought back a lot of memories he'd rather keep buried, if you know what I mean."

Yes, I know what you mean.

"Did he tell you?" I ask. "How he got it?"

"I know," Ty says.

Ty knows?

"He told me that day in the garden, after we went Downtown, you remember?"

Do I remember the night we went Downtown? Yes, I remember.

"He was worried about you. I asked him if you two were, like, *a thing* and he said he wanted to be, but he felt like he should tell you some stuff about his past."

"What stuff?" I ask.

"He pretty much got forced to join a gang when he was thirteen. They were trying to take money from his grandma—you know, like extortion?"

"He told you this?" I'm feeling a little dizzy, so I grab my seat with both hands and grasp tight.

"Kid didn't do anything," Bo adds. "He helped them with some petty theft for a few weeks. They got him drunk and gave him that ugly-ass tattoo, and the first time they tried to make him do some truly bad shit, the kid ran away."

"He told you, too?" I ask Bo.

"He wanted you to know." Barbie leans over to touch my knee. "He wasn't hiding it. He was just so worried he would upset you. He didn't want to upset you."

"I told him to wait and tell you later," Ty says. "I'm sorry. I guess maybe I did the wrong thing, but it didn't really seem to matter much. Phoenix was such a stand-up guy—I mean, he's, like, so honest and real. And, I felt like he was so good for you, and you were so—"

"Oh, baby," Barbie breaks in. "He thought you were just too—"

"Fragile." I whisper. "I was—I guess maybe I still am."

"You're a lot better, Gretchen," Ty says. "Dudes!" He's talking to Bo and Barbie now. "When I first started hanging out with this girl, she was a total wreck—a real basket case."

"You mean, when you bit me in preschool and I had to get a tetanus shot?"

"Nah, I'm talking about once Bree and I got together." He gives me a little shove. "Sorry about that, by the way," he says, grinning sheepishly.

I laugh, and so do Bo and Barbie. "We go way back," I explain to them.

Ty leans forward and exclaims: "See, girl! I'm telling you: you're way better now."

And even though he called me "girl," I'm okay with it, because I know he's right.

"Anyway," I say, "Phoenix's lawyer says he could have a chance of getting asylum in California. I guess the judges out there are nicer, or more lenient, or something."

"And it's just the money that's stopping him?" Barbie asks. "That's not right."

"Not just the money," Bo says quietly. "The boy messed up. He was around when some bad shit happened, and even though he left it behind, he can't forgive himself for letting it go down."

"Do you have any information, maybe?" Ty says. "Did he tell you anything that could help Gretchen convince him to appeal?"

"Information?" Bo leans forward and grabs the edges of Barbie's chair. "Here's what I know. Phoenix Flores Flores is a good kid. But all he sees is the bad—thinks he ain't worth shit—to no one. Thinks the whole world would be better off without him." He pauses and puts his hand on Barbie's shoulder. "I know what that feels like, don't I, baby?"

She looks up at him, takes his hand in hers. "Yes, you do."

"All that boy needs," Bo says, squeezing Barbie's hand, "is somebody to show him what he's worth."

Ty puts his arm around my shoulders, and Barbie pats me on the knee.

"I don't know *how*."

"It's easy, baby," Barbie coos at me. "It's real easy. All you have to do is love him."

I look up at her. She's so kind. "I can do that." I nod. "I can love him. I mean, if he'll let me."

"Yes, you can," she says, "and he will let you. I know he will." She leans over and wraps me in a hug. I stay there for a while, not wanting to move. Her hug feels good. So we hug, and we listen to Ty and Bo talking.

"When's she headed out to California?" Bo asks quietly.

"I don't know," Ty whispers. "But it's gonna have to be soon."

They're quiet for a few seconds, and I'm still resting in Barbie's hug.

"Listen," Bo says to Ty. "Do me a favor."

"Sure, yeah."

"Come by here in a couple of days, before she heads out there. I got somethin' I wanna send out to Phoenix."

"Yeah, absolutely," Ty says, his voice animated. "I can do that."

That makes me feel good, hearing him say that.

We stay for a while, and Bo and Barbie tell us about the first time they met Phoenix, about how he was trying to convince them he was an ex-con, and all they saw was a scared kid. Phoenix talked to them about a lot of things, I guess all the things I never let him tell me, because I was too wrapped up in my own messed-up head. Anyway, it's not easy to hear those things, but it's good, too. It makes me feel like I know him better. It makes me miss him too.

God, I miss him so much.

Ty and I say our good-byes and promise we will keep them posted on any news. He and Bo exchange phone numbers, and Bo says he'll text when he's ready for Ty to come by.

After a few more hugs, we get into Ty's car.

"That was—"

"Great!" Ty says. "Those two are *awesome*."

"Yeah," I tell him. I put on my seat belt and then dig Phoenix's phone out of my purse.

There is one other number in the call history. It's an international number, probably from El Salvador. Phoenix called it every morning at the same time. Usually, he only talked for two or three minutes, but sometimes the calls were longer. I have been trying to work up the nerve to call, or to find a Spanish speaker to do it. I figure whoever he has been calling every day probably doesn't speak much English. And if I want information, I need to be able to say more than *Me llamo Gretchen*.

"Hey, Ty," I say. "You wouldn't happen to take Spanish, would you?"

"Hell, yeah!" he replies. "AP Spanish, baby! Just got a five on my exam."

I laugh out loud, mostly at myself, for getting Ty so wrong. "Wanna do me one more favor?" I ask him.

He nods vigorously, and I hand him the phone.

CHAPTER THIRTY-FOUR
PHOENIX

ARI AND I ARE OUT here getting pummeled by the waves.

It's turned into sort of a thing for us, ever since we got to California. Ari's not in school yet. He starts next week, so we have a little time to explore. We wake up early every morning and walk down to Balboa. We go into Dunkin' Donuts, and I buy him a doughnut and me some coffee. I like doughnuts and all, but I can't put that shit in my stomach before the sun's even up. Especially not the kind Ari gets, those ones with a bunch of icing on the outside.

We take the bus down to Newport Beach. It's a long ride. Ari always falls back asleep, even with all that sugar in his veins. I watch out the window and think about how lucky I am to have this time with Ari. It feels good—moving fast out of town.

I have to get my ticket back to El Salvador tomorrow, so that I can show it to my new ICE officer. She's a lady. She doesn't joke around with me like Officer Worth did, but she's all right. Just doing her job. Since I'm not gonna appeal, I need to go into her office and show that I have a ticket, or else I go back to detention. I'm not going back there.

I have to fly out in three weeks. I'm not sure what scares me more:

getting back on an airplane or landing in San Salvador. Both are gonna suck. At least I don't have to go on the government plane, though. At least I won't be handcuffed, chained to a bunch of strangers.

I'm not letting Sally and Amanda pay for the ticket. They've done too much already. I'm gonna borrow the money from one of the priests who works with Sister Mary Margaret. I used to help out around his parish when I had free time. She's pissed at me for not appealing, so she wouldn't give me his number. I found it on my own, though, and he was pretty cool about helping me pay for the ticket. He owes me, I guess—for all the free labor I gave him, fixing sinks and toilets in that old, run-down church of his.

Until I leave, I can go anywhere in California. I'm still wearing a stupid ankle bracelet, but I have a radius of way more than twenty miles with this one. It doesn't matter. I don't really have anywhere else to go—not yet.

I don't care if people see it anymore—the ankle bracelet. The other day, when I went with Ari to check out his new school, I saw a kid wearing one to registration. The kid was, like, fourteen. He didn't seem embarrassed at all. He wasn't even trying to hide the thing. I guess it made me realize it's not such a big deal.

So I don't try to cover it, not out here. The stupid tattoo, though. That's a different story. There are a bunch of guys around where Ari is living now who would know what that thing's all about. I'm guessing a few of them have the same one. There's not a chance in hell I'm gonna let them see it—and think I belong to them. So I never take my shirt off. Not even out here on the beach.

We like to get here early—it's usually just the surfers and us, down by the pier. They pretty much leave us alone. Today there are a bunch of surfers, because the swells are big. I like to sit on the sand and watch them. It's pretty cool, the way those guys paddle out there and chill on their boards until the right time comes. There are some girls, too.

They're really good surfers, those girls—better than most of the guys out there, to tell the truth.

Ari won't let me watch for long, though. He's teaching me how to body surf.

I'm way out here in California, hiding out from all the things—and people—that scare the hell out of me. So I figure I should probably man up and face at least one of my fears. This one seems like an okay choice. Plus, Ari loves this shit. Every time he catches a wave, he screams at the top of his lungs, which is awesome. I mean, hearing him yell, after all those months of silence. It's worth getting slammed into the shore a few times for that.

Sally was right. It hurts like hell sometimes, but—every once in a while—when you catch the perfect wave, for a few seconds it feels like you're flying.

The first time Ari and I came out here, I made myself a little promise: I was gonna keep at it until I caught one of those perfect waves. After I catch it—after I fly—I let myself go back up to the shore. Ari, though, he wants, like, fifty of them, every time we come out here. It's cool, though. That kid deserves a few perfect waves.

Ari and I are out deep, watching the waves roll in. Usually there are three or four waves in a set. The first is never the best. That's what Ari told me. So we both float over the first one. The second one's bigger.

"Es mia!"

Ari claims it. It starts to break before it gets to me, so I duck under. It's amazing, how even a really rough wave can feel so still if you get up under it. You know all kinds of craziness is happening over your head, but it's calm and quiet down underneath.

I turn around to face the shore before I come back up. I learned that the tough way—a few too many waves slamming into my face. I'd rather not see them coming.

I stand up, and a wave hits the back of my head. No big deal. I jump and look toward the shore, wanting to see Ari cruising out on the edge of that wave, wanting to hear him scream. But the hit must have been harder than I thought, because I'm, like, seeing things.

I'm hallucinating, or something.

She's standing still at the edge of the surf, looking right at me, through the mist coming off all those breaking waves. The sun is on her cheeks, lighting up her orange-blond hair.

Gretchen.

I run my hand over my face. I blink, feeling the sting of salt in my eyes. When I open them, she's still there. Her hand is reaching into the air, and she's waving. At me.

Oh Christ. Gretchen is here, on a beach in California, waving at me.

I move through the surf, feeling it tug against my arms and legs. I'm walking, paddling with my arms to get traction. And then the ocean lets me go, and I move toward her as fast as I can.

I shake the water out of my hair, try to wring out my T-shirt. She's walking into the water, closing the distance between us.

When she gets close, she reaches out and takes my hand in hers.

"Hi," she says. I can barely hear her voice, so soft under the roar of the ocean.

I can't say anything. All I can do is touch her hair, her face.

"I miss you," she tells me, letting her eyes close.

I nod, and then I wrap my arms around her.

My cold, wet body leans into hers, warm and dry. I feel the wind pushing at us, the water splashing around my ankles. I feel the sand under my feet and the salt pulling at my skin. I feel my shirt, heavy and wet against her. I feel a shiver run through her body. I feel *everything*.

I don't want to, but I pull back, worried that I'm making her cold.

"Sorry about that." I'm touching the damp circle on her T-shirt.

She looks down and shrugs.

"I've got a towel." I leave my hand on her stomach for a second. It doesn't seem to want to move from there. I let it drop down to her hand. I wrap my fingers through hers and lead her to the big rock where I always leave our stuff.

I look back, wanting to gesture to Ari, to let him know I'm going to shore. He's way out, though, waiting to catch his next big wave. So I walk with Gretchen to the edge of the beach, both of us looking down at the sand.

"How did you know we were here?" I ask, handing her the faded beach towel we borrowed from Ari's foster family.

"I went to the house where Ari is staying." She wipes her front once and hands the towel back to me.

I wrap it tightly around my chest, under my soaked T-shirt, over the goddamned tattoo. Then I lift the shirt off and lay it out on the rock to dry. I reach into Ari's backpack and grab a dry one. I don't have to think about this. I've done it so many times—changed shirts while still managing to keep the stupid thing covered.

I'm thinking about Gretchen, and about how carefully she's watching me. I wonder if she's seeing that tattoo in her mind, even though it's under the towel. I turn away from her.

"They're nice," she says quietly. "Ari's foster parents."

"Yeah." My back is to her. I'm pulling on the dry shirt over the towel. "Ari's a lucky bastard."

I reach down and pull the towel out from under my dry shirt. The shirt feels good, warm against my clammy skin. I feel her hand on my back. Even through the shirt, her touch is like a wave, pulling me into it.

I turn around to face her, feeling that strange scary swell in my chest. "I'm so sorry, Gretchen. I didn't want to hurt you."

"You didn't hurt me." She keeps her hand on me. I don't think she knows it, but it's right on top of that stupid tattoo. "I was hurt already, and you were trying to help me get better."

"I should have told you—"

"You tried." She's looking at her hand, on my shirt.

"I should have tried harder."

I take her hand from my shirt and wrap it in both of mine. We lean against the rock, looking out over the ocean, not saying anything. Ari's catching a wave, and even though I can't hear him, I know he's screaming. I can tell by the look on his face, the way his hands are thrown out in front of him, like he's Superman.

"I shouldn't have relied on you like that," she says, "to make me feel better."

"I wanted to help," I say, rubbing my thumb across her hand. "I mean, I cared about you—I *care* about you."

"I'm getting help now," she says. "Her name's Janet. She's great."

"I'm so glad," I tell her. And I am. I want for Gretchen to have everything she needs.

"Is that Ari?" she asks, pointing to him. He's struggling to stand up in the shallow surf.

I nod. "Yeah, stupid kid can't get enough of those waves."

She smiles. "Phoenix." She's looking at our hands, wrapped around each other. "I know what happened—how you got the tattoo and everything. There's nothing you have to tell me anymore."

I look over at her, and I guess she sees how confused I am, because she smiles even wider and says, "Ty told me about your conversation in the garden, and we went to meet Bo and Barbie."

This is surprising. "Seriously?"

"Yeah. Is it okay, that they told me?"

I nod, remembering all those crappy fast-food meals around their kitchen table, and how great they were. I miss those guys.

"I wasn't trying to hide anything from you, Gretchen. Maybe at first I was, but—"

"I'm sorry I couldn't be there for you," she says, "in the way they could."

"How are they?" I ask, because I'm not sure how to tell her what I want to say—that she was more *there* than any other person I've ever known.

"Great. Barbie took me over to see her kitchen—the color you picked is perfect. I've got pictures." She digs into her pocket to pull out her phone. "Those two are adorable together; after everything they've been through, they're still totally in love."

Totally in love.

We both turn to look at each other at the same time. My body is shifting toward her, and my hand is reaching over to hold her face. I pull her in toward me and she doesn't resist. She lets me kiss her softly on the lips. She puts her arm around my waist and pulls me in closer. She keeps kissing me, which—after all this—feels sort of like a miracle. To be kissing Gretchen on a beach in California, and for her to be kissing me back.

"Thank you," I whisper. "For coming all the way out here and for—"

"Loving you?" She pulls back, and she's looking me right in the eyes, telling me she loves me.

She's telling me she loves me.

"You make it easy, Phoenix." She touches my face. "*Everyone* loves you—I guess what I'm trying to say is that everyone wants you to be okay. We're so worried about you because we all love you so much."

I feel like I'm gonna explode. It's amazing to hear her say that, and it also makes me really sad. Because all those people loving me—Gretchen loving me—is not gonna make it easy to do what I have to do.

"Let's sit down," she says. "We need to talk."

She drops down into the sand, sits cross-legged. I sit down next to her and stretch my legs out on the beach.

"I talked to Sister Mary Margaret." She's looking at me. I'm watching Ari, who just caught another big wave.

"Yeah, she told me," I say.

"You talked to her?" She sounds surprised.

"Mmmhmm," I look over at her. "I talk to her every day."

"Did she tell you about Delgado? About what he did?"

I don't want to keep looking at her. Not with Delgado in my head. So I turn back to face the ocean. "Yeah."

"And what she did?"

"Yeah." I can't resist shaking my head when I think about it.

Delgado had some of the guys dig two big holes in front of the convent. They were the perfect size for bodies. Then they stuck a big rock in front of each hole with a word spray-painted in black on each rock: *Phoenix* and *Arizona*. They also tagged the wall of the convent, behind the rock. Which was a stupid thing to do.

When the *federales* came out, they thought the whole thing was about a city in the *Estados Unidos*. Sister Mary Margaret knew it was about me and Ari, but she couldn't convince them. So she went over to Delgado's house and confronted him. And she recorded the whole thing with her new iPhone. She's so goddamned proud of that new phone.

Anyway, I guess Delgado said he wanted us dead because I worked for her, when I was supposed to be working for him instead. Something like that. He called me a bunch of names, and he said I was wrong if I thought the church was more powerful than the gang. He said the church couldn't save me. He said *he* ran this town now, and that my rosaries and my novenas weren't going to protect me anymore.

Which is funny, because I've never even prayed the rosary or said a novena—not once in my life.

Gretchen moves back toward me and leans into my shoulder. "Sister Mary Margaret is one badass nun," she says.

"Yeah, she's the best."

I'm kinda worried about her, though. They used to leave the church alone, but now—since the truce fell apart—it's like those guys think they're *gods*, like no one can touch them—not the church, not the government. That scares the hell out of me.

And in three weeks I'm going back there. I might as well just head on over to the convent and climb into that grave they dug for me—save everyone the trouble.

At least Ari won't be climbing in next to me.

"She wrote a letter to the judge, you know?" Gretchen is reaching over to touch my knee. "And she's getting some priest to write one too—he's, like, a bishop or something."

"Yeah, she told me."

She wraps her arm around my thigh and shakes it a little, like she's trying to wake me up. She makes me look over at her.

"Phoenix," she's saying, "this is huge. You know that, right? It's religious persecution. That makes for a really strong asylum case."

I don't say anything. I'm thinking how weird it is that I could maybe get asylum for religious persecution, since I'm not really all that religious. I guess I did pray once—back in that shelter in Texas, I prayed for Ari to make it out here. And he did, so who knows? Maybe I am religious.

"Everything is totally different now. Don't you get that? If you appeal, you'll have a great case, and in California courts, which are supposed to be so much better than Georgia—"

I look away, because I hate seeing that look in her eyes: hope—stupid goddamned hope. She doesn't want me to keep things from her, but she also wants to hope; she wants me to have hope too. That can't happen. What am I supposed to do? I need to make her understand.

"There's something else you should know, Gretchen—I mean, a problem with my asylum case."

"You mean, the torture?"

Oh Christ. "You know about that?"

"Yeah. I know." She rubs my leg gently, like she's trying to soothe me. How can she even touch me? How can she look at me, knowing what I did?

"*Damn.* I wish you didn't know about that."

"It's okay, Phoenix. Some guy named Jesús Monteverde—"

"Blackie?"

"Yeah, Blackie. He was there, right?"

"Yeah." My hand flies to my head, rubbing back and forth, back and forth. I really don't want to think about Blackie.

"Ms. Pérez—she tracked him down. He lives here now, in DC. He's legal and everything."

Another lucky bastard.

"She said he's, like, super-religious. An Evangelical. He goes around trying to convert gang members."

"For real?" I lie back in the sand and look up at the sky.

"Yeah, for real, Phoenix."

"He told Ms. Pérez that you were doing everything you could to make them stop."

"He said that?" The sun is glaring into my eyes. I lift my hand to cover them.

"Yeah. He's writing it all down. He said he'd testify for you."

"Blackie? For me?" With my eyes shaded, I look over at her. She's up on her knees, leaning in toward me.

"It's true, Phoenix. You were only thirteen. You did all you could."

Yeah, I guess I did. But it still happened—all of it.

She's still kneeling next to me, her hands clasped. "Please, Phoenix. Please appeal."

I prop up onto my elbows and look at her. "You know how much that shit costs—to appeal?"

"It doesn't matter. It's only money." Her hands are on my chest, still held together like she's praying, or something. "If you won't do it for yourself, do it for Ari. If you get asylum, you can become a permanent resident. Do you know what that means?"

I nod. Ms. Pérez explained it all to me already.

"You can work, go back to school. You can get custody of Ari!"

"Ari's in a great situation. Those people he's living with are really nice, Gretch."

"Then do it for me."

Gretchen is leaning over me, her hair fanning out across my chest, and she's begging me to stay.

Madre de Dios.

"I want to be with you," she says, pleading. "I'm going to apply for college out here, Phoenix. So I can be here with you and Ari."

"You would do that?" I'm starting to feel dizzy, like, confused. Did Gretchen really just say she wants to come to California? To be with me?

"You can't do that."

"You can't stop me from doing it. That's what I'm doing. I don't care if we have six days or sixty years together; that's what I'm going to do, Phoenix."

I sit up so my face is level with hers. I don't feel dizzy anymore. I feel fine. Better than fine. I feel great. And I know exactly what I need to say.

"Yeah, all right then."

"All right?"

"Yeah, I'll do it."

I can't believe I'm saying it, but I know it's right. Even if they tell me no, which they probably will, even if the whole thing puts me through hell again, I need to do it.

"You will? Really? You'll appeal?"

Her face is all lit up, and she's got this huge, beautiful smile spreading across it.

"Really."

She launches forward and wraps her arms around me. Then she lets out a squeal. "Oh my God," she says. "Thank you."

I'm laughing my ass off, because this girl is thanking *me*. I'm pretty sure that's not right, but I'll take it.

Christ, I will *so* take it.

She's laughing too, but then she kisses me, which shuts us both up. I'm holding her face, and we're kissing and smiling at the same time, which is sort of challenging to do. But neither one of us can stop smiling.

"I love you," I whisper into her ear.

"I know," she says. "I love you too." Then she jumps up, all excited. "Hold on," she tells me. "I've got something for you—stay here!"

Which is kind of a funny thing for her to say, because where the hell else would I want to go? She takes off, jogging toward the parking lot. It feels really good, watching her go, and knowing she'll come back. When she disappears, I look out toward the ocean, and Ari is walking toward me, finally worn out, I guess. Gretchen gets back to me first. She hands me a thick piece of drawing paper, rolled up. "This is for you," she says. "Read it, okay? I'm going to go say hi to Ari, and then we're gonna call Ms. Pérez."

She heads down the beach to meet Ari. I watch them hug. He looks happy, seeing her again. They're talking, mostly with their hands—Ari's English is pretty terrible, and Gretchen really needs to learn some Spanish.

I start unrolling the paper, thinking about how I'm going to teach Gretchen to speak Spanish. Thinking about all the things I'm going to be able to do with Gretchen if she really comes out here to live with us. Maybe we could hike in some of those canyons Ari's foster parents told me about. Or I could take her out for *pupusas*. There are *pupusas everywhere* out here. Or maybe we could go to school together—study at the same university. How nuts would that be? To go to university with Gretchen?

A smaller piece of paper floats out and lands on the sand. I put down the rolled-up one and read. It's a note from Bo.

Phoenix—

That piece-of-shit tattoo is part of you, man, whether you like it or not. Don't go through the pain of getting it taken off. You don't need to do that.

Take this design to Danny at Ink Wizards in Fullerton. I made it special for you. He knows you're coming. He'll fix you up. It's gonna look kick-ass, and nobody will know what's under there.

I know what you're thinking, asshole. Don't worry about the stupid money. I got the bill covered. You earned it.

And one more thing. Barbie wants me to tell you that Gretchen's real good for you. She says don't let that one go.

—Bo

It's amazing. I mean, the design. It's a freakin' work of art. Somehow he made that ugly, horrible hand into a tattoo masterpiece.

Bo's a goddamned genius.

I smooth the paper out flat on the sand, and I study it for a while, all the details. Then I look out at Gretchen and Ari talking to each other. I see the waves behind them, still battering the shore.

The two of them come back and sit down with me, and we look at the design, the bright indigo bird, blue fire below it and long red and orange and yellow flames licking its sides. The terrible, ugly hand is still in there, but it's been swallowed up by the blaze so that the fingers become part of the flames. The bird's wings are spread wide open like it's about to take off, and it looks tough, but not mean or harsh. It's strong and bright and beautiful.

"Do you know what it is?" Gretchen asks Ari.

He shrugs. "A bird?"

"It's a Phoenix," she says, "rising from the ashes."

"*Un phoenix,*" I repeat, "*renaciendo de las cenizas.*"

"Cool." He's trying out his English slang. "Too cool for you!"

I take the little pissant into the crook of my elbow and toss him into the sand. He laughs and kicks and screams, and Gretchen's laughing too.

I let him go, and then I turn to Gretchen.

"Hey," I say. "Can I borrow your phone for a sec? I need to call my kick-ass lawyer and tell her she better file those appeal papers today."

Gretchen smiles and digs her phone out of her pocket. She finds Ms. Pérez's number and pushes call. Gretchen hands me the phone, and I take it because I'll do anything this crazy beautiful girl asks me to do, because she'll do anything for me.

EPILOGUE

FINAL EXAM—SEMESTER TWO
ESOL (English for Speakers of Other Languages)
Level 1
Loma Mission Middle School
Ms. Hernández

Describe your family. Tell about each member of your family: What is her/his name? How old is he/she? Where does he/she go to school or work? What does he/she like? What does he/she dislike? What is one special thing about him or her?

My family is three people: Ari, Phoenix, and Gretchen.

My name is Ari. I am thirteen years old. I am in grade seven in Loma Mission Middle School. I like California. I dislike cold. I am very good swimmer.

Gretchen is the girlfriend of my brother. She is nineteen years old. She goes to university at Los Angeles. She likes math and figs and my brother. She dislikes guns. She is very smart and very nice.

My brother is Phoenix. He is twenty years old. He works in the Home Depot. One day in the future he goes to university again. He likes to kiss Gretchen. He dislikes airplanes. He has a tattoo. It is big. It looks like this:

My family is three people: Ari, Phoenix, and Gretchen. My name is Ari. I am 13 years old. I am in grade 7 in Loma Mission Middle School. I like California. I dislike cold. I am very good swimmer.

Gretchen is the girlfriend of my brother. She is 19 years old. She goes to university at Los Angeles. She likes math and figs and my brother. She dislikes guns. She is very smart and very nice.

My brother is Phoenix. He is 20 years old. He works in the Home Depot. One day in the future he goes to university again. He likes to kiss Gretchen. He dislikes airplanes. He has a tattoo. It looks like this:

ACKNOWLEDGMENTS

I have so much gratitude for the people who made this book possible.

An enormous thank-you to the wonderful and talented Carlos Morataya. Your illustrations brought these characters to life for me. Thank you to Laura Chasen, who continues to be my staunch advocate and dear friend, from all the way across the country. To Erin Harris, my brilliant agent, who always knows just how far to push me. I cherish our relationship. To my editor, Sara Goodman. I am honored and privileged (and still a little bit amazed!) to work with you. To Alicia Clancy, Angie Giammarino, Brittani Hilles, Kaitlin Severini, and all of the talented people at St. Martin's Press. Thank you for loving books, and for taking such good care of mine.

To Becky Albertalli, Aisha Saeed, and all the Atlanta YA authors on this journey with me. It is such an enormous relief to be honest, vulnerable, and real with all of you wonderful people. Thank you to Christine Ristaino and David Jenkins, colleagues and dear friends who bravely shared their own stories with me, inspired me to write unflinchingly, and never second-guessed my unorthodox career decisions.

To Jessica Daman and Kim Dammers, two extraordinary attorneys who offered me your valuable time and knowledge. (I took a few liberties with this story. Please be assured that I accept *all* responsibility for mistakes and inaccuracies.) To Christina Iturralde and Kevin Amaya at KIND Atlanta, and to all of the social service providers and pro-bono attorneys across the country who work tirelessly to advocate for kids like Ari.

To Amilcar Valencia, for your careful lessons on Salvadoran slang, and for welcoming me into your family and community in San Salvador. To Katie Beno-Valencia and Lesley Ediger, for inviting me to join you in El Salvador and waiting so patiently for me to arrive. And to all of my fellow El Refugians (with apologies to the rest of you for the terrible Spanglish). You have taught me so much about how to love with fierce compassion, and how to practice hospitality in the most inhospitable of places.

To The Coven of the Pie Wish: my sister and best friend, the *real* Lee Taylor, who has worked tirelessly for so many years as a guardian ad litem attorney and defender of kids. To my critique partner, Mayra Cuevas. From the moment we met, I knew that you would be a great colleague. I am enormously grateful that you have become a most cherished friend, too. To my mom. Because, because, because. And to the women I hope will join the coven soon: my beautiful and talented cousin, Holly, my extraordinary sister, Carroll Ann, and my dearest friend, Emily.

To Leslie and Tanya Zacks, Kate and Mike Phillips, Araceli and Camilo Morales, Juan and Anja Ramirez. Even though Annie says you're the "not real" family, I know better. You are as real as it gets, and I can't imagine a life without you. To Claire Riordan and Ana Gaby Maldonado. We're so glad you decided to join the family, too. To all the Friedmanns and Marquardts, for continuing to claim me, and for your consistent love and support. And to Beau Redmond, for bringing so much joy to our family, and for giving me awesome new sisters: Ruth and Chris (who made this book so much better!), Sudie, and Laure. I love you all.

I am outrageously blessed to have my own personal entourage: Mary Elizabeth, whose intelligence and passion for justice amaze me every day—thanks for coming up with a math equation, and for doing all the other crazy things I ask of you (generally without complaint). Nate, my creative and compassionate boy—thanks for writing Ari's essay again and again until we got it right, and for creating beautiful music for me. Pixley: your humor and intellect are both beyond compare. Thanks for always remembering the things I forget, and for reminding me to breathe deep and laugh. I can't wait to read your books someday. And Annie, my gregarious and loving baby girl. Thanks for getting out there and making friends for us both. I am so honored to be the mother of you four incredible people!

Most especially, I am grateful to Chris. No distance will ever be beyond our radius.

This all began on a Saturday in May 2013. I walked into a detention center's visitation room for probably the hundredth time, but still my heart broke wide open. As I spoke on a phone, through the glass, with a teenage asylum-seeker from El Salvador, I knew that I had to write this story. To Miguel de Jesús, Darwin, Jonathan, Uriel, César, Isaac, and all of the Central American asylum seekers I have been so honored to know since that Saturday: I have learned so much from your bravery, your commitment to family, and your desire to find a better future. Thank you for trusting me enough to tell me your stories, and for sharing with me your own American dreams. I wrote this book for you, with the sincere hope that—someday very soon—all of your stories might find a happy ending. Godspeed.

Para Miguel de Jesús, Darwin, Jonathan, Uriel, César, Isaac, y todos los jóvenes centroamericanos en busca de asilo. Ha sido un gran honor conocerles. De ustedes he aprendido la valentía verdadera, el amor que une a sus familias, y el deseo para un mejor futuro. Gracias por confiarme sus historias y sus sueños americanos. Escribí este libro para ustedes con la esperanza de que todas sus historias tengan un final feliz. Que Dios y la Virgencita les acompañe siempre.

ABOUT THE ILLUSTRATOR

John Lunsford

Carlos Alfredo Morataya was born in Guatemala and lived there until 2009, when at the age of eighteen, he moved to Georgia. He graduated from Horizon Christian Academy in Cumming, Georgia, and he currently attends the University of North Georgia (UNG), where his major is Art Education. Carlos is an active member of the Latino Student Association at University of North Georgia. He enjoys photography and art.